Karma Bites

by
Stacy Kramer
and Valerie Thomas

🐦 sandpiper

HOUGHTON MIFFLIN HARCOURT
Boston New York 2010

www.hmhbooks.com

SANDPIPER and the SANDPIPER logo are trademarks of
Houghton Mifflin Harcourt Publishing Company.

The text of this book is set in Bembo.

Library of Congress Cataloging-in-Publication Data
is on file.
ISBN 978-0-547-36301-1

Manufactured in the United States of America
DOM 10 9 8 7 6 5 4 3 2 1
4500242107

To Sadie, Eli, Amelia, and Jack

Karma Bites

Don't Blame Me, Blame the Butterfly Effect

Ever heard of the butterfly effect? It's part of chaos theory, which we learned about in sixth grade science. For the record, calling it *chaos* is a huge understatement. It's more like total flipping madness. The butterfly effect is this mind-bending idea that one small change in the world, like a butterfly's wings flapping or a panda turning over in its den, can trigger a crazy, unexpected chain of events that can lead to something huge and unpredictable like a tornado, an earthquake, or, in my case, spontaneous combustion in middle school.

Let me break it down. A panda turns over in its den, and that's it, deed done, the panda goes back to sleep and absolutely nothing in the world has changed, right? Uh, wrong! Totally wrong! Turns out, that panda can rock the whole world with one innocent roll of its fluffy little body. Because when the panda turned over, its furry butt nudged a small stick out of its den; the stick began to roll; it knocked a rock loose, which in turn dislodged a bigger rock, which caused an avalanche of rocks to cascade down a mountain and into the sea, leading to a huge tsunami that hits the shore in Japan and wipes out an entire seaside village.

Crazy, right? But it can happen. Trust me. I know. It happened to me. One little bitty thing knocked my whole world out of whack, metaphorically speaking. And I'm still recovering from it . . . But wait. I'm getting ahead of myself here. Before I go any further, I need to go back. Two months, to be exact, to the night before the first day of school.

Chapter 1

Code Blue

I PULLED THE TOWEL from my head and stared into the bathroom mirror. No. Flipping. Way. I had a code blue on my hands. More specifically, on my head.

"Franny, I think we left it on *poquito mucho,*" Joey Chang, one of my two besties, said, squinting at my head.

"Ya think?" I replied.

"Look, you're overreacting," Joey said calmly. Easy for her to be calm. My hair was neon orange and perched atop translucently pale skin that was under attack by freckles after a summer spent in the sun. I looked like a Creamsicle.

"I. Am. Not. Overreacting. Are you even looking at my head?" I demanded.

"How can I not? It's *très* compelling," Joey responded.

"I do not want *très* compelling hair on the first day of seventh grade."

As usual, Joey was popping European words into her sentences. Ever since Joey discovered that Penélope Cruz speaks six languages, she's been teaching herself new vocabulary words in various foreign languages. She's not getting much closer to fluency in any other language, but she is starting to make a lot less sense in English.

"I'll grant you, it's not *ideal* ideal," Joey offered. "But it's really not that bad. Kind of funky. And fun. A whole new you." Joey was trying to be sympathetic, but this sounded like a lame sales pitch on QVC.

Joey never has to work at her beauty. She's tall and graceful, like a gazelle, with long, black glossy hair. She's Chinese, and her Asian eyes remind me of perfect almonds. Her skin always looks sun-kissed, even in the darkest days of winter. Joey didn't need a makeover before the first day of seventh grade. I, however, did. But the whole thing had turned out to be a catastrophically bad decision.

"I don't want a whole new me," I said. "I just wanted to go blond. Blondes are supposed to have more fun. But that's obviously not the case here." At that moment, I would have given my left *and* right arms to have my frizzy red curls back.

"Look, maybe this is a sign that you should take more chances this year. Embrace your inner bad girl. Let the orange hair bring it," Joey suggested.

"Seriously, what are you talking about?"

"No idea. But Kate is going to love it. It's so Kate," Joey insisted. Kate Franklin is my other bestie. Unfortunately, she and Joey are very much not besties. They used to be, when we all went to Sunshine Preschool. But when we hit middle school, all bets were off. Suddenly Joey was catapulted into social stardom; Kate was sent into social obscurity; and I was stuck shuffling between them.

"Is that supposed to be helpful?" I said. "Since when do you care what Kate thinks?"

"Don't make this about me and Kate, Franny. We're cool. We're just not friends—due to circumstances beyond our control. But that doesn't mean I don't appreciate Kate's *savoir-faire* and her *je ne sais quoi*. I think it's . . . sweet."

I was sure I detected irony. "Okay, you're just messing with me. And I'm not in the mood. We need to fix this. Now!" I was maybe one minute away from complete and total hysteria. Joey sensed it and immediately snapped into action. Which is so Joey, and it's why I love her. She's grace under pressure. Unlike me, a mess in stress.

"*Aaaannnnaaa!* We've got a situation," Joey yelled as she left me in the bathroom and charged through the house in search of my mother. I lumbered after her.

"*Annaaaaa,*" Joey repeated since the first rebel yell hadn't gotten results. We waited and . . . nothing.

"That's weird. Your mom is always hanging in the kitchen or her office. Where do you think she is? She'll know what to do."

"*Mooooooooommmmm!*" I screamed. Still no response.

Joey and I finally found her in bed, under the covers. It was seven in the evening.

"Are you sick?" I asked Mom, momentarily forgetting my own impending social doom.

"No," she responded, her head still under the covers. I peeled her blankets off. She wore ratty old sweats. Her thick brown hair, which she usually pulled into a nice tight ponytail, hung loose and covered most of her face. This wasn't at all like Mom.

"Your hair is orange, Fran. And orange is not a good color for you, sweetie. Tell her, Joey." And with that, Mom pulled the covers back over her head.

"What's up with you?" I asked.

"When I told you to do the laundry this morning, I meant this morning, not next week some time," Mom barked inexplicably. Okay, that really came out of nowhere. I was going to have to let that pass because Mom was clearly in crisis. Suddenly, my mom was no longer the cool mom, she was the psycho mom.

"Mom, I have an emergency here, in case you haven't noticed. So while I hate to be competitive with you, I think my bad day beats your bad day!" I exclaimed.

"I kinda have to agree with her, Anna," Joey chimed in.

I turned to Joey. "What happened to living dangerously and embracing my inner bad girl?"

"Yeah, well, on second thought, I'm not convinced that's the way to go."

"I'm sorry, Franny," Mom said from under the covers. "I wish I were in a better state. I've got writer's block and I'm under deadline. I just need to sleep it off. Maybe you should talk to Granny about it."

Talk to Granny? This was unprecedented. Granny is . . . well, Mom calls her *idiosyncratic,* which basically means she's totally wacky. Three weeks ago Granny moved in, just like that. Mom said it was because Granny was getting old and needed the company, but I knew it was because of Mom and Dad's divorce. Did she really think shipping Granny in would distract me from the fact that my parents were no longer together?

The thing was, I barely knew Granny. And what I did know didn't exactly make me want to enlist her help. In fact, it made me want to put myself up for adoption. Granny had spent most of my life traveling around the globe, going to meditation retreats, visiting shamans, and trekking in the mountains of some unpronounceable country. Ever since I could remember, we'd seen her twice a year: on the Fourth of July and Christmas. Which was just fine by me. Especially since Ouiji boards, ghosts, séances, and aliens were only a small part of Granny's strange repertoire.

Granny is the type of person who says things like, "If you're a Leo, you might want to avoid tomatoes, especially if there is an Aquarius in the room." When Granny makes comments along those lines, we all just nod, because, really, how can you respond to that? Mom wants Granny to vacuum the living room or give the twins their bath. Instead, Granny gives astrological readings or tells the twins stories about her previous lives. Granny has been an Egyptian slave, a Navajo princess who died from a snakebite, and an ocelot, though I can't recall the actual order. This is not someone to entrust with hair repair.

I stared down in horror at the bulge under the blanket that was my mother. A lump formed in my throat, and tears welled up in my eyes. I was doomed. Positively doomed. How could I possibly show my head at school tomorrow? I was going to have to research boarding schools abroad, nunneries, monasteries. Anywhere that I could hide myself away until my natural color returned. Joey put her arm around my shoulder and gently guided me out of the room.

"Okay, so your mom's having a little meltdown. My mom melts down every half-hour. Your mom not so much; maybe she's overdue. Let's give her a moment and go find your *Grossmutter*. She's old. Maybe she's wise as well." I was worn down to a little nub, with no will of my own. I let Joey lead me to my very uncertain fate.

En route to Granny's room, we glimpsed Armageddon in the kitchen, and at Joey's urging we made a pit stop. Pip and Squeak had been left to their own devices, a sure-fire recipe for disaster. Pip and Squeak (that's what I call them) are my annoying eight-year-old twin brothers (real names: Chase and Elias). Food was everywhere, and Pip was sitting on Squeak, attempting to choke the life out of him in an effort to retrieve the remnants of a Pop-Tart.

"What is going on here, boys?" Joey asked.

"I'm hungry," said Pip. "And Elias is eating the last Pop-Tart." Pip stopped crushing Squeak long enough to stare at my head, and then he burst out laughing. "You look so ugly!" I had the urge to pull his thumbnails out very slowly, but I took the high road and ignored him.

Joey foraged for treasures. "Here you go, boys: graham crackers, some marshmallow fluff, and gummy bears," Joey said as she threw sugar at the wildebeests. I was pretty sure I heard them growl as we left the room.

We peeked into Granny's basement cove and found Granny sitting at a table peering into a huge bowl of something nasty; she was blissfully unaware of the storm brewing upstairs. She was so focused she didn't even notice us at first.

"What's in the bowl?" Joey whispered to me.

"Gruel? Sewage? Not sure I want to know," I whispered back. It was a steaming mustard-colored stew, and it smelled kind of rank. "Granny just came back from some sort of herbal-cleansing seminar at the adult extension school—"

Joey held up her hand. "Enough said."

Granny dangled a crystal pendant over the bowl and chanted some gibberish that sounded like English spoken backwards. Joey giggled, at which point Granny turned to see us standing in the doorway.

"Francisco and JoJo, my two favorite twelve-year-olds," Granny said, and then she caught sight of my hair. "Wow, Franny, what the heckle-jeckle threw up on your head?"

"Bad dye job," Joey volunteered.

"I'll say," Granny said. "What exactly were you trying to do?" She studied my head, confused.

"She wanted to go blond," Joey offered.

"Why would you want to be blond, Francisco? People would kill for your red hair."

"Blondes have more fun." That was my story and I was sticking to it.

Granny took a ladle to the yellow sewage, filled two mugs with the lumpy substance, and thrust them at us. "Drink up, girls, it's yak butter tea, and I tell you, there's nothing like it. The Bhutanese have discovered the secret of life. You will have the healthiest bowel movement you've ever experienced— really cleans you out, trust me."

I'm working hard on not being sarcastic all the time because it's so clichéd, especially in middle school, but what am I supposed to do with a comment like that?

"Sounds tempting, but I'm good," I told Granny as I placed the mug on the table.

"Thanks," Joey said, polite as ever, taking the mug from Granny. "How thoughtful of you." Joey faked a sip and gingerly placed the mug down.

Granny had a huge scarf wrapped around her head; I think it was supposed to resemble a turban. She grew up in Cincinnati and for years was the mild-mannered manager of a dentist's office. But then one day she signed up for a transcendental meditation course, and the rest is history.

"I say live with it for a few weeks. Don't do anything now," Granny suggested.

Granny had recently dyed her own hair a shade of blue,

and she looked like an exotic bird. It clashed loudly with her daily uniform of hot pink sweatpants and bright green Crocs.

"I need to do something now. Right now!" I said.

"I'm just about to do a little yoga and get my Zen on," Granny said. "Let's chat afterward."

"Can you get your Zen on a little later, Grans?" I said, losing whatever was left of my cool. "The twins are running wild, and Mom is lying in bed comatose with severe writer's block, and if someone doesn't help me turn my hair back to normal before tomorrow morning I will have to skip seventh grade!"

And just when I thought the world was going to spin right off its axis, Granny took me firmly by the arm, looked me in the eye, and said with tremendous authority, "Franny, I know exactly what to do." I didn't question her for a second. When someone throws you a lifeline in a hurricane, even a flimsy little thread of one, you take it.

Granny locked the door behind us, which was a little extreme for my taste, but whatever. This was her show. She charged into her closet and closed the door. We heard a lot of banging and what sounded like a glass breaking, and then Granny started talking to herself. Joey and I shot each other a look. I couldn't help but wonder if insanity was hereditary.

After a few moments, Granny emerged from the closet holding a sheet of paper and a beaker. She scurried into her bathroom, grabbed numerous bottles and jars out of the medicine cabinet, and then proceeded to pour things into the beaker like some kind of mad scientist.

"Can one of you get me some olive oil from the kitchen?" Granny called out.

Joey hustled off and returned in minutes with the olive oil. We watched as Granny added the oil and then furiously shook the beaker. A little smoke wafted out of it.

"Uh, smoke. Should we worry?" Joey whispered to me, a little freaked.

"I don't know. Please don't mention this to anyone in school," I begged.

"It's in the vault," Joey promised. And I knew I could trust her because Joey was as good as her word, sometimes even better.

"I'm so, so sorry about this," I said, deeply embarrassed.

"It's kinda cool. It would never happen at my house."

It would never happen at anyone's house, unless, of course, Granny was visiting.

Granny approached me with the beaker. "This is a tincture made of . . . well, there's no need to go into all that. Cures what ails you. Cures what doesn't ail you. I'm going to massage the tincture into your hair and it should neutralize things lickety-split. Let's head into the bathroom," she said. Desperate times call for desperate measures, so I followed Granny into the bathroom without question.

Granny took the beaker and poured the mixture over my head and massaged it into my scalp. It felt like someone had put salsa on my head, extra hot and spicy salsa. My scalp tingled and throbbed and then I saw a few sparks. Sparks?

"Is my hair on fire?" I yelled.

"Calm down, sweet pea, it's just a little alchemy."

"Alchemy? You mean magic?" I whispered so Joey wouldn't hear. Joey had already been privy to waaay too much weirdness in my house.

"I think that's overstating it. It's just outside help."

"Outside help? Granny, what are you talking about?"

"Outside the known universe," Granny said mysteriously. "Well, all righty, Aphrodite, the hair is returning to its natural state. Won't be long now. Joey, come have a look-see."

Joey appeared in the bathroom. "Oh, *mon dieu*, it's totally changing color. That's amazing," Joey exclaimed.

Granny held up a mirror for me. To my shock and relief, Joey was right. My hair was transforming before my eyes. There were a few rogue highlights here and there, but they actually looked good. I had no idea what the stuff was or how it worked, but really, who cared? I could lead a normal life again and that was all that mattered.

"Problem solved, Frans. Your *Grossmutter* rocks," Joey said, hugging Granny. "And now, this is where I get off. I've got a ton of stuff to take care of before school. I'll text you later."

After a series of kisses on both cheeks, Joey was off; relieved, I was sure, to be getting out of the asylum. I, however, was stuck in downtown Crazyville with Granny, who had suddenly become the only sane member of my family.

"You said magic, Granny. It's not really magic, is it? I mean, that's crazy . . ."

"Is it?" Granny asked.

"Just tell me what's in it. I promise, what happens in your bathroom stays in your bathroom."

Granny laughed. "Sorry, sweets. No can do."

"Why not?"

"Because you're not ready."

"Why not?"

"Because I said so," Granny said firmly. Oh no. *Because I said so.* There was no arguing with that. I'd been down that road many times with Mom and I knew it led right to a cul-de-sac.

"There may be a few side effects. Nothing dramatic, just a little tingling here and there. But it should all wear off in a day or so. This kind of recipe rarely has long-term effects . . ." Granny gave me a strange lopsided smile. She looked like she wanted to say more but her voice trailed off.

Granny was a mystery to me. Each time she visited, there was always some unexplained and bizarre force swirling around her. Like the time she brought a "spiritual presence" back from Africa and we found her out in the backyard in the middle of the night talking to herself—or rather, to "the spirit"—in an effort to convince it to return home. In the morning, the garden was torn apart. Granny insisted the spirit was angry, and though we all found her explanation ridiculous, we could never pin the ransacked garden on anything else. This was all easy to ignore when her visits were few and far between but slightly more troubling now that she was living with us. Middle school was not a time for strange behavior and unexplained events; it was a time to hunker down, shed any eccentricities, and fit in at all costs, so I'd have to keep Granny at a safe distance from school. Still, I made a mental note to rifle through her closet when she wasn't around to see what I could find.

"All right, whatever. Don't tell me. Anyway, I really appreciate it, Granny. You saved my life." And then I gave Granny a hug, which was not something I normally did. She held on tight. And for the second time in the span of an hour I felt my throat constrict and my eyes well up. This was getting embarrassing. I really needed to get a grip.

"Are you worried about seventh grade?" Granny asked me.

"No . . ." I said, choking up. Tears started streaming down my cheeks. And then I was crying, full throttle.

Granny took both my hands in hers. "Tell me, sweet pea."

"It's just . . . sixth grade was horrible since Joey and Kate can't be friends because peaks and beeks don't talk and I spend my day running between their two groups so there's barely time for lunch." I paused, breathed, and dived back in. "And then there's Elodie, who's scary mean but Joey hangs out with her anyway, and the rest of the peaks circle around her like planets because she's beautiful and has huge breasts." I took another breath and continued. "And I touched Alden Timkins's elbow at the pool this summer and thought maybe we had a chance but Joey said that Janet Scully has her eye on him, which I just can't believe is true—" One more big breath. "Sometimes I feel like I have no one because Joey has the peaks and Kate has the beeks but who do I have?" Granny handed me a tissue. I paused and blew my nose.

Granny opened her mouth to say something, but I wasn't done. "And don't even get me started on Mom and Dad. I mean, when are they going to come to their senses and stop acting like spoiled children—"

"Slow down, sweet cakes," Granny interrupted. "You are getting ahead of yourself here. Let's take a deep breath. In and out. In and out. Two counts in. Four counts out. Feel better?" Granny asked.

"Not really. I want to like middle school, not be trauma-tized by it. Is that too much to ask?"

"Listen, Frans, we all make it to the other side. And we're better for the experience. I know middle school can be trying at times. You just need to figure out a strategy for survival. For me, that meant being myself and listening to my gut. I still live that way, and look how I turned out."

I bit my tongue.

"How about you go to school tomorrow with a new at-titude? You need to believe in your heart that you have the power to change things. Because you do. We all do. Don't ac-cept the status quo. You deserve better. Promise me you'll do one thing to make a difference tomorrow."

"I'm not sure what that even means. That just sounds like something adults say when they don't know what else to say."

"Franny, you are a hoot and a half. I am so glad I'm finally getting to know you. Your spunk will serve you well."

"When? Because it's doing absolutely nothing for me at the moment," I said.

All of a sudden, I was feeling crazy tired. Granny must have sensed my total and utter exhaustion because without another word she walked me up to my room, helped me into bed, pulled the blankets over me, and kissed me good night. I guess I fell right to sleep because the next thing I knew my alarm clock was beeping up a storm.

Fix-It Formula*

¼ cup olive oil
2 tablespoons jojoba oil
1 tablespoon neem oil
3 tablespoons fresh lime juice
4 drops rosemary oil
Pinch of black pepper

1. Pour olive oil, jojoba oil, and neem oil into a small container. Cover and shake.
2. Add lime juice and rosemary oil. Cover and shake.
3. Sprinkle a bit of black pepper into mixture. Cover and shake.
4. Carefully drip the oil onto the scalp and massage thoroughly with fingertips, using circular motion. Focus on desired outcome as you massage, clearing your mind of all thoughts for 1 minute.
5. Leave on hair from 1 to 24 hours, depending on damage. The longer the formula is left on the hair, the more it conditions.
6. Follow with shampoo and conditioner.

* Add 7 drops of sandalwood oil to hands and massage scalp to blunt the effects of formula.

Chapter 2

Geeks, Smeeks, Beeks, Peaks, Govs, Juvies, Loners, and Me

"'Sup, F-ster?" Kate asked as I entered the kitchen the next morning. Kate might as well pay rent, she hangs at my house so much. She was standing on her ubiquitous Razor, occasionally flipping one end up and down.

Kate was listening intently as Granny explained the benefits of a monthly enema. Kate lives for people like Granny. Her family is so normal I don't even have to describe them (two kids, dog, white picket fence, lawyer father, stay-at-home mom), which is all richly ironic, considering what Kate's like. In a word: *extreme.*

"Your grans is riptizzle, dawg. She told me about the cleansing rituals of the Tibetan monks. I'm down with it. We should go with her sometime," Kate said.

"And you're, uh, riptizzle too, Katie, dear," Granny offered with a smile.

Kate inspected my hair. "Slammin' neon orange streaks. You own it, F." I guess the highlights were more noticeable than I'd thought.

Mom was nowhere to be seen, which I assumed meant she was still battling her writer's block under the covers.

"We need to bounce, F," Kate announced.

I had been delayed by seven outfit changes. But I had finally nailed the perfect first-day look: skinny jeans, silk slip dress, a blue beret, and pearls. Kate, as usual, had not. I stared at her, horrified, because we'd talked about this. In fact, I'd spent the better part of last week explaining the importance of blending in as opposed to Kate's irritating compulsion to practically wear a sandwich board that screams *I'm a freaking weirdo, look at me!*

Kate's outfit shouldn't have come as a surprise, since she's been wearing some variation of it for the past year, ever since she became obsessed with the new thrift store in town. Still, I had naively allowed myself to believe that for once Kate would take my advice, get a freaking clue, and not show up in what she refers to as her "Einstein meets skater gurl" uniform. It consists of a black, baggy man's suit with the legs cut off above the knees and the sleeves of the jacket cut off at the elbows, a black bowler hat, a rocker T-shirt, a paisley tie, bright purple tights, and storm trooper boots. To make matters worse, today her hair was in mini buns, ten of them. It looked like a bunch of White Castle burgers plastered to her skull. Taking it all in made my head hurt.

This wasn't rocket science. There are plenty of ways to distinguish yourself in middle school; clothing should not be one of them. Kate insisted on being outrageous in every possible way. She pushed everything that could be cool to its illogical limit where it became strange and bizarre. Sure, an old-school Razor scooter could be a perfectly acceptable mode of transport, unless of course it was painted lime green and carried on her back in a homemade sling all day. Wearing a man's suit and a necktie could be totally hip, if done right. Which, in Kate's case, it wasn't. The pants and sleeves had been lopped off at uneven angles; threads were dangling; the necktie was about six inches too long and in a neon paisley print. And properly using the latest slang could lend you a certain cachet in middle school, unless, like Kate, you let it get totally out of hand and become some kind of crazy parody of itself.

"Let's roll it out, Ms. Thang."

"Can't you just say 'Let's go,' like a normal person?" I asked her. Kate's slanguage, as I called it, mostly amused me, but this morning I was irritated by it. She's the drum major in middle school band, why can't she talk like one?

Kate stared at me for a beat and then said, mock serious, "Absolutely, Francine. But how tedious would that be?"

I laughed. Kate was a true original. I felt bad for snapping at her. Mostly, I get a big kick out of what makes Kate Kate. She collects birds' nests, Thelonious Monk albums, vintage high-top sneakers, and coins from Portugal, and she's so smart the school invented a separate English class for her, her own little Academy of Genius.

I met Kate in preschool a day before meeting Joey. Ever since then, she's stood by me, through thick and thin. I'm forever loyal to Kate for many reasons, but the fact that in third grade she bit Tabitha Barson's forearm while Tabitha had me locked in a chokehold has been etched on my memory forever. She's a true friend, just like Joey. And I was pretty sure I'd go to my grave trying to recapture the threesome we once were.

☺☺☺☺

"I'm totally crushing on James Singer," Kate confided as she scooted back and forth in front of me on the way to school.

"A gov?" I said, surprised. "You're really branching out." James Singer is in student government and, strictly speaking, not part of Kate's band-geek—beek—crowd. Actually, the govs are free agents. But crushing outside of your social circle is a dangerous game at Jefferson, punishable by taunting or the dreaded silent treatment.

Unlike everyone else at school, I'm not really in a group at all. I'm what they call a border crosser. It's a very rare position, assigned by the most popular kids in school (in my case, Joey). As part of the ruling class, Joey was able to spare me from the social wars of Jefferson Middle School, understanding I could never choose between Joey's group, the peaks, and Kate's pals, the beeks. There are only one or two border crossers per year. Max Clarick is the other seventh grade border crosser. His two best friends are Angus Braun (peak) and Patel Vashki (smeek). Max and I can travel from group to group with impunity, unlike most of the others, who must stay within the limits of their carefully defined social boundaries.

It's supposed to be a rare privilege, but it feels more like a booby prize. I'm forced to split my day between Joey and Kate and their respective buds. I walk to school with Kate and then I leave her to go hang with Joey until the bell rings. Free time, lunch, and yard are split between the two. And there are constant negotiations for vacations, summer camp, and birthdays. Between my parents' divorce and Kate and Joey, it's a miracle I can remember where I'm meant to be at any point in the day.

I know, I shouldn't complain. People all over the world have it a whole lot worse. But the thing is, I'm twelve. I live in suburban Fall River, New Jersey, not Gaza. Must my life be so difficult on a daily basis? Aren't I entitled to a more carefree existence, at least until I turn thirteen and the real problems begin? I spend so much time making sure everything is even-steven between Joey and Kate, I haven't made a new friend in years. Sometimes I think I'd rather be a geek or a juvie, just so I'd have someplace I could call my own.

"I saw James yesterday, with his mom at Walmart," Kate said. "I know he saw me, dawg. He did that crunk thing guys do when they don't want you to know they're looking. He looked *everywhere* but at me. He was totally macking on me," Kate insisted. "I'm so not feeling the beek dating sitch. I need to be with a homey who rules."

"Well, he rules. Literally. He's vice president," I said, trying to sound upbeat. But I felt a lump in the pit of my stomach.

"Let him rule all over me," Kate said. And then we both burst out laughing.

We turned the corner and there was Jefferson Middle School in all her glory, looming large like some kind of haunted house on the hill. Like most public schools in New Jersey, Jefferson is a huge brick building that screams *mental institution* or *white-collar prison,* not *nurturing center of learning,* as it should. As we approached the building I saw Joey standing at the top of the stairs.

Intimidating and infuriating all at once, the stairs were a microcosm of Jefferson society. Walking up those stairs was like walking the plank. They're long and wide, leading right up to the front door, with each stair representing a rung on the social ladder. When we studied the caste system in India, I thought, *Jefferson could give that place a run for its money.* Sure, they've got the lepers, the garbage pickers, the working poor, and the ruling class, but I bet a washerwoman has a better shot at becoming prime minister than a beek has at becoming a pom. As I took in all the various groups, quickly settled into their exact spots from last year, I knew that nothing was ever going to change. It simply wasn't in our adolescent nature.

"Later. Peace out," Kate said to me as she joined her beek posse at the bottom of the stairs. Owen and Jane, Kate's other best friends, began a wildly complicated secret handshake with her as I walked away. They looked pretty crazy, but just try to tell Kate that.

With the beeks behind me, I caught sight of the geeks (self-explanatory), who lurked about on the sidewalk because they're not even allowed on the stairs. Clinging together, they somehow found meaning in their shared misery. As I strolled past them, prepared to ignore them like I usually do, my head suddenly started to tingle, just as it had when Granny poured the mixture on me the night before. And then, for some inexplicable reason, I found myself waving to Johnson Otis, who has lived next door to me since we were nine. He laughed nervously, turned bright red, and started maniacally scratching his arm. Even though he's my neighbor, we haven't interacted in years, but suddenly it just seemed rude to snub him like I usually did.

Sitting a few feet from Johnson was Marsha Whalley, the pariah of Jefferson. She's too smart, too strange, and too everything to really fit in anywhere, so she sat alone, slumped underneath a decrepit oak tree, looking around nervously as though hiding from someone. While I've always felt bad about Marsha's solitary confinement, I simply accept it as part of the social landscape. Though in my darkest hours, I have to admit, I feel a strange sort of simpatico with her. We are both rudderless, in our own way.

"Hey, Marsha," I called out. Did I just say that? Or was it my socially suicidal twin? While I may have privately identified with Marsha in my weakest moments, it certainly wasn't something I wanted to share. I really couldn't tell what had come over me. My brain seemed to have a mind of its own. And it was really starting to get on my nerves. Meanwhile, the tingling on my scalp was turning into more of a prickly-heat feeling.

When Marsha heard her name, her whole body convulsed. She dropped her head and sort of collapsed into herself, like a turtle. Jeez, she's really got it bad.

"Hey, Mallory, how was science camp?" I found myself asking a lanky, dark-haired girl with braces whom I'd never spoken a word to in my entire life. Flip me out. What was going on? Why was I talking to these people?

"Awesome. We learned quantum theory," Mallory reported excitedly. Mallory is a smeek (super smart geeks, like science and math nerds), and they're on the landing across from the beeks.

Diagonally and up to the left was a clump of juvies (juvenile delinquents and general rule breakers) and the loners (not really a group at all, more a gang of isolated misfits). As I made my way up the stairs, I couldn't stop myself from interacting with people. Suddenly, I had become Little Miss Chatterbox. I tried to zip it, but my mouth was having none of it.

"Hi, Sophie. Is your brother still teaching guitar? I'm thinking of taking lessons," I said. After seeing Sheryl Crow in concert last year with Joey, it was true, I had flirted with the idea of starting my own rock band, but that certainly wasn't something I wanted to publicize. Maybe this year wasn't going to be exactly the same as last year. Maybe it was going to be worse, if I couldn't shut my big trap.

Sophie is a big bruiser of a girl with the nastiest mouth in school. She spent all of last year in detention. Normally, I would have absolutely nothing to do with her.

"Who friggin' knows what the frick he's up to. I don't give a crap, call him," Sophie offered. Whoa! That was an impressive mouthful, even for Sophie.

I know my limits as a border crosser. Beyond the peaks and beeks, greetings were fine, but conversation was not, and it potentially endangered my precious status. So what was up? The tingling had spread to my neck and I was having this weird out-of-body experience, like I was watching myself from above, unable to control my actions. Which led me to the only logical conclusion: Granny! This whole thing reeked of Granny. Suddenly I was flooded with images: the weird play dough Granny brought back from the Amazon that could miraculously heal cuts and bruises; the strange plant Granny picked up in Ghana that ended up eating my goldfish; the lucky bandanna she'd given me two years ago before my big race that enabled me to beat all school records in the fifty-yard dash. I was sure that the mystery liquid she had poured on my head was somehow linked to my strange behavior. Granny had quite a bit of explaining to do. Unfortunately, I had to get through the next seven hours of school before I could get any answers, and at the moment, that seemed like an eternity.

I saw Joey waving excitedly to me from the tippy top of the stairs. I took the steps two at a time, hoping that if I went fast enough my legs would outpace my mouth. The peaks reside at the top of the stairs, lording it over everyone and literally blocking the entrance to the building. *Peaks* is a general term encompassing the coolest and most popular kids in school, from poms to jocks. And Joey, as head pom, is at the center of it all. Don't get the wrong idea: poms don't just jump around in little skirts, cheering. They perform feats of near-impossible daring involving aerial flips and human pyramids, and they get their fair share of injuries. Despite all of Joey's glaring perfection, she manages to pull it off without making you hate her. Which sometimes kind of makes you hate her.

Kate, on the other hand, had chosen to play the drum during the first week of sixth grade, and she'd embraced band-geekdom with alarming enthusiasm, eventually becoming their leader and thus cementing her social irrelevance. She did manage to make her lasting mark on the whole school when she demanded the cafeteria accommodate vegans. Naturally, the cafeteria refused, and so Kate marched through the halls with a poster-size picture of a bloody slaughtered cow. Students were repulsed, the administration caved, and now nuts, seeds, and tofu are permanently on offer at the salad bar. But Kate's reputation took a huge hit. Luckily, the beeks rallied around her, celebrating her eccentricities, which only encouraged Kate to kick things up a notch. It was right after the cafeteria incident that Kate started to cultivate the "Einstein meets skater gurl" thing that would eventually become her signature look.

While a secret part of me would have loved to bail on the beeks so I could immerse myself in the champagne-and-caviar world of extreme popularity, I love Kate like a sister and could not imagine life without her. I can't quit Kate. And I can't quit Joey, so I'm stuck in this horror show I call border crossing.

"Hey, Frans, your hair turned out great. It actually looks better than ever," Joey said as I approached. "And, listen, word up: *vergessen*." Joey arrived each day armed with a new Western European vocabulary word. Her theory was that she would learn faster if we all learned along with her. "It means 'to forget' in German. Use it or lose it," Joey chirped, kissing me on both cheeks, as is her Continental way.

"I'll try, but I can't make any promises."

"Guess what! Elodie's dad thinks he can get us amazing seats for Justin Timberlake at the Meadowlands in October," Joey said excitedly.

"No way? That's awesome." If only Elodie Blain didn't have to go. But alas, all silver linings have their clouds. One of the perks of peakdom is the access, and Elodie is a key part of that access. Her father is some kind of big shot in Manhattan and can pretty much get tickets to anything. Over the last two years, Elodie has shot up like a rocket into the social stratosphere, acquiring more and more power, thanks to her annoying babeliciousness and her father's connections.

Elodie Blain is awful, simply awful. But she is an indisputable babe, with her long blond hair, perfect figure, fab wardrobe, and B-cup breasts. And babe trumps awful any day in middle school. Especially when that babe can hook you up.

Elodie rules the school with the glee of a tyrant. She is loud, bossy, and mean; she has a gold-and-Swarovski-crystal-plated cell phone, which she wears like a diamond engagement ring; she teases Jason Billings mercilessly because his left arm is shorter than his right; she refers to herself as La Principessa, which she says while snapping her fingers in front of her mean little face. She went to Italy last summer and came back with this new nickname, claiming her mother has Italian royal blood in her. And she flunked geometry last year but her dad called the principal and Elodie's grade miraculously morphed into a B minus. The idea of making nice with Elodie just to get my hands on a ticket felt really wrong. And yet I did it, time and time again. Because . . . well, because it's Justin Timberlake, and I'm twelve.

Joey and Elodie have been friends since before they were born. Their mothers went to college together and then they got pregnant within three weeks of each other. Joey remains the only person at school who can rein Elodie in, because even though Elodie is the self-proclaimed leader of the pack, Joey is the people's choice, and crossing her would be certain death even for Elodie. When Joey talks, everyone listens.

"Big news," Elodie yelled out in her booming voice to all the peaks, interrupting everyone. "It's official. The govs will be part of the peaks this year. We're opening things up. But not too much. So we're starting and stopping with the govs. We think they'll be an awesome addition to our crew." A bunch of peaks high-fived at the news.

And just like that, my day got worse. School hadn't even started yet and things were rapidly going downhill. Now Kate had absolutely no chance with James Singer.

Joey turned to me, immediately sensing something was wrong. "What's up? I thought you'd be happy. We're trying to be more inclusive."

"Kate has a huge crush on James Singer," I said.

"Bummer. I don't see beeks getting folded in anytime soon." Joey sounded sympathetic, but I knew her hands were tied. Luckily, the bell rang.

Elodie had designated herself the reigning queen of morning entry. You simply did not enter the school until she allowed it. Once when Kate needed to get to school early for a science project, she tried to sneak in before Elodie arrived, but one of Elodie's lieutenants appeared out of nowhere, at 7:00 a.m., and latched on to Kate's foot with a death grip until Kate coughed up a ten-dollar early-entry fee.

"Joey, how about doing the honors?" Elodie turned to Joey.

"*Bien sûr,*" Joey replied as she graciously opened the front doors while at the same time waving to the crowds below. "Let the games begin," Joey yelled. And with that, peaks filed into the building, me included, followed by govs, then juvies, then beeks, and so on and so forth. I know the metaphor of kids as sheep has been way overused, but at that moment it seemed so apt I wanted to scream. We might as well have been bleating as we mindlessly moved in a pack, following the one ahead of us, never veering from the path, never questioning the journey.

As I entered the school, I caught sight of my crush, Alden Timkins, standing about an inch too close to Janet Scully. What on earth was Alden thinking? Janet is a pom of the worst sort, incapable of an original thought. Once I witnessed her try to come up with something vaguely intelligent to say in Mr. Hardwick's English class. Her little face quivered with fear; she was overwhelmed by the task. Eventually she just sat down and started giggling, worn out from the effort.

Crazy as it may seem, I'd truly thought Alden and I had a chance this year. I mean, we connected this summer, literally, at the Fall River pool one afternoon: Alden's elbow brushed my forehead underwater. It was electrifying. I was sure Alden felt the charge as well. And yet there he was, leaning into Janet, with a stupid smile pasted on his face and his brown curls falling over his green eyes. What about us, Alden? What about the delicate flower of our love that blossomed this summer? Did that not mean anything to you?

Heartless cad, I thought. Or at least I thought I thought it. Alden and Janet stopped talking and stared at me, perplexed. Wait a minute. Did I just say that out loud? No. Flipping. Way. My head was tingling again, and my mouth wasn't filtering things. Man, was I annoyed at Granny. I smiled at Alden, mortified, then turned and scurried around the corner, running smack into Elodie.

"Walk much?" Elodie snapped.

Oh no. Oh no. Oh no. I could not deal. Not now.

"Nice much?" I snapped back. I wasn't just flirting with disaster; I was heading down the aisle with it. Stuff just came flying out, like heat-seeking missiles. I reached with both hands to scratch my scalp. Elodie tilted her head and stared at me, sizing me up.

"Got lice?" Elodie snickered.

"Of course not!" Immediately, I took my hands out of my hair.

"Watch your step, Franny Flanders. La Principessa is watching," Elodie warned.

Before I could respond, Joey whisked me away.

"What was up with that? You know how cranky Elodie gets on the first day of school," Joey said.

"What do you mean 'on the first day of school'? She's always cranky. I hate her."

"Just ignore her." Joey stared at me like I'd lost my mind. "What has gotten into you?"

"Nothing, I'm just, I don't know," I said, and honestly, I really didn't know. Something from Granny's vast inventory of the strange and inexplicable had taken hold of me, but oddly, it was something else that shook me—emotions buried long ago seemed to be rising up from some forgotten corner of my heart. I could detect the rumblings of a shift deep inside me, somehow begun by Granny's potion. The stupid stairs, where everyone congregated, never once stepping outside the carefully defined areas, felt like a demilitarized zone. How had we come to live this way? How had we let Elodie accumulate so much power? I shook my head to free myself of these thoughts. Nothing good could come of this kind of thinking. Seventh grade was hard enough without trying to overthrow the whole darn system. I had no interest in having a mind of my own. I just wanted to bleat along with the rest of them.

Chapter 3

Things Go From Bad to Worse with Sloppy Joes and *Beowulf*

I HEADED TO ENGLISH CLASS and actually felt a spark of happiness. I love to write; I love to read. What could possibly go wrong with English? Ms. Posey. That's what.

"We will begin the semester by reading *Beowulf*," Ms. Posey announced. "We will read it as it was meant to be read, in its original text. I want a summary of the first five chapters, written in Old English, on my desk by tomorrow morning." She was an evil tormentor of children.

Ugh. I had picked up the book last year hoping for extra credit. But I couldn't crack it. If that was Old English, I wanted no part of it. I was all about new English.

"Not *Beowulf*," I said out loud. Are. You. Flipping. Kidding. Me? It. Was. Happening. Again. When would the madness end? It felt like tiny little needles poking into my scalp. There seemed to be no rhyme or reason to its will.

"Franny Flanders, do you have something you'd like to add?"

"What happened to reading fun books like *Sounder* and

Gulliver's Travels? *Beowulf* is a waste of time." I jammed my fist into my mouth, hoping for a miracle.

"Congratulations, Franny. It's the first day of school and you've already earned yourself one strike. One more and I'll give you an additional paper to write this semester. Two more and I'll lower your grade." Ms. Posey stared stonily at me in a sort of otherworldly manner. Her eyes never blinked. It gave me the creeps.

"Yessh, Msshs. Posshhey," I said, fist still in mouth. Finally the bell rang and I made my way to Spanish, hoping things would go a little smoother.

"Mesero, hay una mosca en mi sopa," we all repeated after Señorita Canana, our Spanish teacher. We must have said the phrase five times. It meant "Waiter, there's a fly in my soup."

"If there was a fly in my soup," I blurted out, "I wouldn't hang around the restaurant and chat up the waiter. I'd get myself to a better establishment." People sitting nearby giggled. No way. No way. My head was tingling. It was happening again.

Señorita Canana stared at me. "If you have something to say, Franny, try raising your hand." And then . . . saved by the bell. I raced out of class and made my way to lunch, expecting the worst. And let's just say, I wasn't disappointed.

The deal was, I ate my entrée with Joey and the peaks and my dessert with Kate and the beeks. I grabbed some food and rushed over to sit with Joey. Elodie had a few sixth grade geeks bussing the table when I arrived. I tried not to make eye contact with Elodie. My head was still tingly and I couldn't trust myself to not say anything risky.

"You're eating the sloppy joe?" Elodie said, aghast. Peaks turned to stare at my plate, and as they did, I noticed that everyone else had chosen the mac and cheese.

"It was the only thing left," I muttered, staring at the floor. What did it matter? All the cafeteria food tasted the same. From tacos to mashed potatoes, it all had the bland, institutional flavor of day-old oatmeal. I could never understand why all peaks must choose the same entrée.

"Geek." Elodie pointed at a scared-looking sixth-grader. "Go into the kitchen and get Franny some mac and cheese." Oddly, Elodie didn't seem to be holding a grudge against me, but I think it was only because she got such a charge out of ordering a sixth-grader around.

I needed to be exceedingly careful around Elodie. With a few swift blows, she could ruin my life. Last year, Sandy Smithson dated Elodie's ex-boyfriend before the specified six-month waiting period (a ridiculous rule instituted by Elodie, of course) was over, and within three days Elodie had kicked Sandy off pom and banished her to the girls' bathroom for lunch. Within two weeks, Sandy was so thoroughly shunned by everyone at school that Sandy's parents yanked her out of Jefferson and sent her to a boarding school in Montana, fearing for her personal safety. Joey got a postcard from Sandy that said she spent most of her time brushing the resident buffalo's fur and making snowshoes.

"I texted you about the mac and cheese," Joey said.

"I forgot my phone," I mumbled, staring longingly at Joey's roll.

"Start with this." Joey handed me her roll. It was dry as chalk and lodged in my throat. I nearly gagged on it. Marta Stevenson must be the worst middle-school chef in the history of the world. The rumor was she'd worked in a prison before coming to Jefferson. Somewhere, convicts rejoiced while we suffered.

"I'm sure the mac and cheese will be out any minute," Joey offered. I didn't have many minutes left. Time was ticking away. Lunch was thirty minutes; I was already ten minutes late; and I needed to get to Kate's table in five.

"Have you managed to use the word of the day yet?" Joey asked.

"Uh, no. I've been kind of busy," I said.

"She *vergessen*," Alexi Butterworth cut in. Alexi is captain of the boys' soccer team. He is a total hottie, with his sandy brown hair and impossibly blue eyes, and he knows it. He and Joey are an item, of sorts. Joey isn't interested in being a full-time girlfriend. She wants more of a part-time gig. Alexi is just happy to have any association with Joey, Inc. He has been in love with her since sixth grade. Part-time, full-time, internship—whatever kind of time Joey is willing to put in, Alexi can accommodate her.

"She *vergessen*," Zach Haus repeated. "Dude, you the man." Zach high-fived Alexi.

"Brilliant, people. Truly inspiring use of language," I snapped. Zach, Alexi, and Joey all stared at me.

"Harsh, Franny," Alexi said.

"Yeah, dude." Zach seconded the emotion, as that was his role in life.

"Sorry, I've had a bad morning. Don't take it personally," I offered.

Zach Haus is also a soccer player but not nearly as fine as Alexi. He has a spit-showering lisp and an annoying habit of using *dude* in every sentence. Inexplicably, Alexi has taken him under his wing. Zach mostly stands in Alexi's shadow, hoping for leftovers.

"Guys, first party of the year's at my place. Friday night," Joey announced to the table. There were high-fives, low-fives, and fist-bumps all around.

Zach Haus turned to me. "Franny, we've decided to fine any uninvited guests at our parties this year. We think we could make some serious bank off the whole thing and use the money for a crazy blowout at the end of the year. So keep up the good work."

Zach was referring to my unsuccessful attempts to sneak Kate into a peak party last year due to her having had yet another crush outside beekdom. I turned to Joey and must have looked like I was about to lose it because she said to me, "I will *auto parar* things, *chérie*."

I think she said she would stop the car. It made no sense but it didn't matter, because when Joey talked people listened.

Even if they didn't entirely understand what she was saying.

"*Vergessen* that plan," Joey said to Zach. "It's lame and childish. Nobody's getting fined." And then Joey turned to me. "Try not to rock the *bateau* so much, Frans."

Rock the boat? I never rocked the boat. I was all about keeping the boat steady.

"I had a *fantastico* idea for Fall Fling." Joey squeezed Alexi's hand as she spoke. "I'm going with Alexi. And I was thinking it might be fun if you went with Zach, and then we could double-date."

"Uh, yeah. Can I get back to you on that?" There was very little I wouldn't do for Joey. But go to the Fall Fling with Zack Haus? No, thanks. I'd rather bludgeon myself. Fall Fling was *the* event of seventh grade. I was hoping against hope that Alden would ask me. But with Janet Scully in the picture, I wasn't so sure. Still, I'd rather go alone than with Zach. I had to figure out a way to let Joey down gently. Luckily, I was saved, for the moment, by the mac and cheese. The sweet little sixth-grader scurried over with my lunch. I thanked her profusely, scarfed it down, said my goodbyes, and zipped over to Kate's part of town.

When I got there, Owen was in the middle of a rousing appeal to take over the peaks' section of the cafeteria. The peaks had controlled prime cafeteria real estate since middle school began. They were closest to the food. It was time for a change, Owen insisted. He was calling it Operation Shove 'Em Out.

All this strife makes for great drama, I'm sure, and maybe one day I will channel it into some kind of artistic expression and end up living in a huge loft in Tribeca with my model boyfriend and my paintings will be exhibited at the chicest galleries in New York and sell for millions of dollars. But for now it was just a bigtime bummer. Even though my dream is to become a real artist when I grow up, I'd rather suffer from a lack of material than endure all these petty school politics.

Kate leaned into me and whispered, "Saw my boy in French today. He said *à bientôt* to me. Yo, that's deep, right?" I didn't have the heart to tell Kate that her chances of dating James Singer at this point were about as good as my chances of winning *American Idol*. (I'm tone-deaf.)

Mom always says what doesn't kill you makes you stronger. But what if it kills you? No one mentions that part. All the people who died trying . . .

❦❦❦❦

After lunch ended, I dragged myself out to yard, where I found Joey kicking around a soccer ball with a few of the jocks and govs. Kate was huddled in a corner with the other beeks, discussing the latest in drum technology, no doubt. I stopped at the water fountain, which is when I caught sight of Marsha Whalley flattened like a pancake against the wall as a bunch of jocks smashed into her while playing catch with a Nerf ball. Against the blackened wall, her frizzy hair and pale skin looked like a stain. Poor Marsha Whalley. She really got the short end of the stick at Jefferson. She ate lunch alone, her nose in a book, and walked the halls with her head down, never making eye contact. I felt kind of lame for whining about Joey and Kate when Marsha was dangling precariously over the social cliff.

Elodie appeared, laughing a little too loud, and lurched menacingly toward Marsha. Elodie, like an animal of prey, could sniff out weakness from miles away. I really didn't want to get involved. I had enough on my plate. But my head and neck were pulsating as I took in the scene and I was compelled to do something, against my will and better judgment. With an obvious death wish, my body made its way over.

"Hey, Marsha, how was your summer?" Elodie purred, all fakey sweet.

Marsha now had two jocks within inches of her; they threw the Nerf ball back and forth, skimming her head with it. She was trapped. Elodie moved in closer. Marsha's eyes bulged. She didn't respond. She just stared at Elodie, panicked.

"Marsha, did you hear me?" Elodie screeched. "La Principessa is talking to you."

Marsha knew she had to answer Elodie or the torture would go on forever. "My summer was fine," she mumbled as the jocks bounced the ball off her head. A little crowd of people had gathered around to stare, as if they were watching a reality show on TV.

"So, Marsha, did you have any hot dates this summer?" Elodie said mockingly.

I had seen Elodie in action thousands of times, and I'd always turned away. It was like looking at a total eclipse of the sun; I didn't want to burn my retinas. But that day I couldn't look away. I stood on the sidelines watching. My whole body was buzzing. I begged myself to leave. Walk. Away. But my body was having none of it. I looked at Marsha; her face was pale white, and her hands clawed her books. I could see how frightened and humiliated she was.

"Uh, why don't you just leave her alone, Elodie?" I said, barely audible.

Marsha looked at me as if I were Jesus and had just walked up and laid a healing hand on her. I got a charge out of it, to be honest. It was kind of heady stuff.

"Since when do you care about Marsha Whalley, Franny?"

"Since now," I squeaked out.

Elodie took a giant step toward me. She was standing two inches away from my face. I could feel her breath on me as she bored into me with her electric blue eyes. Man, she was fierce. Why would anyone want to mess with her? And yet here I was, messing. Marsha took the opportunity to slip away, and then it was just Elodie and me.

All over the yard, people stopped what they were doing and turned to watch me and Elodie, who continued to bear down on me. Now that Marsha was no longer under direct threat, I was really at a loss for what to do. Luckily, Joey rushed over.

"Hey, Elodie," Joey said, shooting me a look as she nudged me aside to talk to Elodie. "I'm wondering if you could come with me to the mall after school. I'm trying to decide between boyfriend, skinny, or boot-cut." Elodie fancied herself a blossoming stylist.

"I'm not feeling the boyfriend jeans at all," Elodie responded. As Elodie launched into her denim theory, I snuck away. Joey had saved my butt. Again. I'd have to thank her later. For now, I was just relieved to make it out alive. I sat down on the ground, closed my eyes, and breathed in and out calmly, like Granny had taught me. I could feel my heart rate slowing down.

When I opened my eyes. I caught sight of Marsha sitting alone by the Dumpster near the parking lot. The all-too-familiar tingling flickered at the base of my neck, and soon I was up and heading toward her like some kind of zombie, ignoring both Kate and Joey, who were furiously waving me away from Marsha as they stood on opposite ends of the yard.

I plunked down next to Marsha, and people from every part of the yard tuned in to watch. Kate and Joey stared at me wide-eyed. Elodie had her back turned at the moment and was jabbering into her cell phone, but I knew it was only a matter of time before she caught sight of me. You only live once, I thought, even if it all comes to a screeching halt at twelve.

"Hey, Marsha," I said. "What're you reading?"

Marsha stared at me, thoroughly confused. For the third

time that day, there I was, at her side. It must have seemed like I was stalking her.

"I'm reading *The Phantom Tollbooth*," she said cautiously. "I needed something to rinse the bad taste of *Beowulf* from my mouth."

I chuckled. Marsha had made a little joke.

"You can go now, Franny. You asked a question. I responded. Communication was successful. You've done your good service."

It turned out Marsha not only had a bit of a 'tude, she also had a lot on her quirky mind. I didn't leave. I stayed and hung with Marsha through the rest of yard while Joey and Kate looked on, annoyed. I found out that Marsha also thought Señorita Canana was a cretin, that vegetarian lasagna with eggplant rocked her world, and that Zac Efron was a little too pretty to be a real heartthrob. We had a perfectly nice conversation, and when I got up to leave, I did not have lice or Ebola, and I didn't feel one iota less cool than I had before I sat down. In fact, I felt pretty good.

Kate nearly tackled me as I headed back into the building. "What do you think you're doing, Franny?" she said. "You've got to swear to me you won't do anything stupid like that again. Marsha Whalley is dead to you. Do you hear me? Dead!" Kate was seriously freaking out. So much so that she wasn't even using slanguage. I knew she was only saying this out of love, but it irked me. For the first time in middle school, I had dared to color outside the lines. Even though powers beyond my control had forced my hand, it still felt great to challenge the status quo.

"She's kinda cool," I shot back, defiant. "We should all hang out sometime." When I said this last bit I knew I was really pushing it, but I didn't care.

Kate looked at me, deadly serious. "You've got first-day jitters; it happens to the best of us. But you really need to get a grip before you go too far, Francine. If you're not careful, this could be your demise. No more border crossing. And then what do we do? How will we work things out?" I had shaken Kate to the core. But I knew she had a point.

When I got to gym class, Joey was waiting for me in the locker room, looking traumatized. She pulled me into a bathroom stall as soon as she saw me. "*Vergessen* Marsha Whalley," Joey warned.

"Wow, that's like the fifth time I've heard you use the word of the day. Impressive," I said, hoping to change the subject.

"Listen, Franny, I think everyone is willing to give you a pass on this one. People make mistakes. Just don't do it again. Marsha Whalley is a black hole, quicksand. If you get too close, you'll be sucked in. It's certain death. Stay. Away. At some point, my hands will be tied and I will no longer be able to help you."

Luckily, we didn't have any more time to talk since Ms. Makepeace, our ancient gym teacher, hobbled into the room. The rich irony of a gym teacher who could barely walk was just so Jefferson. Despite her frail appearance, though, Ms.

Makepeace was one tough cookie. She didn't even accept a doctor's note as an excuse for missing gym. Only death was good enough for Ms. Makepeace.

"All right, people, let's haul butt," Ms. Makepeace shouted as she shuffled us out of the locker room and into a mean game of dodge ball.

Elodie and Owen were team captains. It was an intense fight for players. Owen had first pick and got Alexi Butterworth, the best dodge ball player in school, which threw Elodie into a scary state. I got picked second to last, and not by Elodie, no doubt because of the Marsha Whalley incident. I knew Elodie wanted to slam me, and I had to muster every resource I had to defend myself.

The game was vicious. Elodie hurled the ball at Owen's head, nearly decapitating him. I stayed close to the bleachers, trying to keep my distance from the ball. Before long, there was a sprained ankle, a dislocated thumb, and a black eye. Elodie had whipped the ball at me several times with a force that defied gravity. While I managed to escape unharmed, I was trembling as I headed back to the locker room, got dressed, and dragged myself to homeroom, where I waited for the strangest day of my life to end.

Chapter 4

Outside the Known Universe

I STORMED INTO THE HOUSE after school, on a bullet to find Granny. She wasn't downstairs in her lair, so I went room to room.

I finally found her perched on the side of Mom's bed. Mom was still in bed. I guessed she'd been there all day. It had been more than twenty-four hours; that couldn't be good. Granny was sitting next to Mom, holding her hand. I peeked into the room to check out the situation. Neither of them noticed me, so I stood quietly outside and eavesdropped.

"The new book is due next week and I haven't even started it yet." Mom's voice cracked, and then she burst into tears. *Please. No. Make it stop.* Mom seriously needed to pull her junk together. Mom writes kids' books and normally she can bang them out. She had obviously come down with a bad case of writer's block, something that hadn't happened in years. Still, that was no excuse. It was one thing for me to burst into tears. But Mom crying? This was the last thing I needed after the day I'd had.

Granny reached down and picked up a plate from the

floor; it held something that looked like coffeecake. "Eat up, Anna. It's banana bread. I think a little comfort food will help with your writer's block," Granny insisted as she fed Mom.

"It's delicious. Tastes like lavender." Mom sounded groggy. She finished the bread and then slid back under the covers.

"Go to sleep, Anna. I'll take care of things," Granny promised.

"All right. Night-night." And with that, Mom was out.

"Franny? I know you're out there," Granny said as she stood up and waltzed over to where I was standing just outside Mom's room. "Are you spying on me?"

"Maybe," I said, hedging. "What are you feeding Mom? Are you trying to brainwash her with carbs or something? Isn't that how the Hare Krishnas do it?"

Granny laughed. "The Hare Krishnas are actually a lovely group of people. They're into whole grains, not necessarily carbs. Anyway, don't you worry, sweet pea, it's just a little banana bread to help her get over the hump." Granny headed downstairs and I followed.

"Are you helping Mom like you helped me?" I said.

"What are you talking about, Franny?" Granny asked.

"We need to talk."

"Okey-dokey. Let's talk," Granny said, sitting down at the kitchen table as the twins rummaged for snacks.

"Not here. In private," I insisted.

"Sounds very mysterious. I love it. Let me just set up the twins, and you and I will chitchat."

Granny put out food and games for the twins and then we headed to her room.

"What's up?" Granny said as she plopped onto her bed. She patted the spot next to her but I stayed standing. My body was rigid with tension. I couldn't even think of reclining at a time like this.

"What did you do to me last night?" I asked. I was ready to explode at this point.

"It was just a little alternative therapy, no biggie."

"Actually, it *was* a biggie. A very *big* biggie. You could even call it ginormous. I really don't think I'm exaggerating when I say you may have ruined my entire life with your little tincture."

"Honestly, Franny. Aren't you being a tad dramatic?"

"Don't play all innocent with me. You mentioned magic, outside the known universe, and all that other stuff yesterday. What were you talking about?" I demanded.

"I really can't go into it. All I did was return your hair to its natural state, with a few fabulous highlights as a bonus. You're welcome, by the way."

"I wasn't thanking you. There is nothing natural or fabulous about my current state," I said, finally losing it. "I've been acting crazy all day. I managed to go face to face with Elodie Blain *and* Marsha Whalley, which means that whatever social standing I have, whatever small foothold on happiness and coolness, will soon be gone. And you and your hair tincture are somehow to blame. Because there is no other logical explanation for my bizarre behavior and the pine needles prickling my scalp all day."

Granny stared at me. "Hmmm. This is all a bit unexpected."

A bit unexpected? That was not what I wanted to hear. It was hardly reassuring.

"Okay, tell me precisely what happened," Granny urged.

"Precisely what happened is I've been telling people exactly what's on my mind, which is a terrible idea in middle school. The key to survival is never to mean what you say, and now suddenly I say everything I mean."

"Well, maybe that's not so bad. It's good to have conviction."

"Not in middle school!"

"I'm going to have to get back to you on this, Franny."

"Get back to me? I don't think so. I need to know exactly what is going on. Right now. What did you put on my head? And what does it have to do with what's in your closet?"

"Trust me, you can't handle the truth."

"Bring it." And then I walked over to the closet. I threw open the door with maybe a bit more force than necessary, as the door flew back and the knob went right into the wall, denting the plaster. Oops, my bad.

Granny rushed over and slammed the door shut again. "I'm going to have to stand firm, Franny. This is not for kids. The tincture came from a box I brought back from Bhutan. A monk passed it along to me. I'm still working out some of the kinks. And that's about all I can say for now."

A box? A monk? This was so Granny. "Maybe you should have worked out the kinks before using it on me."

"Maybe," Granny offered, which only further frustrated me.

"Did you get the bread for Mom out of the box as well?"

"Yes," Granny said, refusing to elaborate.

"I can't believe you took the bread out of some old box. How safe is that? I mean, how long has the bread been sitting in there? Mom could die from botulism or hepatitis."

Granny put her arms around me and walked me out of her room and up the stairs. "Frans, I baked the bread. I don't actually want to kill your mother, I have to assume you know that. And I didn't want to make your first day of school any harder than it already was. As for the box in my closet, it just contains instructions for treating some common ailments, universal truths from Lama Tensing Pasha. That's the monk's name. Calm down, sweet pea. It's going to be okay. I've got it under control."

Why can't my grandmother make scrapbooks and play bridge like Kate's grandmother?

"I've already said too much," Granny said. "I suggest you try a little more of that deep breathing, sweetie. Very healing stuff. And then you should probably get started on your homework." And with that, Granny walked me into my room and left me there.

❀❀❀❀

I spent the next two hours immersed in homework, and then Dad called to check in about the first day of school. I wasn't in the mood to get into it so I lied and told him everything was fine. We had a perfectly nice chat, except that Dad casually mentioned his new friend Naomi at least five or six times during the conversation. Lately I'd been hearing a little too much about this Naomi person. A horrible thought suddenly occurred to me: Had Dad gone out and gotten himself a girlfriend? For about the hundredth time that day, I felt my stress levels rising.

How could Mom and Dad get back together if there was a girlfriend in the picture? I know, I sound wildly naive for believing my parents will get back together. But it happened with Maya Lifton's parents, and it was going to happen with mine. It had to. Because the alternative was incomprehensible.

I had always thought we were the perfect family. A well-oiled machine. Humming along. And then one day we conked out. With little warning, everything broke. Or at least that's what it felt like. I guess I ignored some of the signs along the way. Indicators that things might not be running as smoothly as I thought, that we might need a little bit of maintenance. The late-night fights. The silent treatment that followed. The dirty looks Mom and Dad gave each other at dinner some nights. But why dwell on that? Everything was working well enough. Until Dad moved out. At which point we might as well have put up a big Out of Order sign and closed up shop, because nothing would ever work properly again. Even though we see Dad a lot, I still have a huge raw hole in my heart. It physically hurts sometimes, and there's nothing I can do to stop it except wait for Mom and Dad to come to their senses and get back together.

I really needed to talk to Mom, writer's block or not. I poked my head into her bedroom only to discover her bed was empty and neatly made.

"Where's Mom?" I asked Granny, whom I found in the kitchen playing solitaire.

"Working."

"No way. No way."

"Way," Granny replied. "I'm a lot wiser than I look."

"Perhaps," I said, withholding judgment.

Just then, Mom sauntered into the kitchen singing. Yes, singing. "Umbrella" by Rihanna, no less. She looked transformed. Calm, peaceful, and happy.

"Just knocked off three chapters. And while I hate to toot my own horn, it's brilliant. Could be my best work yet," she chirped. Mom pulled me into a tight hug. "How was your first day of seventh grade, Fran?"

"It was fine. I guess." I was too distracted by Mom's miraculous transformation to talk about myself. "Uh, how're you feeling?" I asked.

"Great. Never better," Mom responded. She was a little too happy for my taste. Granny was beaming. Had the wacky banana-bread concoction actually worked?

I took in Mom's outfit. "You're wearing a miniskirt and, like, six feet of beads," I said, slightly appalled. She's forty-two. This grab at youth was embarrassing and perplexing. Mom is more the jeans-and-T-shirt type.

"I know. Isn't it cute? I totally forgot I had it in my closet. I just felt like wearing something different for a change," she said. "I'm going to get back to work. I'm really on a roll." Mom practically floated out of the room.

"Granny, you need to tell me what's going on right now or I'll . . ."

"You'll what?" Granny asked, amused.

"I'll . . . I'll . . . call the cops," I said, mustering my authority.

"Call the cops? Wow. You're not messing around, huh?" Granny laughed.

She was mocking me. I needed a different tack. "Look, if I'm old enough for you to give me the hair tincture, I'm old enough to know where it comes from."

"I'd really rather not, Franny. I don't think it's in your best interest."

"You are going to have to learn to trust me if we are going to live together successfully." It was my best shot. Granny looked up at me and gave me a long stare. "And if I betray your trust, you will have learned a valuable lesson," I added for good measure.

Granny laughed. "All right, you make some valid points. Let's go to my room," Granny said, rising from her chair.

I couldn't believe that line had worked. I think I heard it

on *Gossip Girl*. Never let adults tell you that television is a waste of time.

I followed Granny into her room. She shut the door and locked it.

"Listen, Frans, your mother's just got a bit more spring in her step, but things should settle down soon. With you, I'm not quite sure what transpired. I just e-mailed Lama."

"The monk has e-mail?" I asked, surprised.

"Don't be condescending. Everyone has e-mail," Granny chastised me. "In fact, Lama has an iPhone *and* a BlackBerry."

"Sorry, I had no clue monks were so hooked up."

Granny looked distracted; she talked more to herself than to me. "This is perplexing. The hair tincture wasn't meant to stay in your system. In fact, I added a bit of sandalwood after I was done, just as Lama told me. Five drops of sandalwood to blunt the effects. Or was it six? Maybe I got the number wrong."

"What do you mean, it wasn't supposed to stay in my system?"

"The recipe has an antidote. Some recipes do. Some don't. If you don't counteract the effects, the recipe can stay in the system."

"For how long?" I asked.

"Magic is an art, not an exact science. Results can be unpredictable."

"You just said *magic*."

"Yes, I did."

I stared at Granny for a long beat. Where did I go from here?

"Can I trust you to be prudent?" Granny stared back hard at me.

"Absolutely. Prudent is my middle name."

"That's rich, Frans." Granny chuckled.

I *could* be prudent. I usually chose not to, but I could be.

And this is where things went right off the rails. I wish I'd kept my little mouth shut and gone on my merry way because Granny was right, information can be a dangerous thing. And, honestly, Prudent is not my middle name, Elinor is.

Without another word, Granny walked over to her closet, pawed through the mess on her shelves, and pulled out a dark brown wooden box—not unlike a pirate's treasure chest—about the size of a shoebox. It had a big lock on the outside, and there were bands of thick metal across the lid. On the front of the box there was a thin drawer, a few inches long, with a faceted orange stone affixed as a knob.

"This has to stay between us, Frans," Granny warned me. "Do not repeat any of this to anyone. Is that understood?" She could be such a drama queen.

"Tell anyone what? Is that the box?" I asked, pointing. And as I said this, I saw the orange stone flicker with a tiny pulse of light.

"Yes. This is the Hindi help box," Granny said, sitting

down and holding the box on her lap. "There used to be many of them scattered throughout Asia. Shamans use them for healing. But now only a few remain," Granny said excitedly.

"How did you get one?"

"Lama Tensing Pasha and I had a very intimate spiritual connection. And I also beat him at poker."

"Poker?"

"Yes. He bet the box during a heated poker game at the monastery."

"And what does the box have to do with what's happening to me and Mom?"

"The box is filled with recipes, formulas, and helpful hints for almost any problem. The stuff I applied to your head came straight from a recipe in the box. It's a basic cure-all elixir called Fix-It Formula, and as you can see, it worked wonders. The tingling, however, was a surprise, as was your behavior today. For the most part, the recipes are meant to give you a little astral boost. Help you on your way when you're stuck and traditional solutions aren't working."

"It wasn't just tingling, Grans. I was acting strange. Not at all myself. Like, I talked to Marsha Whalley. And no one talks to Marsha Whalley."

"And how did that work out for you, talking to this Marsha Whalley?"

"She's actually kind of cool. I mean, it made me wonder why no one's allowed to talk to her," I said. "And it felt kind of great to break a few rules."

Granny was staring at the box. "I guess I got the sandal-wood wrong and the formula kept working on you. Anyway, the Fix-It Formula was just supposed to fix your hair. But it seems to have penetrated a bit deeper. It appears to have been working on an emotional level, which might explain your behavior. If no one talks to Marsha Whalley, that's a problem that needs to be fixed, no?"

"I'm not sure I follow."

"Well, it obviously bothers you that no one talks to Marsha, right? So, with the formula still in your system, your mind was forced into action to fix what was broken at school, meta-phorically speaking."

"I also talked back in Spanish and English class, which didn't fix anything. It just created new problems."

"Maybe, maybe not. Let's wait and see what happens."

Granny walked over to her bedside table and plucked a small glass bottle from the bevy of containers by her bed. She emptied a few drops of the liquid into her hands, rubbed them together, and then sat down next to me and began to massage my head.

"A little more sandalwood oil for good measure and you should be back to normal by tomorrow," Granny promised.

"This is too crazy, Grans. A Fix-It Formula from a moldy old box possessed my mind and body?"

"Looks that way."

Pass the crackers. It was all too cheesy. I didn't know what to make of it. "And what's happening to Mom?"

"I made your mom Be-Brilliant Banana Bread to get her writing again, which it obviously did. Though it also seemed to produce this Polly Perky side effect, which, I'll admit, is a tad annoying. The point is, this is an amazing resource to have around the house for little emergencies. Come have a look-see."

Granny yanked hard on the lock, and the chest snapped open. I sidled over and peeked inside. There were scraps of paper, all different sizes, covered in writing and sketches.

"It's a mess in there. How on earth can you even find anything?"

"It finds you," Granny said eerily. Her whole voodoo vibe was wigging me out a little bit. "There's a deep spiritual energy here. Can you feel it?" Granny had her hands on the sides of the box.

"Uh, not exactly," I said, not sure what deep spiritual energy felt like.

"Place your hand in the box, get a feel for things," Granny instructed.

I plunged my hand deep into the box, and as I moved it around, little sparks of light bounced off the sides, as if a small sparkler had been set off. I yanked my hand away.

Now I was officially freaked out. "Granny, this isn't funny. What's going on?"

"It's okay, sweet pea, this is white magic. It won't hurt you."

For the record, I don't subscribe to the land of make-believe anymore. Magic, mermaids, unicorns, and fairies aren't part of my vocab. Even Santa Claus left the building a long time ago. I kicked the habit on all that hokeypokey stuff when I was six, and I haven't looked back. But this was different. Very different. I was in way over my head here. Granny pulled me close, sensing my concerns.

"This is your first exposure to magic. It's normal to feel a little scared. But don't worry. Nothing bad will happen if the magic is used responsibly," she said, trying to soothe me. "This is how it works: Close the box. Get a picture in your mind of a problem, and then try to envision the solution. Once you've got it, hold it in your mind for one minute, and then tell the box your need and it will respond," Granny explained.

Okay, things were getting weirder by the minute. Now I had to talk to a box? Whatever. I took a deep breath and steeled myself for the task.

"I want you to think outside the box." Granny stopped and began giggling uncontrollably at her own joke. "Get it? Outside the box? Sometimes I crack myself up." Granny collected herself. "Okay. Think big picture, Franny. Think about something that could help a lot of people, something that has nothing to do with you."

Wait a minute. Stop. Rewind. A problem that had nothing to do with me? What was the point of that?

"I have loads of problems, Granny. How about we start with me and then tackle the world?"

"It's my way or the highway," Granny said.

All right, fine. I would take the high road, for now. *World peace,* I thought. Go ahead, top that. I tried to picture happy, smiling people holding hands around the globe, an image I lifted from a UNICEF card on the refrigerator. It was all I could come up with on short notice. I had trouble keeping a grip on that vision. A minute is longer than you think. Beyoncé and Kate Hudson crept in there, and a dream I once had about a wolf choking on a cracker, and there was a momentary blip of Alden Timkins, but I shook my head to clear my thoughts and returned to the image.

"Ready to make your request?" Granny asked, beaming like a madwoman.

"As ready as I'll ever be. World peace," I said to the box, which felt really weird because I was talking to a box, and that was so not normal.

After a few moments, the drawer on the front of the box slid open, kind of like when an ATM card pops back out of the machine. I nearly jumped a foot into the air. Inside the drawer was a square piece of paper. The paper looked about a thousand years old, gray with age and frayed at the edges. I picked it up. At the top, in an old-fashioned script, were the words *Lovely Life Lotion.* Below that was a list of ingredients, a recipe of sorts, with things like coconut oil, rosemary, and something called wild frankincense. But that was all I saw because Granny yanked the paper out of my hand.

"Hey, what are you doing?" I demanded.

"That's enough for today. I'm proud of you. A very unselfish request. My guess is that this lotion, if used properly, would help people be more compassionate toward their fellow man and promote a common understanding throughout the world. But that's just a guess. And world peace is way too big of an issue for you or me to even think about tackling," Granny said.

"Okay, so let's start with something more practical." My mind was racing with the possibilities. Maybe this was crazy. But maybe it wasn't. "C'mon, Grans. Let's solve a small problem. Together. It'll be fun. You've wanted to do something with me since you moved in. Now is as good a time as any."

"Francisco, when you want something, you are relentless. You remind me of myself." Granny smiled. "But when I was talking about spending time together, I meant going to a museum or to lunch. And you weren't interested. I may be old but I'm not stupid."

"You're right. I'm sorry. I should have taken you up on your offer. It was selfish. Let's have some together time now and do something we'd both enjoy, like chatting with the box." I had a lot to talk about with that box. There was a whole world of possibilities inside that musty wooden container. Things that might come in handy for me and my big world of problems.

Granny shook her head. "I think you and the box have had enough conversation for one day. This isn't a toy, sweet pea. We gave your mom a little boost. And you got an unintentional one as well. That's enough for now."

Be-Brilliant Banana Bread

8 tablespoons (1 stick) butter, at room temperature

⅓ cup sugar

2 eggs

1 cup unbleached all-purpose flour

2 teaspoons baking powder

¼ teaspoon salt

1 cup whole wheat flour

3 large ripe bananas, mashed

1 teaspoon dried lavender flowers

1. Preheat oven to 350 degrees.
2. Grease a 9x5-inch bread pan.
3. Cream butter and sugar until light and fluffy. Add eggs and beat well.
4. Sift all-purpose flour, baking powder, and salt together. Add whole wheat flour; stir. Add to creamed mixture; mix well.
5. Stir in mashed-up bananas and dried lavender flowers.
6. Place hands on bowl, close eyes, remove all thoughts from your brain (as much as humanly possible), and concentrate on desired outcome for 1 minute. Add no more than 30 additional seconds for especially tough cases.
7. Follow with a quick jig around the bowl. Jig should last no more than 30 seconds but should be executed with exuberance.

8. Pour batter into greased pan. Bake for 45–55 minutes, until golden brown. When a cake tester or thin knife placed in the center of the bread comes out clean, it's done.
9. Let cool in pan for a few minutes, then remove from pan by running a butter knife around the edges, loosening the bread.

Chapter 5

Blissful Buddhist Bracelets

Granny had just shut me down. I couldn't believe it. Her door was closed and she had started her tai chi. How could she dangle magic in front of me and then just whip it away? It was cruel and inhumane. I sat down outside her room and decided to wait it out. After about five endless minutes, Granny emerged. She could sense me lurking.

"Have you ever heard the expression 'patience is a virtue'?" Granny asked.

"Yeah, I'm not a big believer."

"How about 'good things come to those who wait'?"

"I'm not feeling that one either."

"You're not, huh?" Granny smiled. She was softening.

"Granny," I implored, "you cannot do this to me! You cannot introduce magic into my life and then ask me to forget about it. I mean, if this box can do what you say it can, then I don't think I'm overstating when I say this is the biggest thing that's ever happened to me in my entire life. You've got to at least let me try one recipe."

"I have to hand it you, Frans. You have a real stick-to-itiveness that, while annoying at the moment, is admirable," Granny offered.

"So what do you say? Can we try something that might actually work in my life? C'mon, just one. I'll be prudent. I promise." I was buzzing with intensity. "I'll go to a museum with you, followed by lunch. Or anything else you want. You name it."

Granny stared at me for a minute, debating. "Fine, we'll try one on for size. But just one. I need to get a better handle on how things work. I don't have antidotes for most of the recipes. I haven't gotten that far yet. So we have to be careful what we ask for."

"Careful. Got it." I would be whatever Granny needed me to be.

"And I'm taking you up on your offer to spend some time together. We'll go see a Balinese puppet show and then out for an Indian feast."

"It's a deal."

"Okay, so what're you thinking?" Granny asked.

I was picturing all sorts of ways I could dramatically improve my life. "How about Joey and Kate become best friends and then everyone stops talking to Elodie—"

"Did you hear anything I said, Franny? We need to be cautious. And, most of all, we need to use the box to make the world a better place. And only when all traditional means have been exhausted. Have you even tried talking to Joey and Kate?"

"It wouldn't work, trust me. You don't understand."

"Believe it or not, I was actually young once. I do understand. And I know that talking solves a lot more than you think."

Yeah. Right. Granny didn't have a clue. She hadn't done time in the trenches at Jefferson. Talking was not an option. It was war. I needed firepower.

"You're going at this all wrong. The Hindi help box is about fostering love and understanding on a much greater level," Granny said.

Suddenly, this didn't sound like quite as much fun.

"Let's think of something generous, noble, altruistic . . ." Granny stopped talking and stared hard at the ceiling. I was pretty sure she was going to come up with an idea that would be of absolutely no use to me at all. I had to act fast if I was going to protect my own interests.

"I know," I blurted out. "Let's find something that will help the twins get along better." It was genius. It seemed incredibly selfless while in truth it was wildly self-serving.

"I love it," Granny stated enthusiastically. It was the perfect ruse. If the box could make the twins get along, then whatever it came up with could be used on Joey and Kate. And then, *voilà* (a word of the day last year), all my problems would be solved, which would certainly make *my* world a better place.

Within moments, Granny was off and running. She grabbed the box out of the closet and we sat down on the bed together, the box nestled between us.

"Okay, let's do this." Granny put out her fist.

"What are you doing?" I asked.

"A fist-bump. What? You've never heard of it?"

"Of course I've heard of it. I just didn't know you'd heard of it."

"I try to stay current."

I laughed and we fist-bumped. Maybe having Granny around wasn't going to be so bad after all.

Granny closed her eyes and I followed her lead and closed mine as well. I have to admit, I couldn't keep them closed. I had to peek to make sure I wasn't missing anything.

"Bring the twins together in love and harmony," Granny said to the box with the zeal of a true believer.

Once again, the drawer slid open, revealing a piece of paper. I scrambled over to read it: *Blissful Buddhist Bracelets*. Bracelets? On the paper were instructions for woven friendship bracelets, the kind I used to make in third grade, when Joey, Kate, and I were all still friends. We wore ten bracelets on each wrist until they got so dirty they actually grew mold and Mom made me cut mine off.

The instructions were fairly straightforward—nothing very exciting. No frog skin or newt bladders. And frankly, I was a little disappointed. I don't know what I expected, maybe some gutting of the neighbor's hamster or removing of the heart of a dog. Certainly not a bunch of string.

Granny could barely contain herself. She got off the bed

and started pacing. "Franny, this is going to be *so* much fun." She did a little jump into the air. I hadn't seen her this pumped since she made contact with her dead mother.

"You've had a change of heart," I said.

"I've never done bracelets, but I've heard talk of their powers. I've been hoping to conjure up a bracelet, and we've done it. This should be extremely illuminating. Since the bracelets can be removed, there's more control here than the other formulas have provided."

I was so out of my element I was at a loss for words, which was pretty rare.

"I feel blessed to share this little wonder with you, Franny. I know you can handle it. I see the strength in you every time I read your aura." Granny rummaged around in her messy drawers and pulled out some string, scissors, and tape. She cut eight pieces of string, divided the string into two bundles of four, tied the four into a knot, taped each bundle to a book, and then handed me one of the books.

"All right, let's begin knotting," Granny instructed.

We followed the arrows and instructions on the paper, working as quickly as we could. We labored in silence, both of us completely focused. Twenty minutes later, we were both done and we had two colorful string bracelets.

Granny extracted the bracelets from the tape and placed them on her desk. She took both of my hands in hers and stared into my eyes. "Time to give our spirit to the task at hand. We need to free our minds of the things that tie us to this earth and commit ourselves to that which cannot be explained."

I tried to conjure my most serious solemn expression by thinking about the time my fish died and we'd had to flush it down the toilet.

"Now, join me in a tree pose." Granny proceeded to lift her right leg, stick her foot under her crotch, and clasp her hands and thrust them into the air above her head.

"What are you doing?" I asked.

Granny looked like a cross between a stork and a church steeple.

"It's a yoga pose. It's on the paper. It helps seal the deal. Follow me."

I forced my limbs into the same awkward pose as Granny, but while she stood perfectly still, I wobbled all over the place. After a few moments, I completely lost my balance and did a face plant onto the carpet.

"All right, we're done," Granny said as she gracefully came out of her pose and then peeled me off the floor.

"Can I try one on?" I asked, fingering one of the bracelets.

"Nope. It's just for the boys," Granny responded.

"Please. I just want to see if I feel anything," I whined.

"Franny, didn't you learn anything from what we talked about?"

"Uh, yeah. Sure. Of course."

"Okay, what?"

"What what?"

"What did you learn?" Granny said with measured patience.

"Uh . . . well . . ." I paused. What exactly *had* I learned? I couldn't do a tree pose to save my life and I couldn't put the Hindi help box to good use as long as Granny was in charge. Was I missing something? "How about you help me out here so I don't get the answer wrong" was what I said instead.

"This offering is special. It's only for the person or people who need it. I don't know what would happen if you shared it. And I certainly can't take any chances."

"Oh, right, that's what I learned," I said. That was no fun at all. As always, with Granny, nothing was ever as simple as it seemed.

"Now let's go find your brothers."

We made our way upstairs. *Crash, bang, blam.* We just followed the sounds of mayhem and destruction and they led us to the beasts' bedroom. We opened their door to find them somersaulting like wild baboons on their bunk beds, swatting and whacking at each other.

"Elias started it. He took my book," Pip said to Granny.

"It's Chase's fault. He spit on me at school this morning," Squeak countered. I watched as Granny maneuvered her way between them, careful not to get smacked on the head, and slipped a bracelet onto each one's wrist. They barely noticed.

After a few minutes, Squeak slowly untangled himself from Pip and sat up. Pip's body relaxed and he lay down and stared at the ceiling. Squeak walked over to the bookshelf, pulled out a few *Star Wars* books, and offered one to Pip.

"Wanna read with me?" Squeak asked.

"Sure," Pip responded.

And then they settled into the bottom bunk and started reading. Together.

I'd never seen them get along so well. This was powerful stuff. I was seriously spooked. And seriously stoked. Flip me out. I had real live magic in my house. And strange as that was, it was also totally, utterly, majorly major. Sure, Granny wanted a kinder, gentler approach. But I had different ideas in mind. Magic could come in superhandy in middle school. Opportunity had knocked and I was going to open the door and let it charge on in. We left the twins cuddling in their Buddhist bliss and headed downstairs.

"It works. It works!" I screeched, bouncing up and down like a rabbit that'd had way too many Red Bulls. My mind was spinning. If eight little strings could tame the beasts, imagine what they could do for Joey and Kate. And me. Me. Me. And the horror show I called middle school.

"I never doubted for a moment it would work," Granny exclaimed. "When you need the universe to reach out a hand to you, simply open your heart . . ."

I wasn't listening. I was laser focused on me. Me. Me. But I needed to get Granny off my trail. I had to assure her she could trust me, even though I was pretty sure she couldn't.

"Granny, that was amazing. You are a powerful healer," I said, looking her right in the eye. "I want you to know, your secret is safe with me."

"I'm impressed with your restraint, Francisco. It's nice to know I have an ally around the house." Granny smiled. I felt bad, but she had forced my hand.

"The recipe said to wear the bracelets for two weeks for best results. But we're just testing the waters. I think we'll start with three days and see how they adapt. Now I'm going to put the box away until I get a better handle on things. And I'm going to finish up my tai chi, if that's okay with you."

"By all means."

Once Granny disappeared into her room, I made my way toward Pip and Squeak's room. The twins were still sitting on the floor, quietly turning the pages of a book. It was like something out of a television show from the 1950s. My plan had been to remove the bracelets from their arms right then and there, but I decided to put it on ice. Timing was everything, and I couldn't afford to slip up.

❦❦❦❦

It wasn't until everyone had gone to bed that I felt safe returning to the beasts' burrow. They were both asleep in their bunk beds, and slipping the bracelets off them couldn't have been easier. Joey's party was on Friday. It was the perfect opportunity to test the potency of the bracelets. My plan was to invite Kate, who under normal circumstances was entirely *verboten* (a word of the week this summer), and present a bracelet to both her and Joey as a token of our friendship. And then I'd kick back and revel in the harmony that would follow. For a moment I struggled with my conscience. I didn't want to disobey Granny and I didn't want to cause chaos. I mean, Granny had flipped out when I wanted to try one on. Would something weird happen if I gave them to Joey and Kate? It was a nagging thought and it took some effort to wrestle it down. But wrestle it down I did. I rationalized it like this: Pip and Squeak, Joey and Kate—to me they were the same thing, warring parties who needed to be brought together in peace and harmony to make the world a better place. Hopefully, Granny would see it the way I did, as just a teeny-weeny, itsy-bitsy detour from her original plan. Better yet, maybe Granny wouldn't see it at all.

Blissful Buddhist Bracelets

4 pieces of embroidery thread, each about
   two feet long (various colors)
Masking tape
Hardcover book

1. Hold your thread so that the ends are even. Tie a knot about four inches from the top of the bundle.
2. Secure the knot to a book with masking tape.
3. Spread your threads out, and starting on the left, count them 1 through 4. Hold strand 2 tight as you take thread 1 and loop it over and around. Pull the end of thread 1 up and through to make a small, tight knot. Then make a second knot directly under the first.
4. Go down the line and double-knot strand 1 around strands 3 and 4.
5. Use strand 2 to make double knots around the other threads.
6. Continue double-knotting with strands 3 and 4, and repeat the entire process until the bracelet is long enough to fit around a wrist.
7. Make a knot at the end of your bracelet using all four strands. Trim the ends, leaving enough room to tie on wrist. Make a knot on each strand end to keep them from fraying.

8. After bracelet is complete, follow with a tree pose by bending right leg and placing foot firmly at top of inner left thigh. Put both arms in the air, clasp hands, intertwine fingers. Hold for one minute, focusing on desired outcome. Keep bracelet on for two weeks.

Chapter 6

My New, Hassle-Free Existence

I woke up and actually leaped out of bed, ready to greet the day. I felt like I had a secret weapon in my pocket, or rather in my backpack. The Hindi help box, as nutty as it was, might save my middle school butt. And if it did, I would be eternally indebted to Granny. How exactly I would return the favor was a mystery. But I could think about that later. Much.

I had two days before I could unleash my superpowers at the first party of the year. Until then, I would have to carry on as though everything were normal. I didn't want Granny to suspect a thing. I bounded into the kitchen, where as usual I found Kate polishing off a huge bowl of cereal and chatting up the twins.

"Lucky Charms are beat, bro," Kate said.

"Lucky Charms rule," loudly proclaimed Squeak.

"Frosted Flakes are way better. You don't know anything," Pip railed at Squeak. And within seconds Pip was out of his chair and right up in Squeak's face. Clearly the twins weren't getting along so well. Operation Bracelet Removal had set us back a bit in the bliss department.

Mom grabbed Pip and placed him in his chair. "I've got a little news flash for you, boys: neither of you controls the truth. You're both entitled to your opinions but you need to keep them to yourselves if you want television privileges this weekend.

"Eat fast, Franny. I don't want you going to school without breakfast," Mom insisted in her very Mom way. So everything was back to normal. Mom was forty-something again, having unloaded her scary tween double; the twins were at each other's throats; and my scalp wasn't tingling in the slightest. I breathed a sigh of relief. Aaaah, home sweet home.

Granny entered the kitchen and gave me the hairy eyeball. "I could hear the twins fighting from downstairs."

"It's early for them to be going at it," Mom said.

"Franny, can I have a quick word with you?" Granny asked me.

"Uh, we're kinda running late," I said. "How about we chat after school?"

"This won't take a second." And with that, Granny grabbed my arm and led me out of the room and into the hallway.

"Where are the bracelets?" Granny wanted to know.

"What do you mean?" I said, feigning innocence.

"The twins aren't wearing them. And they obviously weren't on long enough to have an impact."

"Oh no." I raised my eyebrows and acted surprised. "Maybe they fell off during the night. Maybe the twins ripped them off in their sleep."

"Maybe," Granny said warily. "Or maybe you're behind this."

"I'm not behind anything. I don't know what you mean." I made a mental note to plant facsimiles of the bracelets somewhere in the twins' room to divert suspicion. I was a little too good at criminal activity. I couldn't help wondering if I should worry.

"Really? Because this isn't child's play. You can't use them willy-nilly. You can upset the delicate balance of the universe. And you really don't want to do that. Trust me." Granny stared at me through narrowed eyes. I stared back, unblinking. Because I was pretty sure that at a moment like this, you just can't blink. It was a sign of weakness. And Granny was looking for any sign. It was hard. Granny held my gaze for a few seconds, eyeing me suspiciously.

"I hear you, Granny. And I have no interest in upsetting the universe. I already upset too many people yesterday. I don't need the universe on my case." I smiled, to lighten the mood.

"All right, sweet pea. Like you said, we have to trust each other. I'll go look for the bracelets. I'm sorry to give you the third degree. I just don't want you doing anything you might regret."

"I know, Grans." I gave her a quick peck on the cheek, grabbed Kate, and we were off.

Kate talked nonstop about James Singer on the way to school as she circled me on her Razor. Would he ask her to the Fall Fling or not? Should she ask him? I didn't have the heart or stomach to level with her. Besides, all bets were off once the bracelets came out to play. Who knew what the ripple effect would be? I nodded and smiled and provided general companionship en route while secretly fantasizing about my new hassle-free existence. I wondered what I would worry about when all my social anxiety was gone. I was sure I'd come up with something.

"So, how chewy is that, F-ster? You'll be there, right?" Kate asked.

"Be where?" I hadn't heard a word she'd said in the last fifteen minutes.

"The Battle of the Bands. September twenty-fifth. It's crescent fresh. We're gonna throw down," Kate said.

"Uh, sure," I answered. I certainly didn't have plans for October 1, at this point. It was September 8. I was pretty free for the rest of my life. Except for Joey's party on Friday night.

When we got to school, Joey didn't even wait for me to leave Kate and walk up the stairs. She came skipping down, trailed by Samantha Ross, hanger-on and social wannabe of the highest order. She was so enamored of Joey and Elodie that she followed them around like a puppy dog and tried to act and dress like them, though she was always a few days behind. It was so irritating it made me want to boil her in hot oil and then throw myself in as well.

"*Pollo,*" Samantha said to me, inexplicably.

"It's 'chicken' in Spanish. It's the word of the day," Joey explained. "It's good to know when traveling in Spain."

"Yeah. Right," I said. "The closest I'm getting to Spain is Señor Rosa's on Orange Street." We never seem to go anywhere since Mom and Dad divorced.

"Well, you never know, could come in handy with your gardener or something," Samantha said. What a tool. My gardener? You mean my mom? Yeah, that would be really handy, calling my mom a chicken while she's pruning the bushes. Where do people like Samantha Ross come from? Pods? Underneath rocks? On the bright side, much as I wanted to give Samantha Ross a piece of my mind, my head wasn't tingly and I seemed to be in complete control of things again. So I filed my opinions away, as usual.

"Big news," Joey said.

"The poms are going to the semifinals," Samantha chimed in.

"So save September twenty-fifth," Joey trilled. "It's the citywide pom competition. We're going to kill."

Uh-oh, September twenty-fifth? I distinctly remembered booking that date, like, a half-hour ago. The only two things on my social calendar for the rest of my life, and they fall on the same day. So typical I had to laugh.

"You're going to be totally pomtastic," I said, recovering.

"Pomtastic. That's brilliant!" Joey shrieked. I would work out the details of how I'd get to both events later.

"Pomtastic. Love it! I'll get the word out immediately," Samantha promised Joey.

I walked into school alone. I was wondering how someone could see fit to schedule pom and band competitions on the exact same day when Principal Mackey's booming voice came over the loudspeaker announcing that Pom and Band would be competing in their respective citywide competitions. Yeah, did she really have to rub it in?

❂❂❂❂

The next two days were a blur; just the usual territorial battles, insurgencies, and friendly fire that make up middle school. But it rolled right off me, now that I knew things were about to change. I kept my head down and plowed through, biding my time until Friday night.

The high point of the week occurred during my first art class on Wednesday. Alden Timkins was in art class with me. And Janet Scully was not. I was pretty sure Alden glanced over at me, approximately sixteen minutes into class. I tried not to make too big a deal of it but I couldn't help thinking it meant something. Did Alden secretly pine for me? Was he just toying with Janet Scully, waiting for the right opportunity to break up with her and ask me to the Fall Fling? I realize this theory didn't entirely make sense, but the heart wants what it wants. Love and logic don't go hand in hand.

Then there was Call Me Jeff, our new art teacher. Teachers didn't let us call them by their first names. But Call Me Jeff was different. He looked more like a surfer dude than a teacher, with his baggy jeans and ratty, paint-splattered blond hair. And he couldn't have been much older than twenty-five. But he was wise beyond his years, as evidenced by the fact that he picked right up on my talent. At the end of art class, he called me over.

"Franny, your work is really impressive," he said. "I think you should start on a landscape painting in class that we could submit to the Fall River Art Fair in October. They'll be picking ten student paintings from local schools. You've got two weeks to finish. So you may have to work on it at home as well."

Wow. Me? Franny Flanders: world-famous artist at twelve. Youngest person ever to have her work in the permanent collection at MoMA. I was getting a little ahead of myself. Still, submitting a painting to the Fall River Art Fair was nothing to sneeze at. I would get on it immediately and begin my rise to stardom ASAP.

When I walked out of the art room, Elodie was waiting for me, her cherry red Juicy Couture capri pants blazing like the sun.

"What was Call Me Jeff talking to you about?" she sniped.

"He thinks I should submit to the Fall River Art Fair," I said proudly. I refused to let Elodie be a buzz kill.

"He told me I should submit something as well. Like, twenty minutes before he said anything to you," Elodie snarled. "So don't think you're all that, Flanders."

"I don't. Don't worry." I had no interest in getting into it with Elodie. One tussle a week with La Principessa was plenty.

"I've been taking art classes since I was three and if anyone's going to get her painting into the Fall River Art Fair it's going to be La Principessa." And with that, Elodie turned on her half-inch heels and marched down the hall, huffing and puffing. Her long blond ponytail bobbed up and down with such bounce it looked alive.

After art class, I wouldn't have minded skipping out on the rest of the day (or the week, for that matter) and hanging in my room, sketching ideas for my landscape painting as I waited for Friday night to roll around. But I'm no juvie, I play by the rules. So I kept trudging through, hoping that things would be different next week, postparty. After school, I pasted on a smile and hauled myself to pom and band practice, just as I'd promised Joey and Kate I would.

With the competitions coming up, they wanted my input on their respective routines. As usual, my own interests would have to wait. Somehow pom and band always took a front seat, and despite my best intentions, both Kate and Joey always seemed to think they'd gotten short shrift on the spectating front.

At the end of the day, I spent exactly twenty minutes watching Joey perform mind-boggling feats of physical daring as she somersaulted and backflipped her way onto the top of the pyramid. Dang, those poms were talented. I had to hand it to Joey and the pom squad: they worked their tight little butts to the bone. If they didn't win the competition, they certainly deserved an A for effort.

Joey smiled all the way through the routine, barely breaking a sweat. She waved to me from her perch on top of the pyramid, giddy with the thrill of it all. It kind of made me wish I had an activity to call my own. Of course I didn't, because I spent so much time ferrying between pom and band and then offering up my critical commentary. I should have probably stopped this madness at the beginning of last year, when Joey and Kate first insisted I watch their practices. But that's what friends do for one another. Though I couldn't help but wonder if Kate and Joey would do it for me.

I slipped out of pom practice and made my way to the gym, where I watched the marching band rehearse. Taken individually, this strange group of misfits weren't much to speak of, but together they could rock the house; they played a rousing rendition of "Boogie Wonderland," with Kate joyously leading them. Man, she was into it as she marched from side to side, her baton held high. Her enthusiasm was infectious; it even had me tapping my feet in time to the music. I made sure to watch for exactly twenty minutes. No more. No less. I knew Kate would be clocking it.

En route home, I stopped at the store to pick up some string, which I planned to destroy beyond recognition and then offer up to Granny as exhibit A in the Missing Bracelets

Mystery. I didn't need Granny sniffing around the house for clues. I wanted to put this baby to rest.

I placed the shredded string under the twins' bunk beds and then sat down at my desk for a little me time. But I wasn't five minutes into sketching some ideas for the art fair when Kate texted me, wondering why I hadn't stayed for the Beatles medley and wanting to know if I ran out in order to catch more pom practice. Then Joey called to tell me I'd missed the synchronized handstand splits that she'd choreographed. She was sure I'd spent more time at band practice. Jeez, people, give me a break.

◎◎◎◎

Friday night arrived with little fanfare. In fact, I wasn't even sure I'd make it to the party since Mom had a dinner and Granny had a trapeze class (whatever) and suddenly everyone was looking to me to baby-sit. I tried to remain calm about the whole thing but finally burst into tears, so Mom called Dad into service and that was the end of that.

I spent the next half-hour deep breathing with cucumber slices on my eyes in order to get the swelling down from my crying jag. Mom lent me some powder and even allowed for a bit of blush and lip-gloss. Then, feeling bad about my whole freak-out, she let me wear mascara for the first time. Wow, mascara rocks. A brilliant invention. My eyelashes looked about ten miles long. There is no going back once you've experienced mascara. I don't think I'm exaggerating when I say I looked unrecognizably good. Alden Timkins, you watch out, boyfriend.

I triple checked that the bracelets were in my back pocket and then went out to the corner to wait for Kate. I was feeling very anxious about things and started biting my nails, a bad habit that rears its ugly head during times of high stress. I was starting to question my whole plan. Did I really know what I was doing? Had I made an enormous error relying on magic to solve my problems? What if things backfired? As I saw Kate approaching, I shook my head to clear out the bad juju. Showtime. *Let's do this,* I told myself.

"Yo yo yo, F-ster!" Kate greeted me wearing, once again, one of her freaky black suits. This time around she had little skull pins all over her pants, and she had stuck a bright green feather in the band of her bowler hat. Her whole ensemble made me want to enroll in a Swiss boarding school far, far away.

"Ready?" I asked.

"Fo shuggidy, my weeble," Kate replied.

"I have no idea what you just said. How about you lose the slanguage tonight?"

"I could. But that wouldn't be nearly as vexing for you. And, ergo, not nearly as much fun for me." Kate smiled. I had to laugh. *Ergo?* At heart, Kate was such a geek. "I'm not going to conform to some peak-approved standard of behavior to win James's heart. I'm going to be me with all the trimmings and win him anyway. And the peaks can bite me if they don't like it."

"Don't hold back. Tell me what you really think."

"I don't want to hang with Joey and her peak posse. But what can I do? It's basic math. James is going to be there. I want James. So I have to be there."

"Great. Why can't you talk like that?"

"Because I don't want to. And you can't make me. It's not the way I roll. Don't hate on me, dawg." Kate smiled at me again. "And, by the way, thanks for the invite."

"Sure. Whatever." I decided to move on. "Let me see your wrist," I said.

"Why?"

"I have a present for you."

Kate stuck out her arm, and I slipped one of the bracelets around it and tied it tight.

"I made it."

"Bangin' wrist cord. Kind of Rasta meets Dylan meets preppy. I'm loving on it."

I would not have described it that way, mainly because I had no idea what she meant; I was just relieved I had successfully made the transfer of bracelet from pocket to wrist.

෧෧෧෧

We arrived at Joey's to find Jane and Owen waiting for us, which was not part of the plan.

"Yo yo yo, K bro!" Owen said.

"Yo yo yo, J bro." Kate echoed Owen's greeting in what was, I assumed, some kind of homing signal for the band.

"What are they doing here?" I whispered to Kate.

"They wanted to come," Kate stated matter-of-factly, as though it were the most normal thing in the world, bringing a bunch of beeks to a peaks party. "Besides, you said you had a foolproof plan for getting me in."

"I said you, not your entourage," I whispered, freaking out. I could see the sweat marks spreading on my new silk shirt. As I was trying to decide what to do about this wrinkle, the door flew open and Joey appeared.

"Hey, you look awesome," I managed to squeak before Joey came out, closed the front door, and dragged me off toward the bushes.

"Okay. What. Is. Up?" Joey looked distressed. "Why are they here?" She pointed at Kate and her beeks.

"I brought Kate, it's true, " I said slowly. "But she brought Owen and Jane. Oh, I almost forgot, I made this for you." I grabbed Joey's wrist and quickly tied the other bracelet on. "It's a symbol of our friendship. Do you realize we've been friends now for nine years? Can you believe it? I'm so lucky to have a friend like you." And then I threw myself at Joey, engulfing her slim frame in a tight embrace. "I love you," I exclaimed. It wasn't exactly what I had planned, but you've got to be nimble on your feet, or you go down quick.

Joey stared at me. "Are you okay, Franny?"

"I'm great!" I said, sounding a little too manic.

Joey looked at her wrist. "The bracelet is *incroyable* and it's really sweet of you, but what am I supposed to do about the beeks? I told you, govs are in, but that's it. It's the most I can do."

"We can all leave, if you want," I said, stalling for time, hoping the bracelet would do something, anything, to change the situation.

"I don't want you to go . . . but I don't see how they can stay. It's going to cause madness, which is no one's idea of a fun night." Joey looked like she felt bad. "You remember what happened last time?"

My last attempt at mixing social groups was such a disaster I blocked most of it out. Frankly, now that it all came to me like a horrible flashback, I couldn't believe I was actually trying it again. I had snuck Kate into Joey's Christmas party, since Kate had been crushing on Sam Fituri (yearbook staff; they had been briefly folded into the peaks when Elodie wanted to join, but she later reconsidered and they've since been cruelly discarded and now hang with the theater nerds). To make a very long story very short, Kate and Jane, who had snuck in on Kate's heels, ended up chanting, "Peaks stink," while Joey and her friends yelled, "Beeks blow." Then several of the jocks pelted the beeks with Hershey's kisses, and the beeks fought back with Christmas cookies. Joey started crying, her mom freaked out when she saw the mess, and I ended up locking myself in the second-floor bathroom until everyone went home. I swore I would never, ever invite Kate to one of Joey's parties again. But never say never . . .

"Let's blow this Popsicle stand," Jane said angrily. "I know when I'm not wanted." Jane marched down the path toward the street. Owen followed, but Kate stood her ground.

"What are you doing, Kate?" Owen asked.

"I . . . I don't know. I, uh, don't think we should bounce yet, dawgs." Kate looked at me. I looked at Joey. And then Joey and Kate looked at each other for what seemed like an eternity. Was the magic working? This wasn't how it had happened with the twins, but then again, the twins were a simpler target. With Kate and Joey, there were layers of tension, wrapped in discord, with a soft, hostile center, all of which I expected two silly string bracelets to cure. What was I thinking? It would be easier to solve world hunger.

My shoulders slumped. I felt defeated as I watched Kate walk away. Owen and Jane escorted her down the path, toward the street. Joey stared after them but did nothing. Without much choice, I turned and followed the beeks. So much for alchemy. The four of us were halfway down the street when Joey came running after us.

"Wait. Come back." Joey panted, out of breath. Was something shifting or was Joey just feeling guilty?

"I don't know what I was thinking. You guys can totally party with us. Let's rock it out," Joey said. And then she and Kate high-fived. They high-fived. Blow my mind, why don't you?

"Yeah, let's own it. Let's do it. Let's be it, girlfriend," Kate said, beaming at Joey. And then Joey grabbed Kate by the arm and the two of them practically skipped back into the house. Okay, this was weird. Even though it had been my plan, it was still extremely strange to see it in action.

"Loving your look, *chica,*" Joey said to Kate as they made their way back into the house, arm in arm. The bracelets were working.

Owen and Jane looked like they'd each just been hit over the head with a blunt object as we all followed Kate and Joey into the house. But they didn't ask questions. Because where Kate leads, they will follow. She is their leader.

Joey burst into the party with Kate on her arm. Owen, Jane, and I brought up the rear. Poms, jocks, govs, and the rest of the peaks greeted us with shock and dismay.

"What are *they* doing here?" grumbled Elodie.

"Who invited the beeks?" Josh Toling asked.

"I did." Joey smiled at everyone, blissfully unaware of the storm of protest that was brewing. Joey picked up the remote, blasted the music, and began to dance with Kate. Kate pulled Owen and Jane into the circle, and Joey pulled me in. Everyone kind of froze, watching in horror. Should they follow Joey's lead, which was what they always did, even if what she was doing was beyond comprehension?

Alexi Butterworth joined us immediately, always happy for an excuse to dance with Joey. Max Clarick, my fellow border crosser, hurried to us as well, eager to be part of whatever group crossover was happening. I could see the hope in his eyes as we shared a look. It was immediately clear that, like me,

Max had been suffering in silence about having to divide his time between Angus and Patel. I could almost feel his relief. He must have wondered if this was just a blip or a subtle social shift with the power to change his life forever, which was exactly what I was wondering.

Zach Haus and Angus Braun tried to stare down the beeks, but Kate, Jane, and Owen were oblivious as they rocked out to the Plain White T's. Joey and Kate had invented a little dance move that involved flinging their arms into the air at the same time, and soon Alexi, Jane, and Owen were following along. They were so immersed in the music and their dance, they didn't notice peaks glaring at them from every corner.

Zach and Angus gawked at us, trying to make sense of it, then they finally gave up and joined in. After that, Samantha Ross sidled up next to Joey, copying her every move. And then one by one, the dominoes fell. Everyone was taking his or her cues from Joey. For once, the sheep mentality was working in my favor.

I danced alongside Joey, keeping an eye on things. This train had left the station; I just had to make sure everyone was on board. I pulled two more poms onto the dance floor, Hannah Bellweather and Sophie Lang. And then Alden Timkins joined us. He danced right next to me. Maybe even with me. I couldn't be sure because everyone was dancing with everyone. At one point, Alden's elbow poked my ear for a full two seconds. I was pretty sure it was his way of expressing the deep and abiding love he felt for me but couldn't act upon due to circumstances. It's okay, boyfriend, I hear you.

I saw James Singer snake his way toward Kate. I crossed my fingers and . . . bingo. Before I knew it, James and Kate were dancing together. Like, *together* together. He leaned over and whispered in her ear. Kate giggled and they moved even closer. It was unbelievably, superfantabulously awesome. Better than Disney World.

Everyone was on the floor now except Elodie. She stood in the corner, fuming. But I was having too much fun to care, because for the first time since middle school began, everyone was getting along, dancing, talking, and laughing. It was a historic night as beeks, poms, jocks, and govs partied together as one.

Operation Bracelet was a huge success. All I had to do was keep those bracelets on Joey and Kate for two more weeks (according to the recipe) and we were good to go.

Chapter 7

From Fantabulous to Suckopolis

I WOKE UP WILDLY EARLY Saturday morning. I was too excited to sleep. I don't want to overstate things, but I had worked miracles. I was feeling powerful, invincible, like a superhero. Maybe I was getting ahead of myself, but I already had an image of me, Kate, and Joey sitting together at lunch, laughing and talking like the besties we once were so long ago. In fact, this vision went even further—everyone would be mixing and mingling in the cafeteria except Elodie, who would be seated alone, maybe in a little cage, off to the side. I needed to start working the phones. I rolled over in bed to discover that it was 7:00 a.m. Too early to call. So I headed down to breakfast, where Mom was busy whipping up a mad, crazy feast.

"What's up with the banquet meal at sunrise? Is this a Ramadan celebration or something?" I asked.

"Dad's coming by for brunch," Mom said.

"And?" I asked, sitting down. Why was it such a big deal? Dad comes for brunch every Saturday. It's one of the reasons I feel confident my parents will end up back together. They said they needed their "space." But the truth was, they couldn't stay away from each other. Adults could be so dense sometimes. But that was okay. I could wait out their little phase. Let them get it out of their system. Their bond would be stronger for the time spent apart.

After brunch, Dad usually takes me or the twins or all three of us to a movie, ice-skating, swimming, or whatever. It's a day with Dad. More fun than it sounds. And sometimes Mom comes along. But Mom's tone sounded strange this morning. She gave my boxers and ripped T-shirt the serious once-over.

"You might want to change," she said. Which was when things got really weird. Mom put some fancy casserole dish in the oven. She was wearing her skinny jeans, along with a cashmere sweater that I know she only wears on special occasions. And she had makeup on. For breakfast?

"Who cares? It's just Dad. Do I really need to look like all that for Dad?"

"Uh, he's bringing a friend," Mom said a little awkwardly.

"Which friend? I know all of Dad's friends." I was starting to feel alarmed.

"A new friend. Someone he wants you to meet," Mom said quickly.

"It's that Naomi person, isn't it? He told me she was just a friend. And now we've got to meet her. I knew it," I said, jumping out of my chair. My thoughts were racing as fast as my heart was beating. This was very bad news. Possibly the worst news I'd ever gotten. "She's definitely more than a friend. Dad doesn't bring his friends to brunch. This is a girlfriend, isn't it? Count me out." Dad had a girlfriend, which meant it wouldn't be long until we were talking stepmonster.

"I'm counting you in. I need you to try and make it a pleasant brunch."

"I don't do girlfriends."

"I think you're going to have to change your policy."

I could tell Mom was freaked out too. The twins were attempting to dismantle the toaster and naturally hadn't picked up on the fact that Mom was using *the voice*. When Mom is feeling awkward, her voice kind of squeaks and sputters. She sounds like our old VW right before it died. I had to stop myself from bolting from the room, from the house, in fact, and heading to IHOP to drown my sorrows in the banana fudge stack with whipped cream and butterscotch syrup.

"I need you to get dressed and then come back down and help me with brunch," Mom said.

"I'll take brunch in my room this morning." I turned and headed upstairs.

I put my ear buds in and blasted the Fiery Furnaces. I took out my charcoal pencil and began drawing a picture of a hideous troll-like woman. I hoped it was an exact likeness of Naomi. It wouldn't work for the art fair but it went a long way toward making me feel better.

Mom was outside my door, like a minute later. She knocked. I didn't answer. She tried the knob. It was locked.

"Francine, open your door this minute," she barked. Man, talk about a total buzz kill. I had gone from the best night of my life to the worst morning ever. I hid the picture under the bed and reluctantly opened the door.

"Listen, Franny, we knew the day would come when your dad would have a girlfriend. And in time I'll have a boyfriend too—"

"What? Whoa, hold up," I interrupted. We were moving at warp speed now. "Boyfriend? You want to date too?" I could barely get the words out. Mom dating? How were they going to get back together if they were both dating up a storm?

"At some point, yes, I too will date. And maybe even have a boyfriend, if all the stars align and some man finds me attractive—" I put my hand up to stop Mom. Waaaay too much information. Was nothing sacred?

As usual, I didn't have a choice in the matter. I was coming to brunch, and that was that, according to Mom. She can be so hard core sometimes.

ⓒⓒⓒⓒ

Two hours later, the twins and I were dressed and sitting at the breakfast table with Mom. Granny had wisely slipped out, muttering something about a Japanese flower-arranging class. Mom was attempting to make conversation, but I was having none of it. And then Dad burst into the kitchen, all smiley, with a tall, stylish woman with long black hair and skin the color of melted milk chocolate following behind him. Sadly, she didn't look a thing like the hideous troll-like woman I'd imagined. She was way too pretty to be coming to brunch. I could tell Mom was startled by her beauty as well. Naomi was officially a major problem.

"Hi, guys. Everyone, this is Naomi. Naomi, this is everyone," Dad said, as if it were the most normal thing in the world to bring another woman to our brunch.

"Hi." Naomi smiled at everyone. Her perfect white teeth glistened.

I hated her immediately. The twins vaulted out of their seats and leaped onto my dad's back. He shook them both off and they jumped right back on. Everyone laughed. Ha, ha, ha, what glorious fun we were having with Naomi. Not! I glared at everyone and wondered how long I could live off my savings in Canada. Normally I'm not a petulant brat, but in times of real emergency, snarky and ill-tempered is the only way to go.

"Franny, Franny, bo banny. Fee fi mo manny. How is my girl?" Dad plucked me off my chair and pulled me into his arms. When he finally let me go, *she* was practically standing on top of me.

"Hi, Franny, I've heard so much about you," Naomi said. Brilliant line, Naomi. Was that right out of the *New Girlfriend of Divorced Dad Handbook*?

We all sat down to brunch and everyone chatted as if nothing were wrong. Except for me. I barely spoke and avoided eye contact with Dad. Naturally, the twins were unfazed. Unaware that our world as we knew it was in extreme peril, they actually seemed to like Naomi. But then Pip and Squeak always did have the worst taste. They laughed at her lame jokes, listened to her boring stories, and answered her stupid questions.

Mom also seemed to like Naomi. Which was truly frustrating because it really wasn't in her interests to welcome Naomi into the fold. It meant waiting that much longer to get back together with Dad. But there she was, chatting away with Public Enemy Number One. Mom talked about her writer's block, and Naomi was all sympathetic. She even claimed to be a writer herself. A copywriter. Please, I'm so not impressed. Dad kept trying to engage me, but I refused. *Sorry, Dad, I'd love to help you but I guess you didn't get the memo: I don't do girlfriends. Not even a little bit.*

An hour later, the twins were playing outside, the grown-ups had gone into the living room to yackety-yak all over the place, and I was up in my room sulking. I simply could not believe that my life had gone from fantabulous to suckopolis in twelve hours. It must be some kind of world record. Dad was on the verge of getting married and probably starting a whole new family, at which point we could basically count him out. How could we compete with newborn babies? I was practically an orphan and yet everyone was acting as if nothing at all had changed. Our world was crumbling around us and I seemed to be the only one who cared.

I stuck in my ear buds and started drawing a picture of Naomi being eaten by a swarm of red ants when—surprise! Another knock on the door. It was Dad this time. I stuffed the picture of Naomi under the bed yet again and opened the door.

"Frans, can we talk?" my dad asked.

I took my ear buds out long enough to say "I'm not really in the mood."

Dad sat down on the bed and turned off my iPod. "I know it's weird to meet my girlfriend," he said. Ugh, that word again. "But I wouldn't have brought her if she wasn't someone special. I'd like you to give her a chance," Dad continued.

"Okay. Got it. Give her a chance," I said.

"So will you? Give her a chance?" Dad pleaded.

"Don't think that's in the cards."

"Well, how about you keep an open mind and we'll hold off making any decisions right now," Dad said, kind of giving up. "I'm taking the twins to the mall. Wanna come?"

I didn't really want to watch Dad and Naomi suck face in the food court. "I think I'll pass."

"Okay, well, we'll miss you," Dad said and then he gave me a long hug and went back downstairs. I had to hand it to him, he was all about the soft sell, which usually worked. But not today. And not on this issue.

I was about to IM Joey when Mom walked into my room without even bothering to knock. My parents were stalking me. We clearly needed to have a chat about privacy issues during adolescence.

"What did you think of Naomi?" Mom asked.

"I don't want to talk about it," I said pointedly. Mom shot

me one of those looks she gives me when she thinks I'm being a total cliché of a child.

"Sweetie, I know this is hard, but Daddy loves you very much, and his new girlfriend will never change that." And then Mom's voice cracked, like she was going to cry, which totally flipped me out. Hadn't she come in here to make *me* feel better?

"Mom, are you okay?" I asked, not sure I wanted to hear the answer.

"I'm fine, sweetie. I'll admit, it was a little strange to see your dad with someone. But I'm happy for him. I really am. It's just, this is his first serious girlfriend and it's the beginning of a whole new chapter for him, for us, and that's kind of an emotional thing. I mean, I actually really liked her, so that was a relief. It's just—this may sound weird, but I just hope you don't like Naomi better than me. She seems pretty terrific and . . ." Mom's voice trailed off. "What am I saying? This is terrible. It's bringing out all my insecurities. I shouldn't even be telling you this."

"Probably not," I said. If it was possible, I now felt even worse. I hated Naomi not only for my own selfish reasons but because she was making Mom miserable too, and that crossed the line. Naomi had to go and I would have to see to that.

"Don't worry, no one could do better than you. Even when you're bad, you're still better than anything else out there," I said to Mom. She pulled me in tight and hugged me for what seemed like ten years.

Chapter 8

The Universe Will Screw with You

I SPENT THE NEXT HOUR painting my butt off in an effort to distract myself from the Naomi Factor, as I had named my most recent problem. I figured I'd do some practice studies for the art fair. I whipped and banged the brush at the canvas, taking out all my frustrations on the picture, which went from a lovely sunset over the sand dunes to a big old brown mess. I was so wrapped up in painting I didn't even hear the doorbell ring.

"Franny, Joey's here," Mom yelled from downstairs. I raced down to find Joey in the front hall.

"Hey, J," I said. "What're you doing here?"

"I thought maybe you, Kate, and I could hit the Sweet Spot this afternoon and then catch a movie at the Quad."

What? Joey wanted to go to the movies with Kate? I had to pinch myself to make sure I wasn't dreaming. Ouch. A little too hard. I stared at Joey to see if she was messing with me.

"My mom can drive us," Joey offered without any hint of sarcasm. She was completely sincere.

"Yeah, sure. Totally." Oh. My. God. The bracelets had worked, really, really worked. I could barely contain my excitement. Jackpot! I had rolled the dice and hit the mother lode. It felt good to be in the winner's circle for a change. I did a little victory dance in my head.

"Last night was soooo fun. Kate is awesome," Joey declared.

I was triple flipping out. Joey was telling me everything I'd ever wanted to hear and it was kind of blowing my mind, in the best possible way. I looked down and saw the bracelet on her wrist. I wanted to bend down and kiss it.

"Let's go to Kate's and see if she wants to hang," Joey said.

ⓔⓔⓔⓔ

"'Sup, F?" Kate asked, sounding confused and a little testy when she answered the door and saw me and Joey standing there. Maybe she'd only just gotten up and needed a moment.

"We just came to say *hola, chica*," Joey said, leaning in to give Kate a hug.

Kate pulled away. Uh-oh. Kate looked at Joey strangely and then looked at me.

"Can we get some face time, F?" Kate asked, grabbing me by the arm and pulling me inside the house, leaving Joey standing alone outside.

"What are you fools doing, dawg? I'm not feeling this ambush." Kate looked pissed. Panic coursed through my system.

Oh no. Somehow things had gone terribly wrong. Why

was Joey all about Kate while Kate was not at all about Joey? And that's when I looked down at Kate's wrist and saw it. Or rather, didn't see it. No bracelet anywhere in sight. Shoot. Shoot. Shoot me in the head. Couldn't I catch a break? Kate and Joey just had to wear the bracelets for thirteen more days and we'd be in the clear. It was so simple.

"You're not wearing the bracelet I made you," I said.

"Yeah, don't hate on me. I lost it at the party. My bad. Maybe you can make me another one?" Kate said. She really did look sorry.

Kate had lost the bracelet! The bracelet that was going to change all our lives forever. And now I was stuck with a completely lopsided situation. Nightmare.

"No biggie." I had to force the words out of my mouth because Joey was heading our way. I had what was fast turning into another code blue on my hands.

"What's going on?" Joey said, coming into the house.

I grabbed Joey's arm and dragged her back out of the house before Kate had a chance to say anything. "Kate's got tons of homework, so we should go. Bye, Kate, see you later." Joey looked at me, confused.

"No, I—" Kate started to protest. But before she could say much more, I slammed her front door and pulled Joey down the path.

"Kate is dying to hang with us. But you know how intense she can get about homework. We'll have to figure something out for this week. Guess we should have called ahead." I tried to laugh the whole thing off. I could tell Joey didn't know what to make of it all.

I faked stomach cramps and headed home, alone. I wasn't even really lying because at this point, I did feel sick to my stomach. I was defeated, depleted, demoralized, depressed. But there was no time to lick my wounds. I had work to do. And fast. Who knew how long Joey would want to hang with Kate if Kate didn't return the friendship? I needed another bracelet, pronto.

I found some string in the kitchen and tried to recreate the thing. But it was a no-go. I couldn't do it from memory alone! I needed the directions. I had to get my hands on Granny's box. I cased the house. Mom was writing in her study.

"Where's Granny?" I asked her.

"She's at mandolin lessons. Are you feeling better about things?"

"Yeah, it's all good," I responded. I really didn't want to encourage conversation.

"It's all good? You were pretty upset earlier."

"Yeah, well, I rebounded. I'm over it," I said as I inched my way out of the room. I was on a bit of a schedule here. Who knew how long a mandolin lesson lasted? I didn't even know exactly what a mandolin was.

"That was fast," Mom said, eyeballing me suspiciously.

"Since everything's 'all good,' how about you call your dad and plan a time to get together with him and Naomi. I think he'd like that."

I'd really stepped in it now. If I wanted to get to Granny's room this century, I was going to have to agree to a date with the devil. "Fine," I told Mom.

"That's great, Frans. I'm really proud of you," Mom said.

I slipped out of the room.

"Frans?" Mom called just as I'd almost made my getaway.

"Yes?" I said, popping my head back in the room.

"I love you." Mom smiled at me.

"Okay. Good stuff," I said and then bounded off toward Granny's room.

You can upset the delicate balance of the universe. Granny's words rang in my ears as I snuck into her room. Maybe that's what I had done, upset the balance of things. Well, if that was the case, then I needed to rebalance things. Or at least that was how I justified what I was about to do.

I threw open the closet door and searched the shelves. The box was nowhere to be found. I couldn't believe it. Granny had hidden it from me. Why couldn't she trust me? I felt indignant until I realized I was sneaking around her closet looking for it. I guess she knew me better than I knew myself.

Okay, think. Where would Granny hide the box? In a place she thought I'd never want to venture. And lo and behold, there it was in the closet, nestled under a huge pile of laundry, a stinky girdle wrapped around it. I was extremely impressed with my powers of deductive reasoning. As I extracted the box from the girdle, a glass bottle fell from a closet shelf to the floor. It was the tincture Granny had put on my head, safe in its little vial. This was what had somehow installed a pipeline directly from my brain to my mouth. It was dangerous stuff, unpredictable and potentially explosive. I should probably just leave it alone. And yet . . . it beckoned to me. It was just too tempting to resist. Who knew when it would come in handy? Maybe I would just take a little bit and save it for a rainy day.

I went into Granny's bathroom and grabbed one of her mini shampoos from the collection. There were hundreds of tiny plastic bottles in Granny's cabinet, taken from hotels and motels around the world. I emptied out the contents of one and poured in some Fix-It Formula. I placed the rest of the vial of tincture back on the closet shelf. Granny would never know the difference. In the meantime, I'd have a secret weapon in my arsenal, for emergency use only. I jammed the shampoo bottle into my pocket and turned my attention back to the box.

I knew I had to calm down and focus on what I wanted or the box wouldn't work, but my heart was thumping around in my chest and I was gulping air like it was Gatorade after a big race. I sat on Granny's bed with the box in my lap and closed my eyes, trying to picture Kate and Joey bonding, as best friends do. I could see Kate, wearing some crazy outfit and tooling around on her lime green scooter while Joey stood nearby in a bikini, looking like a swimsuit model. I had to laugh. These two didn't remotely look like they belonged together, even in my imagination. Still, if this was going to work, I needed to envision them as the perfect pair. I nudged them closer together, until they were kind of leaning on each other, and then I made them both laugh really hard at the same joke, and then, whoa, they high-fived spontaneously. My imagination had taken on a life of its own. Kate took Joey's long ponytail and started braiding it, and Joey took Kate's headband with the black furry balls on it and placed it on her own head. Awesome! The perfect vision of absolute harmony. I was good to go. I turned to the box.

"Kate and Joey, BFFs," I said to the box.

Pop! The drawer slid open. I grabbed the piece of paper, expecting to get the directions for the bracelet, but instead I got a recipe titled Brassbound Beatitudinous Blondies. No, no, no, no. Not blondies. Bracelets. I needed the bracelet instructions. What was wrong with this box?

I put the recipe back in the drawer, shut it, and repeated the whole exercise, focusing twice as hard this time on Joey and Kate getting along. The drawer opened and . . . the blondie recipe appeared again. Oh no! I tried three more times, but the darn box kept spitting out the same stupid blondie recipe. What. Was. Up?

There was clearly no reasoning with this box. I would

have to get baking. I biked to the store to pick up the ingredients, telling Mom that I needed some school supplies, and then waited until everyone was asleep to get to work. I crept into the kitchen and worked quietly, focused and intense. I baked half a dozen blondies, following the recipe precisely. I couldn't afford mistakes. As with the bracelets, the last part of the recipe was completely wacky. After putting them in the oven, I had to do a headstand for a minute. Thank God for those gymnastics classes Mom had dragged me to. Finally, they had paid off. I flipped myself up against the wall and started counting. Just as I was finishing up, Mom walked in.

"What are you doing?" Mom asked, thoroughly perplexed. "You're upside down and you're baking and it's nearly midnight. There are several things wrong with this picture."

"Uh, I had a craving, and a headache?" I said, groping for a reasonable explanation. "And it's that time of the month," I added for good measure.

"What time of the month, Fran?" Mom wanted to know. "Wait. Oh my goodness, did you just get your period?" Mom started to get all misty-eyed. Oh no, she was getting waaay ahead of herself here.

"No. But it should be anytime now. I mean, I'm practically a teenager. Where is it already? This is getting a little embarrassing. Anyway, maybe this is how it starts. Cravings and weird hormonal swings before the actual thing shows up." I was spinning quite a yarn. Even I couldn't follow my train of thought. Luckily, Mom was too tired to keep up. I plopped back down on my feet and looked up at Mom with a puppy-dog expression. "I love you, Mommy." I threw my arms around her and we hugged it out.

"I love you too, sweetie." Mom smiled at me. "I guess there's no harm in a little baking. Just don't eat too many sweets. You'll get a tummy ache."

I finished making the blondies, wrapped them in foil, and hid them in my backpack.

Brassbound Beatitudinous Blondies

   8 tablespoons (1 stick) butter, melted
   1 cup brown sugar
   1 egg
  ½ teaspoon vanilla extract
  ⅛ teaspoon salt
   1 cup all-purpose flour
  ½ cup white chocolate chips
  ½ cup butterscotch chips
  ½ cup milk chocolate chips

1. Preheat oven to 350 degrees. Grease an 8x8-inch pan.
2. Mix melted butter with brown sugar. Stir until smooth. Beat in egg and then vanilla.
3. Add salt; stir in flour.
4. Add white chocolate chips, butterscotch chips, and milk chocolate chips and stir, focusing on desired outcome.
5. Pour into prepared pan. Bake for 20–25 minutes.
6. While blondies bake, do a headstand for one minute: balance on head with legs in the air, using elbows and arms for support, and a wall if necessary.
7. Remove blondies from oven once they've set in the middle. Cool on rack before cutting into squares.

Chapter 9

Let the Bliss Begin

Sunday was a blur. I spent most of it in bed recovering from the emotional roller coaster of Saturday. I also spent a good portion of my day pondering this blondie/bracelet puzzle. Joey still had her bracelet, but Kate was about to get a blondie. Would that, could that, possibly upset the delicate balance of things even more? I didn't want to risk it. Better to start with a clean slate. I would give both Kate and Joey blondies and destroy Joey's bracelet. And that was that.

I cleaned my room, picking up my jeans and the Fix-It Formula I'd taken from Granny's closet that I'd dropped onto the floor. I figured I should probably use it or lose it. Might as well put it in the backpack, just in case. I was already pretty far down the rabbit hole. A few more steps wouldn't kill me.

Granny popped her head into my room mere seconds after I'd tucked away the Fix-It Formula. Whoa. Close call. The gods were smiling on me for a change.

"Searched the twins' room and I finally found the bracelets under their bed. I guess you're off the hook," Granny said.

"I didn't realize I was on the hook," I said, knowing full

well that Granny would have caught me if I hadn't so brilliantly covered my tracks. In my mind, I gave myself a huge pat on the back. Well done, Flanders.

"No? Well, you were." Granny smiled and raised one eyebrow at me. How did she do that with just one eyebrow? "But now you're clean. Sorry I doubted you."

"That's okay. I totally understand your position."

"Well, good night, sweet pea." And with that, Granny was gone.

☾☾☾☾

I texted Kate first thing Monday morning: *Running late. C u @ skool.*

I was like a spy embarking on a really dangerous mission. I had to be supercareful. I didn't want any witnesses.

Mom dropped me at school a few minutes before the bell rang. As I headed toward the stairs, anxious and nervous, I stopped suddenly at the sight of Owen and Susan Blackly, hands intertwined, lips touching in a . . . kiss? A kiss? If I were a cartoon character, my eyes would have popped out of their sockets and bounced like tennis balls up to Owen.

Owen, as one of Kate's best friends, is a die-hard beek (he plays the clarinet like nobody's business), and Susan Blackly is a smeek who will likely win the Nobel Prize in Chemistry as a teenager, but as far as I knew, these two had never spoken. And now they were kissing? I was unable to avert my eyes. Then I saw it: Owen was wearing Kate's friendship bracelet.

Mystery solved. Owen had obviously found Kate's bracelet and was now under its influence.

"Owen, where did you get that bracelet?" I asked, getting right up in Owen's face. Susan continued to cling to Owen's waist like a gecko. I could tell she was freaked out by me, but I didn't care. I needed to get that bracelet back on Kate's wrist.

"Franny, we're kind of in the middle of something here," Owen snapped, turning his attention back to Susan. What an emo boy. I wanted to flick him in the nose.

"Owen, you need to give that bracelet to me this instant! Do you understand?" I sounded exactly like my mother, which kind of weirded me out. I was a little too young to be turning into my mother.

"I'm not giving you the bracelet, Franny. It's mine. Finders keepers."

"We're not going to play it that way, Owen. It's a family heirloom and I need it back."

"It's macramé, Franny. And it's polyester, which was invented in, like, the sixties, so how can it be an heirloom?" Susan asked unhelpfully. What a tool.

I needed that bracelet, pronto. This way I wouldn't have to bother with the blondies, which were a bit of a wildcard. I reached out and grabbed the bracelet. Owen pulled his arm back but I held on with a death grip. We tussled for a moment, drawing the attention of the smeeks and loners nearby. Finally, I yanked with all my might, and the bracelet snapped off, breaking in two, leaving a red welt on Owen's wrist. Oh snap, and I meant that literally. Guess I'd have to go with the blondies after all. Well, better to destroy the bracelet than have it out in the world working its magic.

"Ow, that hurt, Franny. What is your problem?" Owen asked, annoyed.

"It's just, this bracelet is really important to my family. It comes from my great-grandmother in, uh, Russia. Sorry to bother you. Just, uh, carry on," I said, smiling sweetly. They both stared at me as though I had just landed in a spaceship from the planet Xenon.

Susan sidled up to Owen but he pushed her away, kind of hard.

"Uh, sorry, Susan, I have chemistry, I've g-got to go," Owen stammered, turning beet red and then slinking away. Poor Susan. She looked crushed. I felt kind of bad. No bracelet, no love. It was definitely the last time for a long, long while that she would kiss a boy outside her social circle, and she knew it. I rushed away to spare her any more embarrassment.

I found Kate and Jane on the stairs, and right away Kate could tell something wasn't quite right with me.

"You cool, F? You look tweaked. You need to chillax."

"I'm fine. Just worried I was going to be late," I said, covering.

I reached into my backpack and pulled out the package of blondies. Looking back on it, this was probably one of those crossroads where I should have taken the other path, the one of self-restraint and modest ambition. Instead, I barreled forward, determined to pull Kate and Joey together one way or another.

"Have a blondie, I baked it just for you," I said, shoving the Brassbound Beatitudinous Blondie at Kate. "Have two. They're really good."

"Can I have one?" Jane asked.

"No!" I yelled. Jane jumped a bit and stared at me, bug-eyed.

"That's kind of mean, Franny," Jane said, looking hurt.

"I'm sorry, Jane, it's just, I only made enough for Kate and Joey. How about I make more tomorrow?"

"Okay, whatever," Jane mumbled. I felt bad, but what could I do? It was really in her best interest. Look at Owen.

"Bracelets, blondies. You're like Santa Claus, dawg."

"What can I say? I give until it hurts." I laughed nervously and then went in search of Joey. I found her near the front door, texting.

"Hey Frans," Joey said, "I was just about to go find Kate, want to come?"

"Yeah, in a minute," I said as I looked down at Joey's wrist. There was the bracelet, wrapped tighter than ever. How the heck was I going to get the thing off without making a scene? I didn't want to give her the blondies while she was still wearing the bracelet. Who knew what kind of trouble that would bring?

"Can I, uh, have the bracelet back?" I asked Joey. "I want

to add some beads to it that Grans got in Bali. It looks kind of unfinished without them."

"It's perfect as it is," Joey said, admiring her bracelet.

"It would just make me feel better if I could finish it properly. I want it to be totally perfect. I mean, it's a friendship bracelet, and right now, it's kinda bland. And our friendship is definitely not bland."

"This bracelet is so not bland. It's *parfait* just the way it is. But that is such a sweet sentiment. Franny, you're the best."

I don't know exactly what I was at that moment, but I definitely wasn't "the best." With little choice, I moved on to plan B, mixing blondie with bracelet. I crossed my fingers and hoped it would all work out.

"Here, have a blondie. I just made them." I shoved a blondie into Joey's hand. "Have two." What's the worst that could happen? Joey would like Kate more than Kate liked Joey. Whatever. I was getting a headache thinking about the whole thing.

"Yum, can I have one?" Angus came over and said.

"They're for Joey. Besides, when did you ever bake me anything?" I asked as I stuffed my blondies back into my pack.

"Franny, you need to take a chill pill," Angus replied.

"Maybe I do," I said, thinking that maybe he was right.

"Thawnks, shweetie, id's delitius," Joey said with a mouthful of blondie.

The deed was done; I had successfully stuffed magic blondies down both Kate's and Joey's throats before the bell rang.

Elodie opened the doors and I bolted inside, thankful that classes were about to begin.

The day was pretty much like all other days where I bounced back and forth between Kate and Joey. I couldn't help but wonder what had gone wrong. Why weren't the blondies doing their job? But then, at the end of the day, as I approached Joey's locker, I found her standing in the hall with Kate. Kate was whispering something to Joey. Joey whispered something back and then they both cracked up. At the exact same time. Elodie was glaring at them from about ten feet away. The blondies were kicking butt and taking no prisoners.

I watched as Kate took off her favorite black blazer and handed it to Joey. Joey slipped it on and smiled. Elodie made a gagging sound from across the hall. My work here was done. It was time to kick back and let the bliss begin.

Chapter 10

I Don't Do Girlfriends, Not Even a Little Bit

AFTER SCHOOL, I hung out at pom practice where—wait for it—Kate joined me for a little, while she waited for band practice to begin.

"They're totally crunk," Kate said as we watched Joey flying through the air in a dazzling display of athletic skill. "I always thought the poms were major lame."

Wow. Those blondies were clocking serious overtime. I was so psyched, I put my arm around Kate and gave her a squeeze.

"'Sup with all the lovin', dawg?"

"I guess I'm just feeling it today."

"Whatevs. I gotta roll to band."

"I'll come with," I said.

"Chillax with the poms. It's all gravy. We're just doing the same-old same-old."

"You don't care if I watch band today?" I asked Kate, incredulous.

"Check us tomorrow, dawg." And with that, Kate was off.

❀❀❀❀

I practically skipped home. And I haven't skipped since I was five. But I was over the moon. Waaaay over the moon. The recipes worked like magic because, well, they were magic. Finally, I could start having fun and stop feeling like a human rope in a constant tug of war.

I was walking toward the house making a mental list of all the things Kate, Joey, and I could start doing as a threesome when Mom stopped me. She was outside pruning the bushes.

"Your dad called," she said. "He wants to take you to dinner tonight. With Naomi."

A total freaking buzz kill to an otherwise stupendific day.

I started to protest but Mom stopped me before I could even get going.

"I know you don't want to go, Frans. And I'm sure you've got a lot of stuff to do tonight, but you promised you'd try. It's really important to your dad."

"Okay. Fine. I'll give Naomi one chance. But that's it."

"Very generous of you."

"I guess I'm just a fool for love."

"Yep, that's you to a T." Mom smiled. "How was school?"

"Awesome."

"Really? That's great. What happened?"

"Kate and Joey are finally getting along," I offered without really thinking.

"No way, no way," Mom blurted, like she was twelve. "How did that happen?"

Why hadn't I just kept my big mouth shut? How would I

possibly explain this? "They just, uh, decided to put their differences aside and, uh, come together. I guess they kind of figured it was the right thing to do," I said, fully aware that I had officially become a pathological liar. In truth, I wished I could tell her everything. It would be fun to share it with someone. But I was pretty sure she couldn't handle the truth. *I* could barely handle the truth.

"I want to hear every little detail. Did you talk to them like I suggested? I knew you could do it," Mom said.

As difficult as it was to keep my hard-earned victory to myself, that was exactly what I did. Because I'd already said too much. "Can we talk about it later? I need to get on some homework and I should call Dad. And, uh, where's Grans?"

"In the kitchen, I think," Mom said. "And Frans, I'm really happy for you. I'm glad Joey and Kate finally came around. I told you it would all work out if you just gave it time."

Yeah. Time. And friendship bracelets, a few blondies, and a whole lotta monk magic. What Mom didn't know wouldn't hurt her.

I headed into the house, annoyed that the Naomi Factor was back on the front burner. It clearly needed to be dealt with, stat. I couldn't shake the idea of Naomi and my father rushing toward the altar with no thought at all about how this affected me. And Mom. I had no interest in a stepmonster. Or stepsiblings. Naomi had to be disposed of before people started getting too attached. If the box could solve a major problem like Joey and Kate, a minor problem like Naomi should be a breeze for it. First order of business: keep Granny out of her room. I was heady with magical power, feeling a little too cocky after my recent triumph. In retrospect, I probably shouldn't have pushed my luck. But I'm twelve. That's what I do. It's kind of my job.

I found Granny in the kitchen, her rubber-gloved hands immersed in murky water.

"What are you up to, Grans?" I asked.

"I'm tie-dyeing all my winter clothes. I think it's a good way to perk up an old wardrobe. Got anything you want tie-dyed?"

Tie-dye? I wouldn't be caught dead in it, but I needed Granny out of her room. "*Love* the tie-dye idea," I exclaimed. "I've got tons of stuff that could use a makeover."

I hightailed it up to my room and grabbed every raggedy old white piece of clothing that I never wore and rushed back downstairs.

"Here," I said as I plopped a mound of clothing at her feet. "It would be great if you could tie-dye all of it."

"All of it?" Granny looked at the huge pile. "That's a lot, Frans. Could take a while."

"Please? It would mean a lot to me. I've always wanted a tie-dye wardrobe but Mom just wouldn't go for it. You're so much hipper than she is," I added.

"All right, Francisco," Granny said as she turned back to the sink and got to work.

I snuck downstairs and into Granny's room. The box was

right where I'd left it, in the laundry. I pulled it out, sat down on the bed, placed it on my lap, and said to the box, "We have to stop meeting like this." Because really, we'd been seeing quite a lot of each other and if I couldn't get a good laugh out of talking to a magic box, then what's the point?

Then I got serious and concentrated on coming up with a plan. I don't want to say the idea hit me like a bolt of lightning because that's massively clichéd and I try not to peddle in clichés, but really, it was genius.

"Make Naomi irresistible to men," I said to the box, picturing Naomi choosing her new boyfriend from a lineup of highly eligible men. This would free Dad to return to Mom without leaving Naomi boyfriendless. Everyone ended up with someone. It was win-win. I was pretty proud of myself for making Naomi's welfare a key part of the plan. I mean, another preteen with far less compassion wouldn't have spared her father's soon-to-be ex-girlfriend's feelings. But I wanted to stress that I could rise above. Message: I care.

The drawer flew open and there lay a recipe for Sensationally Sexy Smoothie. I didn't even know they had smoothies back in the day, and in Asia to boot.

I dialed Dad, pronto. "Hey, Dad. Mom said you wanted to go out. You, me, and Naomi, and I'd really like that. Would you guys want to go see a movie tonight?"

Dad was ecstatic at the idea of an intimate evening, just the three of us. He was so happy I'd come around that I almost felt bad about my plan. Almost.

I ran to the kitchen; there was no time to waste. Granny was still there, knee-deep in tie-dye. Without much choice, I went about my business, making my smoothie. I mean, a girl can have a smoothie without necessarily being up to something, right? Yogurt, bananas, frozen strawberries, and juice, check. It was all there. I blended everything together until it was creamy, poured the mixture into a thermos, and was about to head back to my room to do the last bit of the recipe when Granny took a sudden interest in my snack.

"What're you making, Francisco?"

"Uh, just a little smoothie," I said.

"Yum. Got any extra?"

The idea of Granny irresistible to men made me a little queasy. "Sorry, Grans. Only made enough for one. Do you want me to whip you up another?"

"No, don't bother, sweets. I've got a little yak butter tea I can have when I'm finished laying out the tie-dye." And with that, Granny trundled off to her room with her bundles of tie-dye. And I snuck the smoothie upstairs to put the final touches on things.

The recipe called for what I think was a chant in Sanskrit, but I'm not sure, because I don't know Sanskrit. All I know is that for about sixty seconds, I stood in the bathroom crooning, *"Om shanti namaste chadaranga,"* over and over again as I turned in a clockwise direction while holding the thermos of smoothie. You'd think a kid from the suburbs of Jersey wouldn't be able to pull that off. But either I had more of Granny in me than I thought or the events of the past few days had changed me in ways I could only begin to understand, because the truth was, I was kind of enjoying myself.

☺☺☺☺

Dad and I met Naomi at the food court in the mall. When we got there, she was waiting for us, all eager-beaver. Naomi gave me a warm hug. They seemed so happy, and Naomi was all interested in me, with her questions about school and the Fall River Art Fair. I actually had a moment's hesitation.

I shook my head to free myself of all the junk that was collecting . . . worry, anxiety, guilt. I needed to stay the course. Once Dad and Mom were back together, we would all have a good laugh about this.

Dad bought popcorn and lemonade, just as I knew he would, and we headed into the theater. The plan was to make sure Naomi got as little lemonade as possible. I had also snuck in some extra salt. I needed her seriously parched. We sat down in our seats and I set about polishing off the lemonade before the movie even began.

"Frans, take it easy on the drink, you're going to drown," Dad said.

"I am *so* thirsty," I said. "I haven't had a drop to drink all day." I slurped up the last of the lemonade just as the lights went down. I had to struggle to remain seated as my stomach started to roil.

I'll go get some more lemonade," Dad offered.

"No!" I said, louder than I intended. A number of people seated nearby turned to look. "It's just, I'm scared. Don't leave."

"It's a comedy, Frans, about a zookeeper and a bunch of talking animals. I think it's pretty mild," Dad said, confused.

"You never know. These days they're always putting something inappropriate in every movie." I stared at Dad, wide-eyed. "Just. Don't. Leave. Me."

"Okay, whatever you say," he said.

"How about I go and get a drink and you stay here with your dad," Naomi offered.

"Oh my God, I almost forgot. I brought a homemade smoothie for you," I said to Naomi. I opened the thermos and poured Naomi a cup. I could tell she was a bit thrown by my offering. I mean, seriously, who brings a homemade smoothie to a movie? So lame. Naomi must have thought Dad had a total nutcase for a daughter. But I've got to give her props, she recovered nicely and graciously took the thermos.

"Thank you, Franny, it smells delicious," Naomi said.

"That looks good," Dad said. "I'll take some too."

"Sorry. Didn't make enough," I snapped. "Why don't you get us more lemonade before the movie starts?"

"I thought you were too scared for me to leave." Dad looked thoroughly baffled. I was coming off like some kind of crazed lunatic. It couldn't have been pretty to watch.

Luckily, the theater completely darkened, the screen lit up, and the sound swelled. We turned our attention to the movie.

I kept one eye trained on Naomi to monitor her progress. She had barely touched the smoothie.

"Bottoms up!" I said, hoping that would goad her into drinking more.

"*Sshhh!*" people around us hissed.

"Don't you like it?" I whispered a few minutes later when I noted Naomi had stopped sipping. "I made it especially for you." Guilt was my best weapon at this point. I stared hard at Naomi until she finished every last drop and then I waited and waited and waited for things to get rolling. Nothing happened for quite some time and I was forced to watch this juvenile movie I had chosen about a bunch of talking animals. Painful. Who writes this junk?

The movie was almost over when the first rumblings finally began. A man in the seat next to Naomi leaned in. "I must tell you," he crooned, "you are perhaps the most beautiful woman I have ever laid eyes on." Bingo!

Naomi shushed the guy, as did many people around us. My dad looked over, curious. Naomi just shrugged and turned back to the movie, ignoring the guy.

Next, a man in front of us turned around and thrust a business card toward Naomi. "You are an absolutely exquisite creature. Maybe you'd like to go out sometime? Call me. Anytime. Day or night. I put my cell, home, and office numbers on there." Naomi looked a little freaked by the sudden attention.

Dad, having overheard this exchange, sat forward in his

seat. "Hey, buddy," my dad warned. "She's with me. And my kid. So lay off."

Dad was going all Rambo. The man didn't have time to respond because right after that, things went completely off the grid. Three men came walking up the aisle and shimmied their way into our row, toward Naomi. Before I knew it, they were pushing and shoving one another, clamoring to get to Naomi. The smoothie was working overtime. Yikes. I had a bit of a 911 on my hands. Maybe I should have started with half a glass.

At this point, the credits began to roll and I hustled Dad and Naomi out of the theater before the three men could get to her.

"What was up with that?" I asked, feigning innocence.

Dad looked really puzzled and didn't say anything. Naomi didn't respond either. She looked like she'd just been side-swiped by a Mack truck. She glanced nervously around the mall.

Trying to buy myself some time in the hopes that the smoothie's powers would weaken, I suggested a snack break at Wok 'n' Roll, my fave spot to chow at the mall. I took the liberty of ordering noodles and egg rolls for all of us.

Suddenly a man appeared at my side. "Let me get this," he said, handing his credit card to the cashier.

"No, I'll get it," another guy offered, shoving bills at the poor, confused cashier.

Then the first man turned to Naomi with a huge smile. "Is

there anything else you want, gorgeous? A little tea, some fried wontons? My name is Frank, by the way."

Naomi didn't know what to make of any of this. "Uh, thank you, that's very kind of you," she said warily. My dad looked positively miserable. My enjoyment level had peaked in the theater and was now seriously on the decline.

"Naomi, what is going on?" Dad said. "Do you know these guys?"

"No, I don't," Naomi stated. Dad and Naomi took a giant step away from each other. There was trouble brewing in paradise.

"Then why are you talking to them?" Dad demanded.

"Because they were talking to me. And it's rude not to respond," Naomi said.

"Well, I'm not sure what to think," Dad said.

"About what?" Naomi raised her eyebrows and shot my dad a harsh look. "What are you implying, exactly?"

"You must have given these guys the impression that you were interested in them. Why else would every guy in town suddenly want to be with you?" Dad asked.

Uh-oh. Dad was in trouble now. This was not the thing to say to your girlfriend.

"You could try having a little faith in me," Naomi said, annoyed.

"Faith in you? That's a bit hard right now."

Things were going from bad to worse. A verrrrry long moment passed where no one said anything. Dad and Naomi stared at each other. The two men stood by, gazing at Naomi. One of the men offered to drive her home. Naomi didn't say anything. I held my breath, waiting to see what would happen next.

"You know what? I don't need to take this," Naomi finally said. "I haven't done anything wrong and yet you don't seem to trust me. That doesn't bode well for our future." Naomi turned to me. "Goodbye, Franny." Then she turned back to Dad. "Good night, Mark." And with that, she walked off.

"Naomi, wait, come on," Dad pleaded, but she was gone.

Dad looked . . . well, it's hard to describe exactly how Dad looked, as I've never seen him like that. Dad is a pretty happy guy. Kind of pathologically happy. No matter how upset I am, he's the one person who's always been able to make me laugh through my tears. But now he looked sad and stunned and hurt as he watched Naomi stomp off.

I know I must seem like a total monster, but I'd had no idea things would deteriorate so quickly. I was hoping for a slow dissolve, thinking the smoothie would allow Naomi to find a more suitable partner, giving Dad time to seamlessly transition from attached to single and then back to attached, this time with Mom. The hurt, the sadness, the anger, weren't part of my plan. The unintended casualties of war, I suppose. I just had to buck up and deal. Because all was fair in love and war, right? I did what I had to do. Dad would bounce back soon. I was sure of it.

Sensationally Sexy Smoothie

    1 ripe banana
    1 cup pineapple chunks
    1 cup vanilla yogurt
    1 cup orange juice
    1½ cups frozen strawberries
    ½ teaspoon vanilla

1. Put banana, pineapple, yogurt, and orange juice into blender and blend well.
2. Add frozen strawberries and vanilla and blend for another minute on low setting.
3. When mixture is well blended, pour entire contents into a pitcher or suitable container; while holding container with both hands, turn in a clockwise direction for one minute while chanting *Om shanti namaste chadaranga.*
4. Pour into tall glass and serve.

Chapter 11

BFF Bull's-Eye

WHEN I WENT DOWN to breakfast the next morning, Kate was nowhere to be found. Weird. In the midst of a lame breakfast of oatmeal with the twins, both of whom looked as disappointed as I was with the morning's meal options, Mom turned to me and said, "Kate called. She's at the Starbucks on Scrubgrass and wants you to meet her there."

Starbucks? Kate hates Starbucks. But I don't. And I was grateful for an excuse not to have to eat the oatmeal.

"I'll get breakfast at Starbucks," I said, jumping up from the table and gathering my things. I waved to Mom and headed for the door.

"Can we get breakfast at Starbucks?" I heard Squeak asking as I exited.

☺☺☺☺

I waltzed into Starbucks and was pleasantly surprised to see Joey and Kate in a corner booth sipping drinks, sharing a muffin, and giggling. Wow. It was the preteen version of preschool.

But better, because we got to have muffins and Frappuccinos instead of juice and cheddar bunnies.

Joey and Kate waved me over.

Joey handed me a drink. "We're all doing Chai Lattes," she said.

I glanced over at Kate to verify this fact, since it was Kate's long-held belief that a Chai Latte was not actually a legitimate beverage and was not to be drunk under any circumstances. Kate was pretty hard core about her coffee, just like everything else. She took her coffee dark. No milk. No sugar. Yet there was Kate, gulping down her Chai Latte as if it were the most delicious thing she'd ever tasted.

"Yo, this is da bomb, dawg," Kate said to me.

"Da bomb, dawg," Joey repeated. "I *love* it. You are so cool."

I wasn't the hugest fan of Chai Lattes either. They tasted like pepper and cloves. I'm more of a Frappuccino girl because I like my coffee to taste like dessert. But I didn't want to mess with success. If Chai Latte was our official group drink, then I would learn to love it.

"We need to figure out some kind of look to, you know, let everyone know we're officially a new group. Like maybe skinny jeans and flannel shirts."

"Sho' 'nuff," Kate tossed off, as though Joey's idea were no big deal. As though Kate hadn't been wearing the exact same wacko outfit for the past year. "But I don't have threads like that."

"No prob. I'll lend you some," Joey offered.

Wow. Kate was finally going to dispense with her crazy uniform. I was so thrilled I wanted to jump for joy right there on the banquette at Starbucks, but I knew I had to play it cool.

"We need a radical name for our crew, J," Kate said to Joey.

"How about the three musketeers?" I asked.

"F, that's kinda foul," Kate said.

"Uh, yeah, Franny, *très* juvenile," Joey added.

Okay, whatever. We didn't need to be called the three musketeers. Because we were the three musketeers. We were back, baby. I didn't care if we called ourselves the Wiggles or the Teletubbies. The only thing that mattered was that we were all friends again.

"Sleepover at my crib this weekend?" Kate asked.

"I'm in," Joey assured Kate.

"Me too." I seconded the motion. My life was complete. I could die happy.

@@@@

When the three of us approached the stairs, our arms linked together, people turned to stare. Joey waved to the peaks and poms as if nothing unusual were afoot. Kate waved to the beeks, equally oblivious. Everyone except Elodie waved back, but no one said a thing. People wouldn't dare question Joey, and the beeks' infinite faith in Kate's wisdom was working in our favor. Still, I could see that every geek, smeek, beek, juvie, loner, gov, and peak was wondering what was up. *Get used to it, people,* I thought. This is the new world order.

Kate and Joey plopped onto the grass to compare schedules. I was about to join them when I caught sight of Marsha Whalley staring at her feet and wearing huge headphones, tuning out the world, completely unaware that Josh Toling and Toby Silverman were standing directly behind her, giggling and pouring Krazy Glue on her hair. My God, these boys were barbarians. I was sure they'd end up locked in juvie hall before high school was finished.

I had tolerated a lot but this prank was beyond the beyond. It was cruel and inhumane. I was outraged, and combined with the fact that I was a bit giddy with my new power, I made the snap decision to take action. After all, I had magic at my disposal, I thought as I remembered the Fix-It Formula in my backpack. Maybe I was overreaching, but wasn't helping someone like Marsha the whole point of the box? It was a completely and utterly selfless act.

I rifled through my backpack and found the mini shampoo bottle stowed away for a rainy day just like this. I was sure that if Granny were here, she would have suggested it herself. I marched over to Marsha. Josh and Toby fled as soon as they spotted me, flinging the Krazy Glue across the steps. I picked up the glue and threw it at them as they retreated.

"Hey, Marsha," I said.

Marsha took off her headphones and stared up at me.

"Why are you talking to me again, Franny?" Marsha was like a soldier who'd seen too many wars; she had given up on the human race.

"I, uh, have something for you," I said, pulling out the tincture. "I noticed that you have extremely, uh, dry hair, just like I do. Believe me, I struggle with it. As I'm sure you do. But ever since I discovered this amazing leave-in conditioner from the Amazon, my hair has become so much more manageable. I think you should try it."

"Franny, you sound really weird, like some crazy infomercial my mom would watch on late-night TV," Marsha said.

"Sorry, it's just, when you find a product you love, you, uh, want to share it. So, can you lean over a little?"

"You want to pour something on my head? Now?" Marsha asked, incredulous.

"*Pour* probably isn't the right word. I'll massage it in. You'll barely notice. Until, that is, you see how smooth and moist your hair becomes later in the day."

Marsha didn't respond. She just gawked at me, not sure what to think.

"I'll be insulted if you don't let me at least try. I feel like dry hair is such a curse and if I can help just one person, I will have done my job." Alas, with my eyes boring into her, Marsha really had no choice but to put her head down and submit to my strange request. I proceeded to shake the tincture onto her head wherever I saw the glue, and then, as strange as it sounds, I began massaging her scalp in circular motions, just as Granny had done, working the stuff in. After a few moments, I was done. I stepped back to inspect. It was hard to tell what exactly was happening in Marsha's huge mound of frizz. Hopefully, the tincture would neutralize the glue.

Marsha didn't say anything. I felt the need to fill the void, so I babbled on. "You're going to thank me for this, Marsha. It's probably the most exciting new product for dry hair on the market. After just a few drops, your hair will feel—"

"Franny. Are you okay?" Marsha interrupted.

As I stared at Marsha's head, I could see her hair loosening up; the glue was melting away. Magic could really come in handy at times. How had I managed to live this long without it?

"I'm fine," I said. "In fact, I'm better than ever."

"Okay, well, uh, good for you," Marsha responded, still staring at me. "My head's really tingly. Is that normal?"

"Totally. Toe-tally. That means it's working. We've got your dry hair exactly where we want it."

"Uh, okay," Marsha said, thoroughly confused.

Uh-oh. Speaking of tingly, my hands were feeling it as well. Must have been the residue from the Fix-It Formula. Oh. No. I hadn't figured my own reaction into the equation. I needed that stuff Granny had used. What was it again? Sandalwood oil. How had I forgotten that? And where on earth could I get sandalwood oil at the moment?

"Let's go inside. What's the point of hanging around down here?" I asked Marsha. I was eager to get to a bathroom and wash the stuff off my hands. Maybe soap and water would work in a pinch. After all, it hadn't been on that long.

"You mean together? Go in together?" Marsha asked, bewildered.

"Yeah. Why not?" Power was a strange brew. I was taking chances I never would have considered taking a few days ago. Thanks to me, Joey and Kate were about to usher the peaks and beeks into a new era of peace and harmony. I might as well take Marsha along for the ride. I grabbed Marsha by the arm and marched up the steps with her, head held high. You'd have thought we were carrying a live explosive or something. Everyone stopped what he or she was doing and stared at us.

When Marsha and I got to the top of the steps, Elodie stood at the closed door like some kind of crazed Secret Service agent, her arms crossed and her chest all puffed out.

"Step off, Flanders," she said fiercely. "Take your little pet geek back where she belongs. *Hasta la vista,* baby."

Elodie had been watching way too many action movies.

"Good job using the word of the day, Elodie," Samantha Ross said. "It's *hasta la vista,* Franny. Did you get Joey's text?"

"It's more of a phrase than a word," I said to Samantha. And then I turned to Elodie, my hands feeling hot and spiky. "Have you ever considered that being mean, petty, arrogant, and shallow just might leave you begging in the streets someday, no friends or family in sight?" Marsha's mouth spread into a huge grin.

I'll admit, it was bold, possibly even insane, but I was on

entirely new ground here, flying by the seat of my middle school pants. Joey and Kate were best friends, so how much longer could Elodie hold on to her power base? If she was going over the edge anyway, might as well give her a little shove.

I reached around Elodie and yanked the door open. Marsha audibly gasped. Elodie grabbed the door and tried to pull it shut, but I outyanked her with no effort at all. Marsha, meanwhile, seemed to spring to life just as the door swung shut behind us. The Fix-It Formula had taken hold of Marsha, and the change was pretty impressive.

"Smellodie," Marsha said, loud enough for Elodie to hear. I'd never actually heard that one, and I chuckled. Through the glass pane in the door I could see Elodie's entire body go rigid with rage as her group of loyal lieutenants swarmed around her.

"Nice, Marsh," I said, and we high-fived. Marsha's newfound confidence was a marked improvement. No sandalwood oil for her.

We entered the lobby and saw that the sign-up sheet for the school play was prominently placed on the bulletin board. Marsha ran toward it.

"You know what? I think I'm going to try out this year," Marsha said. "I've always wanted to but never had the guts."

Wow. Marsha had certainly come flying out of her shell, which I guess was a good thing. I just wasn't sure the school play was the absolute best place for her to reinvent herself. It was a pretty public forum. I wondered if I should discourage

Marsha. I mean, she needed to pace herself. Baby steps. How about making eye contact with a few people, for starters? But I didn't have much time to react because Marsha marched over to the sign-up sheet and scrawled her name across the form. She had just finished when Elodie appeared next to her, grabbed her by the shoulder, and spun her around.

"Smellodie?" Elodie barked.

I could practically see the steam coming out of Elodie's ears.

"Shower much?" Marsha said.

Elodie ripped the try-out sheet off the bulletin board. "What do you think you're doing?" she asked.

"I'm going to play the lead in this year's school play," Marsha stated. And then she broke into song. She began to sing something from *High School Musical*. At the top of her lungs. She was good. Better than good. Great even. But that was beside the point. Singing in public was an express train to the social abyss. Everyone stared at Marsha in horror. I grabbed her by the arm and tried to drag her away, but Marsha was having none of it. She had found her inner showgirl and she wasn't letting go.

"Let's start slow. Maybe you could try out for a part in the chorus?" I said.

"No way, no way, Franny May," Marsha sang out in some made-up tune. "I want to reach for the stars this year. No more living in fear." Marsha spread her arms wide, did a high kick followed by a spin, and then took a bow. She had talent.

Still, the middle school hallway was hardly the place to throw down.

"See you at the audition, Smellodie," Marsha said, and then she scampered off down the hall. Serious stuff, that tincture. Proceed with extreme caution.

Reeling from Marsha's performance, I made a beeline for the girls' bathroom, hoping I could wash the Fix-It Formula away. I scrubbed my hands for a solid ten minutes and then, with no real choice, hurried off to Ms. Posey's English class. I took my seat only to discover, to my horror, that my hands were now burning with an intense heat. I rubbed them on my pants as hard as I could, but it was a lost cause.

"Class, please settle down," Ms. Posey said, which is what she says at the start of every class. "Does anyone have any questions about last night's homework?"

"I do! *Beowulf* is a huge waste of time," I spit out. "Why are you making us read it when there are millions of better books to choose from? Do you get pleasure out of torturing us?" And the deed was done. I might as well have walked up to Ms. Posey and slapped her in the face.

"Congratulations, Miss Flanders, that was strike two. I'm not sure if you're familiar with baseball, but let me fill you in on the rules: one more strike and you are out. You have one week to write an essay on the merits of *Beowulf* and why it has remained a classic for more than twelve hundred years." Ms. Posey glared at me. Man, she was scary. How did she ever end up teaching kids? She was much better suited to the job of prison warden or butcher. I bit my lips, hard, to stop myself from saying anything further. My teeth dug into the skin. Yowza!

Ms. Posey scribbled something, got up from her desk, and walked right over to me. She plopped a note down on my desk addressed to Principal Mackey and stared at me menacingly. "How about you discuss your strong opinions with Principal Mackey and leave the rest of us in peace?"

Did I hear her correctly? Principal Mackey? I had never, ever been sent to the principal's office. I don't mess with authority figures. I play by the rules, get straight As. And yet here I was, heading to the principal's office like some kind of juvie. I shuddered to think what was next for me. Maximum-security prison?

I slunk down the hall toward Principal Mackey's office, not really knowing what to expect. Did they still hit kids with rulers? On the way, I passed the girls' bathroom and rushed back in to scrub my hands a little more. They were red and raw when I finally gave up. I couldn't tell if they were tingling from the excessive washing or the tincture. I prayed for the former and headed off to meet my fate.

I handed Principal Mackey's secretary the note and sat down to await my sentence. A few minutes later, Principal Mackey called me into her office. She read the note and then glanced through my file as I sat frozen in front of her.

"Franny, tell me why you don't like *Beowulf*," she said after studying me for a moment.

Miraculously, my hands had stopped tingling. I didn't know if it was temporary or not, so I dove right in, picking my words carefully. I knew my response could have a wide-ranging impact on my academic future.

"I apologize for treating Ms. Posey with disrespect. Sometimes I get a little carried away with my passion for literature. I will admit, I am not fond of *Beowulf*. I find it a bit dense and old-fashioned, but I also recognize there is tremendous merit to reading books that have stood the test of time, even if you think they're boring." I finished and waited for the ax to come down.

After what seemed like two days, Principal Mackey finally spoke.

"Franny, I'm going to let you go on this one. You've always seemed like a lovely young lady. And you've got a wonderful academic record. I don't know what went wrong this morning but I'm going to chalk it up to a bad day. It happens to the best of us. But I have to warn you, Ms. Posey is not pleased with you, and that is not a happy place to spend the year. Try to get back into her good graces, would you?"

"Definitely, I'll get right on it, ma'am." I had been spared and I was grateful.

⊚⊚⊚⊚

I sat silently through Spanish and social studies. I had an occasional tingle here and there but the magic was clearly on the wane. I was able to control any stirrings by biting my lips. By the end of class, I had a nasty sore brewing on the inside of my lip but at least I hadn't said anything stupid.

I headed into the cafeteria and spotted Kate and Joey sitting alone at the peaks' table, chatting and giggling. Other peaks were standing in a circle around them, not entirely sure what to do. As students streamed into the cafeteria, they stopped and took note of Joey and Kate, eyeing them with a mix of fear and suspicion. There was a lot of rubbernecking as geeks, smeeks, beeks, govs, loners, and juvies walked slowly by, carrying their lunch trays. The scene riveted even Mr. Pandrock, the lunchroom monitor, who was usually comatose.

"Anyone mind if Kate sits with us today?" Joey asked, looking up at the peaks surrounding her.

"Uh, no, I guess not," said Alexi as he sat down next to Joey. And then Zach Haus scooted in as well. Soon, other peaks and poms followed suit and took seats at the table, accepting the new world order as a *fait accompli* (a phrase of the week last year).

Samantha Ross was just about to sit down when Elodie barked, "I mind. Do. Not. Sit. Down. Samantha."

Poor Samantha looked scared out of her brain. She kind of froze, half standing, half seated. Her two leaders were at war. What was a lowly subject to do?

"Dommage," Joey said mockingly to Elodie.

"Dommage. That's tope," Kate said. "What does it mean?"

"'Too bad' in French. I know, like, seven European languages. I'll teach you." And then Joey added, "It's too silly that Franny has to split lunch between the two of us."

"Fo' shizzle, dawg," Kate responded.

"Did you hear me, Joey? La Principessa has a problem with a beek joining us," Elodie told Joey.

"I don't know what to tell you." Joey held Elodie's gaze for a moment, daring Elodie to push it further. But she didn't. She'd never take on Joey in public. She knew it would have critical social fallout. Though I was pretty sure she'd figure out a way to do something damaging behind the scenes. I made a mental note to keep an eye on her. I quietly slipped into the seat next to Kate, letting this scene play itself out. I was actually really enjoying the show.

"C'mon, Samantha, we're out of here," Elodie ordered. She knew Samantha Ross, brown-nose extraordinaire, was her best chance of forming a coalition at the moment.

"Now? But I haven't had lunch," Samantha said.

"Yes. Now. Right. Now. Let's. Go." Elodie stomped out of the cafeteria. With no real choice, Samantha followed her out.

Kate caught sight of Owen and Jane standing by the beek table looking hurt and confused. Kate stood up and waved them over. But Owen and Jane didn't budge. It was at this point that Joey jumped onto the cafeteria table, delicately side-stepping several glasses of juice and platefuls of food.

"Okay, people, the new word of the day is *mingle*," Joey announced. No one moved. No one spoke. You could hear the quiet hum of the air conditioners as everyone stared back at Joey, dumbfounded. "I want everyone out of their comfort zone. Leon, go join the juvies for lunch," Joey instructed a scared-looking smeek. "Mikaela, go sit with the loners," Joey encouraged a juvie. "Jane and Owen, come sit with us, and, Angus, go sit with the beeks."

The recipe had made Joey conscious of the class system and suddenly she was feeling more inclusive. It was an unexpected bonus. I watched in wonder as peaks moved over and made room for Jane and Owen. Leon went over to sit with the juvies. Mikaela joined the loners. Joey had changed the social dynamics of Jefferson Middle School with a wave of her hand and a few simple instructions. Now, that was serious magic.

Her mission complete, Joey took her seat. Joey and Kate smiled at each other and then, at the exact same time, they both said, "Done and done!" And then they both cracked up.

"Jinx," they both said. At exactly the same time. And yes, they cracked up again, only this time even harder.

Wow. Things were working out even better than I could have hoped.

Chapter 12

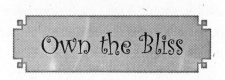

Own the Bliss

The next few days were a blur of bliss. I came downstairs in the morning to find both Joey and Kate waiting for me in the kitchen. They were wearing skinny jeans and flannel shirts, standing side by side, smiling at me, beckoning me, their third musketeer, to join them. Kate looked great. She didn't even have her lime green scooter or the silly knapsack she carried it in. I hadn't seen Kate dressed normally in two years.

As I took Kate in, I felt emboldened and all-powerful, like anything was possible. This is what Moses must have felt like right after he parted the Red Sea. But everyone was acting as though nothing unusual were happening, and that was precisely how I had to act, hard as it was to contain my joy. Humility is overrated. Trust me.

"Kate, love the outfit," I said.

"It's bangin', right? They're Joey's threads," Kate replied.

"Kate and I thought we'd all walk to school together today," Joey said.

"Totally," I said, overjoyed at the prospect.

Mom watched us all, smiling. "I'm so pleased to see you

girls are all friends again. I always told Franny it was only a matter of time."

"You called it, Mom," I said. I let Mom have the satisfaction of thinking she'd been right all along. It was the perfect cover.

Granny pulled me aside. "I gather you finally had that long-overdue chat with your friends?" she asked me, raising one eyebrow.

"Yep. Finally talked it out. Thanks for the advice." I spat out the lie fast so that maybe it wouldn't count.

"I'm proud of you," Granny said, giving me a squeeze.

Kate gave my carefully curated dress and leggings the once-over. "Yo, F, you should go change. We could triplet it out."

Triplets? "You, uh, want all of us to match?" I asked. That was pushing it.

"Fo' sheezy," Joey and Kate said together. Quickly followed by "Jinx." And then gales of laughter.

Okay. Whatever. Triplets it was. I needed to own the bliss. Question nothing.

ⓔⓔⓔⓔ

We arrived at Jefferson to find that people had retreated to their familiar spots. Old habits die hard. As the three of us waltzed up the stairs together, everyone turned to look, realizing at that moment that yesterday was no fluke.

"Kate, we'll see you at music theory after school, right?" Owen called out to Kate as she ascended the stairs.

"Uh, not sure, bro. Kinda living in the moment right now," Kate said.

Owen did not know what to make of this, and neither did the rest of the beeks, who looked on in confusion as we proceeded up the stairs. Frankly, I was a little perplexed myself but, whatever, I was just happy to be part of Kate's moment. At the top of the stairs, Elodie was prowling, eager to make her move. Samantha Ross stood close by, her lady in waiting.

"Hey, Joey, what's the word of the day?" Elodie asked, obviously convinced that the nightmare of yesterday had been erased with a good night's sleep.

"I'm going to have to go with *mingle* again," Joey announced.

"Are you kidding me?" Elodie asked. She looked distraught. I was loving it. So sorry, Elodie. The new Joey was here to stay. Deal with it.

Joey turned around and looked out at everyone. "People, in case I didn't make myself clear yesterday, mix it up. Mingle. Go for it!"

People scrambled off their perches and ventured hesitantly into different crowds. As hard as Elodie was trying to appear in control, her resolve was slipping precariously. She looked like she was going to pull out a shotgun and go completely postal. I had a fleeting whiff of sympathy for her but then reminded myself that Elodie would sell newborn babies to terrorists if she thought she could gain from it in any way.

"Uh, Joey, what's going on?" Elodie's voice rose about eight octaves.

"Nothing. What's going on with you?" Joey replied innocently.

"Uh, I'm not the one spitting out stupid new rules and hanging out with beeks."

"The old rules were the ones that were stupid, Elodie. And Kate is tight. So chillax, dawg." Kate and Joey laughed uproariously at this.

Elodie stared at Joey. And then she looked from Kate to me and back to Joey. "Oh. My. God. You're . . . matching? That is so . . . gross."

Samantha Ross looked devastated as she took in our matching jeans and shirts. With Kate and me matching Joey, Samantha knew she had just been downsized. Elodie was now unequivocally her leader and Samantha didn't exactly seem thrilled with the news.

"Cute, no?" Joey exclaimed. We headed into the building, blowing right past Elodie as she stewed in a vat of her own rage. I kept my head down and followed Joey and Kate inside. But Elodie grabbed my arm and yanked me back out.

"I know you're behind this somehow, Franny Flanders. You're not going to get away with it. La Principessa is watching," Elodie whispered into my ear in a low, raggedy voice. With Joey, Kate, and me back together again, I was too high on life to worry about Elodie. I simply smiled and walked away, which only further enraged her. My whole trajectory had changed. I had gone from an express train to the toilet to a rocket ship to the moon. Elodie could kiss my butt.

@@@@

Things were very good. But they were about to get a whole lot better. I had art that day and I was hard at work on my landscape when Alden plopped down next to me.

"Hey, Franny, how's your sketch coming?" Alden asked me. That's right. Me. Me. Me. Alden Timkins was talking to me. I felt dizzy. I prayed I wouldn't pass out.

"Uh, it's, uh, well, you know, going. It is . . ." Just my flipping luck. I was speaking in tongues. What had happened to my finely honed dexterous conversational skills? On second thought, maybe it would be better if I just passed out. At least I could explain that away. But this . . . collection of incoherent mutterings was inexcusable. I kicked myself in the shin as punishment. The moment of truth had finally arrived and I so wasn't up to the task.

"I'm kind of stuck," Alden said. And then—and I am not lying—he leaned in to me. He smelled good. Boy good. Like grass and sweat and shampoo and a little minty. "I like the way you're filling the paper with, I don't know, different stuff. Everyone else is just doing, you know, trees, beach, houses. But you've got sand dunes and a forest and animals. It's cool, kinda like a collage. You think you could help me with my sketch?"

He was all big-eyed and sincere. I felt warm fuzzies all over. If this was love, then count me in. It felt great.

Alden stared at me, waiting for an answer. I gazed back, lost in his green eyes and his overwhelming hotness.

"Franny, are you okay?" Alden asked.

"Uh, yeah. I was just, uh, thinking about . . . uh, something." What? Another gem out of the mouth of Franny Flanders. I willed myself to get a grip.

"Did I totally disrupt your concentration? Listen, I'll just leave you alone—"

"No! Don't do that," I said, much louder than I meant to. People looked over.

Okay, Flanders, it's now or never.

"Let me show you how I got started." I was speaking fluently again. This was the start of something big. Huge, in fact. I was sure of it.

I explained to Alden how I had used all kinds of outdoor settings in my landscape. I didn't limit myself to one view. Instead, I took different scenes from different places I'd been or seen or read about and mixed them all together. At first, it was a bit of a mess, but then I pulled out the stuff that didn't work and kept the things that did.

"It's kind of the landscape of my mind," I said, hoping I didn't sound too loserish.

"That's awesome. I never would have thought of that. You're really good," Alden said. And he seemed totally sincere. Really sweet. Completely fascinated. Not like he was just humoring me. I bet Janet Scully knows nothing about landscape design.

Alden and I continued to talk quietly throughout the rest of class as we both worked on our projects. I tried to appear casual and cool yet brilliantly artistic and inspired. It was a tricky combination. In the end, I straddled it quite well. I don't think I'm exaggerating when I say Alden was pretty close to perfect. And objectively speaking, I seemed like the ideal girl-friend for him. Toward the end of class Call Me Jeff approached. He gave my sketch the once-over.

"Keep up the great work, Franny. You should be able to start painting soon." And then Call Me Jeff glanced over at Alden's paper. "Alden, nice work," he said, sounding surprised.

"Franny's been helping me," Alden said, giving my arm a gentle squeeze.

I went boneless at his touch. I had to hold on to the table with both hands to stop myself from collapsing onto the floor. He *touched* me. That definitely meant something. I suddenly got an image of Dad walking me down the aisle. I wore a beautiful sleeveless white gown. Alden stood at the altar, wear-ing a well-cut suit. I knew I was getting a little ahead of myself, but whatever. It was my fantasy. I could do what I wanted.

"Keep up the good work," Call Me Jeff said, walking off.

I noticed Elodie glaring at me from across the room. I didn't let her get to me. At least not at that point. Because you've got to pay to play. And if Elodie was the cost, then it was well worth the price.

Alden and I left the art room together and were talking about a million things when we were rudely interrupted by the sudden appearance of Janet Scully. I had forgotten about the ever-annoying Janet Scully. Was she still around?

"Ready to walk to history, sweetie?" Janet giggled like a hyena. If she had a thought in her head, it would perish from loneliness.

Alden turned to me for a split second and held my gaze. "Thanks again, Franny." And then he joined Janet and disappeared down the hall. Still, I felt triumphant. There was no denying that something had transpired between us and it was building momentum. Janet's days were numbered.

ⓒⓒⓒⓒ

"You totally have to get the lip-gloss *and* the blush," Joey told Kate.

"Yeah. It looks awesome," Kate said, staring at herself in the drugstore mirror as Joey finished applying the blush.

Awesome? Kate had said *awesome*. Wow. Maybe she was finally outgrowing the slanguage. It was about time. It was all too good to be true, on top of the fact that Kate was considering a makeup purchase. She's usually dogmatic about makeup, spouting off all sorts of propaganda about how it ruins the environment, maims animals, and does whatever else in the service of corporate profits.

"You look fantastic," I said. And she did. It was amazing what a little blush and lip-gloss could do for a girl.

We were all hanging out on Saturday, gathering supplies for the sleepover party that night. I was in eighth or ninth heaven, having passed seventh heaven a few days ago. After the drugstore, we went to the Burger Joint for—wait for it—burgers! Kate ordered an actual turkey burger. Turkey and all. Usually she just got a bun at the Burger Joint. She was afraid she'd get meat residue off the grill if she ate a veggie burger made where meat burgers had touched down. It was too weird. And too great. All at the same time. Kate no longer seemed nearly as staunch about . . . well, anything. It was a huge relief to watch her relax and slip into the new life I had so thoughtfully designed for her. Thank you very much.

"This is slammin'," Kate said, polishing off the last of her burger. "I don't know why I was so buggin' about the cafeteria."

"No way. You were right to insist on a salad bar. The food sucks. I mean, Marta is the worst chef in the history of the world. Most days, I couldn't have survived without the salad bar," Joey assured Kate.

"I hear you, dawg. She is *the* worst!"

"*Vive la* salad bar," I added for Joey's benefit.

"You know what, Frans, I'm so not into French anymore. It sounds so pretentious," Joey said.

"Got it. Losing the French," I said, thrilled. I hoped that Spanish, German, and Italian would soon follow.

"Have you ever noticed that everything Marta makes tastes like paper? Like even the tacos?" Joey asked.

"I thought it was just the vegan stuff," Kate said.

"Nope. It's the mac and cheese, the hot dogs, the chicken . . ." I said.

"Even the chocolate chip cookies and the apple pie," Kate exclaimed.

We were so in sync, it was eerie. I couldn't believe it had taken a magic box to bring us back together when our friendship was so clearly meant to be. I made a mental note to do a little something to perk up Marta's cooking, in the name of friendship.

We spent the next twenty-four hours in a cocoon of happiness. We watched Kate Hudson movies, stuffed our faces with chili cheese popcorn and Rolos, and then stayed up all night talking about . . . everything. Kate told Joey about her crush on James Singer, and miraculously, Joey encouraged Kate to go for it. I shared my encounter with Alden. Joey and Kate dissed Janet Scully. Neither thought Janet was long for the job. They told me to keep chatting him up in art class and he and Janet would be toast well before the Fall Fling. Joey told us about French-kissing Alexi last weekend, and when Kate and I badgered her with question after question (since neither of us had ever kissed a boy), Joey demonstrated her technique on a pillow and we all cracked up laughing.

We all agreed that Elodie just might be the devil's spawn (though Joey defended her a little), that Patel Vashki was the smartest person at Jefferson, that Marsha Whalley wasn't so bad after all, and that Ms. Posey was worse than awful.

I don't want to overstate things, but it was the best night of my life. And I should have left well enough alone because, really, my work was done. And, best of all, Granny didn't have a clue. It was win-win. All good. The perfect crime. But I didn't stop there. As they say, hindsight is 20/20.

Chapter 13

What Could Possibly Go Wrong?

"IT'S LA PRINCIPESSA," Elodie said when I answered my cell on my way home from Kate's. As if I didn't know. "Normally, I'd never waste my unlimited minutes calling you but you didn't leave me a choice." It was only ten in the morning and she already sounded revved up and ready to go.

"I'm not sure what you mean," I said innocently.

"You know exactly what I mean, Flanders. A juvie texted me over the weekend. A loner invited me to her birthday party and, for the second day in a row, a smeek said hi to me in the hall. And. I. Don't. Like. It. Do I make myself clear?"

"Very," I said.

"I know you're behind this desperate grab at democracy. And I've got a little news flash for you: middle school is not fair. Everyone is not supposed to get along. Things run more smoothly when there's a benevolent dictator in charge, and that's me."

"I wouldn't exactly call you, uh, benevolent, Elodie," I blurted out. It felt good to say that, though I knew I would pay dearly somewhere down the line.

Elodie didn't say anything for a minute. It was the calm before the storm. I braced myself for impact.

"If Joey doesn't start hanging with me and stop messing around with Crazy Kate, you lose all immunity. I never liked you, Franny. I put up with you because of Joey. But if I lose Joey to Kate, I will go after you and everything you hold sacred."

And then the phone clicked off. I pictured myself rooming with Sandy Smithson at her boarding school in Montana, exiled from Jefferson. Would I ever see my family again? Would I have to learn to snowshoe? I felt a cold wave shudder through my body. I hadn't given enough thought to the Elodie factor in all of this. She could easily bring me down if I didn't do something fast. I needed to talk to the box. Hopefully, it would know what to do with Elodie, because I didn't have a clue.

By the time I got home, I was buzzing with intensity, full-throttle focused on solving the Elodie problem. I entered the house on a bullet to get to Granny's room. Unfortunately, Mom and Granny were in the kitchen and stopped me in my tracks.

"Hey, Frans, how was the sleepover at Kate's?" Mom asked.

"Great. Joey was there too!" It popped out of my mouth before I really had time to think about the consequences. I stuffed an Oreo in my mouth to stop myself from blabbering on. I would have loved to tell Mom everything, the way I used to. Before things got so complicated. But that would be opening up a box of another sort: Pandora's. And I didn't want to do that. Certainly not with Granny around.

"Wow. They really are getting along famously these days," Mom said.

"It's a pretty quick turnaround considering they were barely speaking when school started last week," Granny said, raising one eyebrow. Was she onto me? I couldn't tell. I needed to tread very carefully here. And instead I'd sent up a huge red flag that begged for further discussion. I needed to make a quick U-turn.

"I think they were just, uh, you know, doing the sleepover for me. I'm sure it won't happen again anytime soon." I laughed, trying to make light of the whole thing and get Mom and Granny off the scent.

"Well, I'm just glad everyone's getting along again," Mom said.

"I told you middle school wasn't so bad," Granny said.

"You guys were right, grownups always know best," I said. Okay, that was laying it on thick. I think Mom and Granny knew that but they let it pass.

"Ready for some together time, Francisco?" Granny asked.

"Together time?" I asked Granny, horrified at the thought. I wanted time with the box, not Granny.

"You promised together time this week. No time like the present."

Oh, please, no. Not now. How about any other time? I was spending the night at Dad's and I really needed to get my magic on before I left. But it was clearly going to have to wait. How would I get my hands on that box?

Granny bounded out of the room with waaaay too much energy for someone her age. Bummed, I began to follow, but Mom grabbed my arm to stop me.

"You and Granny are getting on like a house on fire," Mom said, smiling.

I gathered that a house on fire was a good thing.

"Granny's, uh, nice to have around," I said.

"You know, I was really worried when I asked her to move in. I thought that you'd be resentful. Or you'd find Granny a little . . . off. I'm glad to see you're able to appreciate her. I know she can be an acquired taste."

An acquired taste? To say the very least. "Yeah, it's all good," I mumbled, distracted, as I tried to come up with plan B.

"Fran, I hate to ask this of you and I wouldn't if any of our regular babysitters were available . . . I know you're supposed to spend the night with your dad but I'm really in a bind and Dad said you could stay over tomorrow instead. In fact, his exact words were 'Any night is good. I've got no plans for the rest of my life.' I don't know what he meant but that's neither here nor there. Anyway, I really need you to baby-sit the twins tonight. Gran has mahjong at Leisure Village with Gladys, I've got a dinner with—"

"Sure, no problem." Mom had just handed me plan B on a plate.

"Really?" Mom looked at me, surprised.

Uh-oh. A little too much enthusiasm. I needed to turn it down or Mom's antenna was going to go up. "You know, I've been thinking about it and I feel like I need to get to know the boys better. Maybe it'll help me understand where they're coming from. Not be so annoyed at them all the time. Joey's been doing more stuff with her little sister and she feels like it, uh . . ." I was really groping here. I had no idea where I was going with this. "Helped them get along better. She said that she gets Jemma now, and she doesn't find her so irritating. And, well, maybe that could happen with the twins."

I had no idea if Mom was buying anything I was selling. But then I looked over at her and saw that her eyes were welling up. Jeez. She could be such a sentimental sucker sometimes.

"Franny, that is music to my ears. I am so thrilled to hear that you want to improve your relationship with your brothers. We'll have to start doing more together. Maybe bowling or bike riding. Let's plan for a hike next week, followed by a trip to the IMAX." Mom gave me a little hug.

More time with the twins? I'd rather light myself on fire.

Granny was wearing a pink sweatsuit and holding two rackets when I got to her room. "I hope you're ready to move your body."

"What do you mean?" I asked.

"We're going to play racquetball, and I'm going to kick your little butt," Granny said, bouncing up and down on her toes. She couldn't be serious. And yet she looked pretty serious. She had sweatbands around both wrists and her forehead. I would have preferred to make yak butter tea. I really didn't have the energy to whack a ball around. But there was no stopping this Granny train.

A half-hour later we were at the gym, rackets in hand. Together time was proving to be a huge thorn in my side.

Granny pulled an impressive stick of incense out of her bag and lit it, inside the court.

"Granny, you can't do that. We're going to choke. Or get arrested."

"It purifies the air. It's the way they do it in India." I knew Asia would figure into this somehow. It always did.

Turned out, racquetball wasn't such a bad idea. I whacked at the ball with a fury and intensity that surprised even me. It was a welcome release. Granny met my force, shot for shot. We went at it for a solid hour. Man, Granny could really haul butt for an old lady. Despite my youth and energy, I could barely get a point off her. By the end, we were covered in sweat and smelled like incense.

"Let's do this again next week, Francisco. With a little more practice, you might actually beat me," Granny said.

I smiled weakly. Everything hurt. I didn't know if I had the energy for much more together time.

☺☺☺☺

Finally, after about two years, Granny and Mom left the house. Alone at last.

"Wanna play Battleship?" I turned around to see Squeak staring up at me.

"No. Let's play Stratego," Pip countered.

Oh, right, not entirely alone. Those darn twins were still here.

"I've got a much better idea," I said as I ushered the boys into the den, turned on the television, and stuck them in front of *SpongeBob*. I didn't plan on speaking to them again until I heard Mom's key in the lock.

I snuck into Granny's room, nabbed the box from its hiding place, and sat down on the bed. I was ready to attack the Elodie issue and while I was at it maybe a few other things as well. It was impossible to resist after my recent success. I knew Granny wouldn't be happy, but if I was going to go back to the well, why not take a good, long drink.

I could change the way I looked and be taller, prettier, smarter . . . breasts! I could make us richer than Bill Gates. I could convince Mom to buy a puppy; heck, why not get a pony and a talking parrot to boot? I had some serious power. Shouldn't I have a little fun with it? Joey and Kate were a raging success. What could possibly go wrong?

And then Granny's words rang in my ears: *You can upset the delicate balance of the universe.* I couldn't shake the image I had of burning comets streaking toward Earth on a path to mass destruction. What if I was responsible for the annihilation of the human race? I didn't want that. If I became a total babe or we became extremely rich or Elodie disappeared, there would be consequences, questions, maybe even jail time. I needed to be cautious. Check out any children's book: magic can wreak havoc.

Still, something had to be done about Elodie, at the very least. I focused and conjured a mental image of Elodie acting nice and generous and gentle, and let me tell you, it would have been easier to imagine the Joker reading *Goodnight Moon* to the twins. I had had the image set for about thirty seconds when suddenly Elodie morphed into an evil monkey, yanked me in tight, and began to throttle me. I shook my head to free myself of the image. I breathed in and out for a few beats and began again.

I concentrated harder than I ever had, so hard that I began to perspire. Finally, I summoned a benevolent Elodie, frolicking in a meadow, picking flowers with a small lamb. *Hold it. Hold it,* I told myself and then, slowly, the drawer creaked open, and out came a recipe for Naturally Nice Nog. Milk, nutmeg, ginger. Totally easy.

I should have stopped there, but I didn't. It seemed foolish to walk away from such an incredible resource. I decided to ask for a recipe that would chill out Ms. Posey and get her off my back. Then, for Joey and Kate, I asked for Marta, the cafeteria lady, to be a better cook. These requests would benefit the whole school. Pretty selfless and exactly the point of the box. I couldn't see how Granny could argue with that. After a few minutes of full-on focusing, out popped Happy Hand Cream for Ms. Posey and Make-It-Better Munchie Mix for Marta.

Now I deserved a reward for all my good deeds. Something small and insignificant, that no one would need to know about; I could go for B-cup breasts on the next go-around. There was this fabulous pair of designer jeans that Mom refused to buy me. (Her exact words were "What does a twelve-year-old girl need a pair of hundred-and-fifty-dollar jeans for? That's obscene.") I conjured an image of myself in those jeans as I stared at the box. And then I waited. And waited. And waited. And ... nothing. I changed tactics and pictured myself buying the jeans instead of wearing them. But still, nothing.

"What is up with you?" I asked the box, which, naturally, didn't respond. "Fine. Be that way."

I moved on from the jeans to a trip to the Bahamas. I pictured us all snorkeling over the reefs, swarms of colorful fish spinning around us. The box refused to budge. I got *nada*. Whatever. I had what I needed for now. I'd try again later.

After a lot of rummaging around in the fridge and the farthest reaches of Granny's medicine cabinet, I managed to cobble together all the ingredients for the three recipes. Our house was a treasure chest of alchemic ingredients. Who knew?

An hour and a half later I had a thermos of Naturally Nice Nog, a small container of Happy Hand Cream, and a big bag of Make-It-Better Munchie Mix. The only confusing bits were counting to ten in Hindi, dancing a jig, and the ten Pranayama breaths. But a quick trip to the Web solved all that. I was armed and ready. And nobody was the wiser.

Naturally Nice Nog

   8 ounces milk
   1 tablespoon vanilla extract
   ½ teaspoon ground ginger
   ½ teaspoon nutmeg
   3 tablespoons sugar
   ½ tablespoon cocoa powder
      Dash of cinnamon

1. Heat milk in a pot until hot, not boiling.
2. Add in vanilla, ginger, nutmeg, sugar, and cocoa powder.
3. Sprinkle mixture with cinnamon.
4. Count to ten in Hindi (*ek, do, teen, char, panch, chhe, saat, aath, nau, das*) while stirring mixture.
5. Refrigerate until chilled. Shake and serve.

Make-It-Better Munchie Mix

3 cups toasted oat bran cereal
1½ cups uncooked quick-cooking oats
¾ cup chopped pecans
¼ teaspoon salt
1 teaspoon cinnamon
½ cup butter
½ cup firmly packed brown sugar
½ cup honey
1 cup sweetened dried cranberries or raisins

1. Combine first five ingredients in a large bowl; set aside.
2. Mix together butter, brown sugar, and honey in a small saucepan over low heat, stirring until butter melts and sugar dissolves.
3. Pour butter mixture over cereal mixture, then stir to coat. Spread in a single layer on an aluminum-foil-lined 15x10-inch pan.
4. Bake at 325 degrees for 20 minutes, stirring once. Stir in cranberries, and bake 5 more minutes.
5. As mixture bakes, dance a jig in a circle in front of the oven for 5 continuous minutes.
6. Spread immediately on wax paper; cool. Store snack mix in an airtight container.

Happy Hand Cream

    2 tablespoons beeswax
    2 teaspoons distilled water
    4 ounces cocoa butter
    4 tablespoons almond oil
    2 tablespoons coconut oil
       Dash of vanilla

1. Melt the beeswax over low heat with the water.
2. Spoon in cocoa butter and blend.
3. Gradually blend in both oils. Add in dash of vanilla.
4. While blending, do ten pranayama breaths: Breathe in deeply, through diaphragm, to a count of five. Hold the breath for a count of four, and exhale for a count of five, pushing all the breath out from the stomach. Repeat nine more times.
5. Pour into glass jar or hard plastic container. The lotion will thicken as it cools.

Chapter 14

A New World Order

I WAS SO EXCITED to get to English and try out the Happy Hand Cream on Ms. Posey, I arrived to class ten minutes early. Ms. Posey was working at her desk and didn't look pleased to see me when I entered the empty classroom. I smiled broadly. She stared at me blankly in return. But I would not be deterred.

"Hey, Ms. Posey. I wanted to ask you about that scene in *David Copperfield* when he mentions a chicken. Do you think it's intended as symbolism or irony?"

The night before, I made sure to read the six assigned chapters of *David Copperfield* more closely than I'd ever read anything in my life. Plus two extra chapters and a bunch of stuff about the book on the Internet.

"Mmmm, and your point?" Ms. Posey was not giving anything up.

"Well, I looked it up and it seems that the chicken may have been a Derbyshire redcap, which was a favorite among chicken breeders in the late nineteenth century..."

Ms. Posey said nothing.

"The chicken's feathers would have been a reddish-brown color. Do you think Dickens intended the color of the feathers to foreshadow the blood that was soon to flow in the story?" I continued.

There was silence as Ms. Posey stared at me for a beat. Maybe she thought she was being Punk'd. I mean, nobody goes the extra mile in her classes; she's just too mean for anyone to want to curry favor.

"Well, goodness, Franny. I'll be honest, I've never considered it from that vantage point." Ms. Posey was softening up. Miracles can happen.

I went on. "Initially, I thought it may have been a common white leghorn, but in that case, I think the white feathers could also have a meaning. They represent purity and innocence perhaps, as does David Copperfield."

"Franny, this is very impressive work." Ms. Posey looked shocked by my enthusiasm for *David Copperfield*. "If you'd like, I would be happy to assign you some extra-credit reading so you could explore some of these themes further."

"I would *love* that," I said, thinking just the opposite.

Perfect. I had her just where I wanted her.

"By the way, I brought in some homemade hand cream today." I pulled out the Happy Hand Cream and massaged it into my hands. "Everyone in my family suffers from such dry skin. Luckily, we've got this amazing homemade recipe we use and, well . . . would you like some?"

I dipped my hand into the cream, brought out a dollop,

and placed it on Ms. Posey's palm. She glanced down at her hand, baffled, and then looked back at me.

"Franny, what on earth are you doing?"

"My mom and I, uh, just made a big batch so I'll leave this one for you," I said. Ms. Posey stared at the big old wad of cream in her palm and then, with little choice, rubbed it into her hands. Bingo. The rest was up to forces beyond my control.

At this point, students started streaming into the classroom. Deed done, I took my seat. Unfortunately, Ms. Posey was her same old grouchy self for most of the class. But as the bell rang and we were filing out, she called, "Have a lovely day, class." We all stopped and turned around to make sure we'd heard her correctly. Ms. Posey stood there waving to everyone, a goofy smile plastered on her face. Mission accomplished. After Spanish and social studies, I would finish what I had started.

When lunch finally arrived, I sprinted to the cafeteria, snaking through the crowds, the thermos of Naturally Nice Nog clasped in my hand. It was showtime. Elodie's and Marta's turns to take center stage.

Perfect. The cafeteria was full of sixth-graders. The seventh-graders had yet to arrive. I grabbed an empty glass, poured in the nog, and went in search of my prey. I found her immediately, a nervous-looking sixth grade smeek cowering at the back of the line.

"Hi," I said to her. "I just need a minute of your time."

"Me?" The girl looked around, hoping I was referring to someone else.

"I've got some exciting news. You've been chosen to bring Elodie her lunch today. Congratulations."

"Elodie Blain? Oh no, I can't . . ." The poor thing looked like she might pass out.

"Sure you can. I can tell, you're made of the right stuff." Okay, pep talk over, time for business.

I took her by the arm and led her toward the food. "Excuse me. Elodie's server coming through," I said. They weren't happy about it, but people made room for the girl.

I placed a tray in her hands. "You need to get Elodie the spaghetti. That's what the peaks are eating today," I said. I set the glass of nog on the tray. "And here's Elodie's special drink. She's always very thirsty. Make sure to hand her the drink first."

The girl looked scared out of her wits. "Why me? I was just minding my own business. Please choose someone else. I, I'm just so clumsy. What if I spill something?" I felt bad for her. I did. But we had a job to do and I wasn't in the mood for excuses.

I took the girl firmly by the shoulders. "What's your name?"

"Cece."

"Listen, Cece, you can do this. I have confidence in you. This is an honor that could change your life." I had to stifle the urge to gag on my own propaganda.

"You're right. I can do this. I can. I can," Cece chanted as she took the tray with the nog and determinedly plucked food off the shelves.

It was perfect timing. The doors to the cafeteria banged

open and seventh-graders poured in. I stood back and watched as Cece carefully advanced toward Elodie.

"I-I've got your lunch, Elodie," Cece stammered, handing Elodie the tray.

Elodie snatched the tray and marched off without even bothering to thank Cece. Cece stood there in Elodie's wake, the sad realization dawning on her that her life was not, in fact, going to change in any significant way. I watched Cece slink off and felt a tinge of regret. But what could I do? This was so much bigger than Cece.

Elodie took a seat at the empty peak table and gulped down the nog. Joey and Kate took seats there as well. I stood off to the side, watching. Elodie tried to get Joey's attention, but Joey was completely immersed in conversation with Kate and ignored her. Owen and Jane plopped down at the peak table and turned to talk to Kate, but she didn't even acknowledge them. She only had eyes for Joey.

Max Clarick, Patel Vashki, and Angus Braun sat at a nearby table hunched over Patel's Sony PlayStation. Mallory, super smeek, sat down with a few juvies. And I think I even saw a pom and a geek sit there as well. Just as I'd predicted, Joey and Kate had set a new tone. People had gotten a taste of freedom and they wanted more. I gazed out at the new world order I had single-handedly created and smiled. But I couldn't enjoy it; at least, not quite yet. I had one last job to do. I wiped my brow. This was hard work, this magic stuff.

I snatched the munchie mix out of my backpack and went

in search of Marta, the head cook. Marta had been running the kitchen for six hundred years; anyway, that was the rumor. People said she put squirrels in the sloppy joes. And I didn't doubt it. It certainly tasted that way. It seemed like Marta's mission was to make the food as inedible as possible. Josh Toling once broke his tooth on one of her hamburgers. I couldn't help thinking there was some larger plan at work. Maybe it was a conspiracy hatched by the school board. The less we appreciated lunch, the more we appreciated learning. Some kind of inverse relationship that only educational specialists know about.

I poked my head through the double doors and into the kitchen, where I found Marta wrestling with a giant can of peaches.

"Marta, I just wanted to let you know how delicious the cheese enchiladas were yesterday. Truly outstanding." Marta stared at me suspiciously.

"They weren't cheese enchiladas, they were potato pancakes." (I rest my case.)

"Whatever. Totally delish," I blathered on. "I brought you something I made at home. I like to cook too and, well, I wanted to share my recipes with you the way you so generously share yours with us." My head hurt. My stomach was growling. Lying was wearing me out. "Anyway, I hoped maybe you would do me the favor of sampling my snack mix and telling me what you think. I'd really appreciate your thoughts."

I handed Marta the Make-It-Better Munchie Mix. To my

delight, she plunged her hand right in and eagerly popped some into her mouth.

"Thanks. I'm starving. The food here sucks." Yes, I couldn't have said it better myself. "Wow. This stuff is great; don't change a thing," Marta said, chewing away.

"Enjoy, there's plenty more where that came from." And with that, I left Marta to her peaches and my munchie mix as I scurried back into the cafeteria.

I made my way over to Kate and Joey, marveling at the scene. Juvies ate with a few geeks, two smeeks chatted up a loner, govs and poms mingled with beeks. And over in the corner, Marsha Whalley was eating at a two-top with Sally McDermott, student treasurer and a gov. They were talking up a storm. Marsha had made a new friend. It was all totally freaky, in the best possible way.

I was about to sit down with Joey and Kate when Max Clarick, fellow border crosser, rushed over to me.

"How crazy is this, Franny? It's like the sixties or something; everyone is getting along. Pretty trippy, huh?"

"It's great," I said, smiling at Max.

"Summer of love, baby. Peace out." Max left to rejoin Patel and Angus.

I squeezed in at the table between Joey and Molly Hastings, pom co-captain. Elodie sat across from us, uncharacteristically quiet. I stole a few glances at her, trying to determine whether or not the nog was taking effect. But she was hard to read.

Then, out of nowhere and seemingly apropos of nothing,

Elodie barked, "Okay, Joey, are you having a brain hemorrhage or what?"

"I don't think so," Joey said calmly.

"Then what are you talking about? You're taking a break from pom?"

Joey was taking a break from pom? What? Joey lived for pom.

Everyone at the table was looking from Joey to Elodie and back, as though watching a tennis match. I had obviously missed something huge.

"Yeah. That's what I said," Joey responded.

"Shut up, Joey. You are so not doing that," Elodie barked again.

"Shut up, Elodie. I so am," Joey countered. "I want time to do . . . other things." At this point, Joey and Kate shared a look. Some kind of secret message passed between them. Something I knew nothing about, which was weird.

"And what about the competition?" Elodie raged. "What about that?"

"I'm over it. It seems so pointless, jumping around in a little skirt," Joey said.

Elodie, her face red, her teeth clenched, her body shaking in fury, stood up, turned on her heel, and stomped out of the cafeteria. Hmm. Maybe the nog took a little longer to work on someone like Elodie. I probably should have made her an extra-strength dose.

"I hear you, J. I'm not feeling band right now," Kate said,

upping the ante. "I'm just bangin' on things. I mean, 'sup with that?"

"What's up with that is we need you. You're the freaking band leader," Owen snapped.

"And we've got Battle of the Bands coming up," Jane said.

"Sorry, I need to shake off the commitments so I can just hang after school," Kate said nonchalantly.

Things had just taken a quantum leap into the great unknown. After the initial shock wore off, I felt relief wash over me. I was thrilled to have pom and band in my rearview mirror. I couldn't begin to count how many hours I'd lost watching Joey and her team flinging themselves around like rag dolls and listening to Kate and company perfect the score of *Godspell* over and over again. Now we could find an extracurricular for all three of us. Something to call our very own.

"Guys, I have a great idea." I could barely contain myself. "Let's join the fencing team. Or the cuisine club."

"I'm not feeling it," Kate said.

"Me either," Joey added.

"Joey and I just kinda want to chillax for a while."

Sure. That made sense. I mean, they had a lot of catching up to do. We could all join something in the spring.

Joey and Kate got up and headed out of the cafeteria. I trailed after them.

"How about we go to the Sweet Spot after school today?" I said, excited that none of us had anything to do after school for the first time in forever.

"Sounds good," said Joey.

"I'm in," Kate added.

As we walked down the hall, James Singer rushed to catch up with us. I got a few butterflies in my stomach on Kate's behalf. After Kate and James had had their little moment at Joey's party, I had been waiting for something more to happen.

"Kate, hold up," he called as he joined us. "I was wondering if, uh, maybe you wanted to get something to eat after school or something." James looked a little nervous.

"Uh, yeah. I guess so," Kate said.

She guessed so? That was so un-Kate. And a little underwhelming, in terms of a response. But James didn't seem to mind, so who was I to argue?

"Great." James smiled at Kate.

"Can Alexi and I come along?" Joey asked.

"Totally. That'd be awesome," Kate responded without checking with James.

James didn't say anything but he didn't look pleased. It was clear he would have preferred time alone with Kate.

"You're cool with that, right, Franny?" Joey asked. "I mean, the three of us can go to the Sweet Spot any day."

"Yeah, no problem," I said, feeling just the opposite. Once again, Joey and Kate had afterschool plans. And I didn't. On one hand, I was superhappy for Kate. But on the other hand, I couldn't help wondering where I fit into the picture.

Chapter 15

Me, AKA the Fifth Wheel

"THIS IS EXACTLY THE WAY she used to do it," Dad said, holding up a bagel. "She would spread raspberry jam on one side, smoothing it evenly with the knife, careful not to let any of the jam spill over. And then she would tear it in half before she took a bite, just like this." He proceeded to rip the bagel in half. "And only then would she eat it." Dad sighed, hard and heavy, as if the weight of the world were somehow resting on his heart alone.

"She's gone. She's really, really gone," Dad said for the millionth time. The fact that he was bemoaning his sorry state to his twelve-year-old daughter was a clear indication of what shape he was in.

He had talked nonstop Naomi for the past hour. I didn't know how much more I could take. I felt bad. I really did. But I couldn't help thinking he was taking this Naomi breakup a little harder than he should have. I mean, they'd only been together a few months. How could she mean that much to him?

"I've tried calling her, but her phone number's been changed. I guess she really doesn't want to hear from me."

"I'm sure you'll meet someone else and forget all about Naomi," I said.

"I don't want to meet someone else," Dad insisted.

"Maybe it's someone you already know. Maybe you don't have to *meet* anyone."

"I don't understand what you're getting at, Franny," Dad said.

"I'm just saying, sometimes the perfect person is right under your nose and you just don't realize it." Maybe this was the time to have that heart-to-heart with Dad about getting back together with Mom.

"Naomi *was* the perfect person for me, Franny, and now she's gone. She's really, really gone. There's no other woman for me. I'm sorry, that's just the way I feel."

Hmmm. Dad was pretty adamant. Better to leave it alone for now. We could have the heart-to-heart another day.

We sat down to watch *Dancing with the Stars*, which was our thing. It's our favorite show. We always made microwave popcorn and fruit smoothies. But Dad had completely forgotten to buy the popcorn and he was out of fruit. So we had lukewarm water and some crackers. Then, to make matters worse, Dad continued to wax on about Naomi throughout the entire show.

"Naomi used to fold the laundry with such care. She had

such delicate earlobes. Such beautiful eyes. She always said, 'That's crazy,' about everything. She was so full of curiosity. She ate spaghetti with a fork and spoon . . ."

Dad was a wreck. He was heartbroken and completely unhinged. And it was all my fault. I reminded myself that I had done it in the name of family. I was fighting the good fight. Dad just needed time to heal and get through his grief so he could turn his attention to Mom. And Naomi would be fine. I had made sure of that. I just had to wait this one out.

I went upstairs and left Dad to his mournful musings. I called Kate to check in. She was on the phone with Joey and conferenced me in.

"How was the double date?" I wanted to know. It was Kate's first real date. The guy she kissed at band camp last year didn't really count. It was one kiss in the woods and then he never spoke to her again. And the kiss was on her arm.

"Fun," Joey and Kate said at the same time. Followed by laughter and then the inevitable "Jinx." And more laughter.

"Can I have some details, please?" I asked.

"Kate totally cracked us up. She was telling stories about all of us in preschool. Like the time we all made sandwiches out of colored paper and play dough—" Joey was laughing so hard she couldn't finish.

Kate jumped in. "And we ate them. My poop was blue and green for two days."

I cringed, wondering how James had reacted to that little nugget.

"Okay, but, like, what did you think of James?" I asked Kate.

"He's cool," Kate said and then, changing the subject, she said, "So, Friday night, Joey and I are thinking horror fest. It's going to be hard core."

"My house. We've Netflixed it already," Joey said.

"Joey and I need to get our horror on," Kate added.

Wait. Stop. Rewind.

"What do you think, F? Horror fest? You into it?" Kate asked.

Horror fest? No! I wasn't into it! I cannot say this strongly enough: I hate horror movies. I think they're horrible. And the thing is, Joey and Kate knew this. At least I thought they did.

"Uh, guys, I'm not a huge fan of horror," I reminded them.

"Dawg, I thought you were over that," Kate said.

"There's nothing to get over. I don't like them," I said, my voice rising.

"C'mon, Frans, horror rocks. Give it another chance," Joey pleaded.

"That's okay. You guys should go ahead without me," I said, feeling like a fifth wheel for the second time in twenty-four hours. But it really wasn't that big of a deal, was it? Joey and Kate had found some common ground. That was a good thing. Right? I could deal with this. I'd dealt with a whole lot worse. The road to happiness was bound to have a few pot-holes. The question was, how many?

☺☺☺☺

When Joey, Kate, and I arrived at the pearly gates the next morning, the stairs looked like a fabulous cocktail party. Everyone was mingling with everyone. It was crazy. Crazy amazing.

Elodie had Samantha Ross on door duty, which was a first. Elodie must have been feeling pretty desperate. Samantha was wearing yellow terry-cloth sweats, identical to Elodie's of two days ago. I kept a close eye on Elodie as we approached. I was dying to know if the nog was working.

"Hi, Elodie," I said in as neutral a tone as possible.

"Oh, hi, Franny," Elodie responded, kind of sweetly. No flipping way. The nog had worked. This might have been the biggest breakthrough of all time. Elodie turned to Joey. "Hey, Joey, I have two tickets for Coldplay this week—"

"Can Kate and Franny come?" Joey interrupted.

"I said two tickets. Did you even do the math?" Elodie raged. "Even if I had four, I would *never* invite Kate and Franny." Uh-oh.

"Then no can do. Sorry, El." And with that, Joey grabbed Kate's arm and the two of them headed into school with no concern for the fact that Samantha Ross was guarding the door and it wasn't time to enter.

Seeing Joey bound into school, disregarding the door rules, other students followed her lead, practically trampling poor Samantha Ross. She had been fired before she'd even really been hired.

I stayed outside to assess Elodie, who was taking in the

chaotic scene with her familiar scowl and mumbling to herself, "La Principessa is not happy!" Elodie sneered. "What are you looking at, Flanders? Get out of my face." Then she pushed me, hard, and stomped into the building.

I followed Elodie into the building and watched as she tripped a smeek, shoved a juvie into his locker, and snatched a chocolate bar right out of a loner's hand. The nog had done nothing at all. The Elodie problem was far from solved. I'd have to try another recipe. Stat.

I entered English to find Ms. Posey waving at me from her desk. I approached her with trepidation. I had no idea what to expect.

"I simply *love* that hand cream, Franny. It was just so thoughtful of you to give some to me." As she talked, Ms. Posey took a big dollop of the cream and rubbed it into her hands. "It's brilliant stuff. I can't get enough of it."

Ms. Posey plucked a paper from a pile of homework. There was a huge red A^{++++} emblazoned on the page.

"I think this is yours, Franny." Ms. Posey handed me my paper.

"I thought we weren't being graded on our first homework assignments," I said.

"I've decided to give As to everyone to help boost people's averages."

"Oh. Okay. Sounds good," I added, backing away and taking my seat.

A few minutes later, Ms. Posey told us we could have a free

period to do what we wanted. And then she passed out cream-filled doughnuts. Flip me out. The recipe may have backfired with Elodie but it was full steam ahead for Ms. Posey.

Becky Mode, theater beek, raised her hand, confused. "Uh, what are we supposed to do now?"

"Listen to your iPods, play on your Game Boys. Whatever's your pleasure," Ms. Posey chirped.

The students were so shocked they sat in silence for most of the hour while Ms. Posey hummed to herself. I was pretty psyched. English was going to be a breeze. When the bell rang, everyone exited in a daze.

"I love you, children. You are all beautiful creatures," Ms. Posey called as we filed out. She was a little happier than I'd intended. But as I was discovering, magic is not an exact science. Things would settle down. I was sure of it.

Next up, art. And my beloved Alden. I knew Janet Scully still laid claim to him, but our connection was unmistakable. It was only a matter of time until we got together, I knew. But as much as I wanted Alden to be my boyfriend, I didn't have a clue what that meant. I'd never had a real boyfriend. I would have to spend some quality time with Google and figure things out.

"Is that Myanmar?" Alden asked, pointing to the right-hand corner of my canvas. I was so busy worrying over everything I didn't know about dating and boyfriends that I hadn't realized Alden had moved his seat right next to mine.

"Uh, yeah. It is," I said. "I thought it would add a more exotic feel to the landscape, you know?"

"Did you know it used to be called Burma?" Alden asked.

Did I know it used to be called Burma? Is the pope Catholic? Enough said. We were so obviously soul mates. "I'm obsessed with Southeast Asia," I said. "I think it's the most beautiful place in the world. My grandmother was there last summer. She promised that when I'm in high school she'll take me to Cambodia and—"

"—see Angkor Wat?" Alden interrupted. "I was there with my family last summer. It was amazing."

We looked at each other and smiled. At the exact same time. My own personal jinx moment. I think I turned five shades of red. My hands shook and I had trouble catching my breath. I felt sick to my stomach. Aah, love. The good, the bad, the nausea.

We spent the rest of class talking about Southeast Asia. Alden's aunt lives in Bangkok, so he'd traveled there twice. He loved the food, the beaches, and the people but hated the mosquitoes and the warm Pepsi. I couldn't help but think he'd make the perfect tour guide.

Elodie kept glancing over at us. I was pretty sure dark forces were gathering strength but I was too stoked to care. We left art class, and as Alden was telling me about hiking in Nepal—he had gone with his brother and his aunt and uncle—we ran smack into Janet Scully, who was waiting in the hall. Alden waved to her but continued talking to me. Janet watched us for a beat, thoroughly bewildered, and then scampered after us. She kind of trailed behind as Alden and I gabbed on and on, until I had to splinter off for Spanish class. Alden smiled that sexy lopsided grin of his and waved to me as I rushed off. I was in love. Janet Scully's fifteen minutes were nearly done. Tick. Tock. Tick. Tock.

At lunch, the cafeteria was a frenzy of activity. People were pushing and shoving each other to get to the food. I rushed over to see what the fuss was about.

Marta was wearing a full-on sushi-chef ensemble, replete with a big black sash around her waist and a huge sushi hat. She even had a young Japanese assistant standing next to her wielding a long knife. Gone were the bowls of gray gluey pasta and slabs of mystery meats. In their place were gleaming plates of sushi and maki rolls.

Marta was a whirling dervish as she churned out roll after roll for an eager audience. She couldn't put the food out fast enough. I plucked a leftover piece of cucumber roll off the shelf and popped it in my mouth. Wow. Seriously good stuff.

"Marta, this is amazing," I said.

"You ain't seen nothing yet. Wait till you see what I've got cookin' for tomorrow. Shrimp gyoza, pad thai, and strawberry rhubarb flan. I'm on fire," Marta said.

Alexi Butterworth squeezed in line behind me. "Can you believe it, Franny? Sushi for lunch. And it's incredible. What is up with Marta?"

"I know. It's wild." I really wanted some kind of formal acknowledgment of all I'd accomplished. The satisfaction of a job well done just wasn't cutting it anymore.

"Hey, have you seen Joey? She's not answering my texts," Alexi said.

"She's not at lunch?" I looked around and was surprised to see that neither she nor Kate was in the lunchroom. Weird.

"James and I wanted to eat with Joey and Kate," Alexi said.

"I saw them in the computer lab a little while ago," Patel offered as he stuffed a piece of eel maki in his mouth.

I exited the cafeteria and headed for the computer room, where I found Joey and Kate huddled over a laptop, whispering.

"Hey, guys. You're missing the most amazing lunch," I said.

"Uh, yeah. We're kinda busy," Kate responded.

"Busy with what?" I asked.

"It's a secret," Joey said.

A secret? Joey and Kate had secrets from me? That kind of sucked.

"You can tell me, can't you?" I was trying not to whine. But I could feel it coming on. I mean, why wasn't I in on their secret?

Kate glanced at Joey. "We should tell her, J," Kate said.

"Yeah, you're right," Joey agreed.

That was more like it. Of course they should tell me. This was ridiculous.

"We're starting a blog," Joey said.

"About our friendship," Kate added.

"That's so cool. I love it. Let me help," I said.

"I don't think you can. It's about *our* friendship, Franny," Kate said.

"Like, Kate . . . and . . . me," Joey explained, speaking slowly as though I were understanding-impaired or something.

Wait. Hold up. Joey and Kate were doing a blog about a friendship that didn't include me? I wasn't even sure what a blog was. But I knew that whatever it was, I didn't want to be left out of it. Kate had called me Franny, which she hadn't done in about a billion years. And she was speaking perfect English. Something felt very wrong.

"It would be cool if you were the first to read it online," Joey offered as some sort of pathetic consolation prize.

Yeah, the first to read your blog that didn't include me. That sounded really fun. Thanks, guys. My head was spinning. Talk about feeling like a fifth wheel. I was the wheel that had rolled down the street, careened over an embankment, and gone into the river.

Joey and Kate turned their attention back to the computer as if I weren't even there. Was this just a blip on the radar as Joey and Kate made up for lost time? Or was it a very bad omen of more to come? How had we gone from three musketeers to two? I didn't have long to contemplate this latest snag because a shriek rang out from the hall. Joey, Kate, and I all rushed outside to check it out.

A swarm of kids surrounded Mr. Sheeplick, the drama teacher, as he attempted to tack a piece of paper to the bulletin board. It was the cast list for *The Sound of Music,* this year's musical.

In schools around the country, this scene plays out with alarming predictability. The same popular kids get the lead roles year after year while all the others slog their way through the chorus. I assumed this year would be the same, with Elodie starring alongside Sam Ling, theater geek extraordinaire. La Principessa interacted with Sam Ling only once a year, during the play. She'd even kissed him in last year's production of *West Side Story,* which was pretty ironic considering the rest of the year she wouldn't even deign to look at him.

Naturally, Elodie was right up front, exuding her usual air of entitlement. It made me want to clock her in the head. I caught sight of Marsha Whalley waiting in the wings for the list to go up.

"People, people, stand back. It's only a musical," Mr. Sheeplick said, tacking up the list and stepping away from the madding crowd. Elodie knocked over two theater geeks as she clamored to get a look.

"What the—?" Elodie roared as she took in the list. She spun around and shoved her way through the crowd until she found Marsha Whalley.

"You. Stole. My. Role! You're playing Maria? What a freaking joke!" Elodie screeched.

This was obviously news to Marsha. She stared at Elodie in shock. Though I saw a flash of a smile on her face as she took in the information. She had done it! She had gotten the lead in the musical! This was perhaps the most unlikely and quickest rise to stardom from total obscurity in the history of middle school.

Elodie was breathing hot dragon flames in Marsha's face. Meaner than I'd ever seen her. Dang! Why hadn't the recipe worked on Elodie? It really could have come in handy right about now.

"There must be some kind of mistake. I demand an answer," Elodie barked at Marsha, who backed away, frightened, trying to keep a grip on whatever confidence she had accrued over the last few days.

Mr. Sheeplick appeared at Elodie's side. "No mistake, Elodie. Marsha is Maria. You're the Countess. It's a great role and I'm sure you'll do wonders with it."

Elodie turned on Marsha. "I'm the only one at this school who can sing and dance and act. You're just going to embarrass yourself—"

Mr. Sheeplick grabbed Elodie by the arm. "For your information, Marsha happens to have one of the loveliest singing voices I've heard in my fifteen years here at this school. I suggest you apologize right now, or you'll be painting scenery for the play."

Elodie knew she had made a huge tactical error by attacking Marsha in front of everybody, especially Mr. Sheeplick. In a matter of seconds, she transformed. Her tight little scowl slipped away, and she smiled and turned to Marsha. It was one of the freakiest things I've ever witnessed.

"I'm sorry, Marsha. Mr. Sheeplick's right. I totally lost my temper. You don't deserve that kind of treatment. No one does. I was out of line. It won't happen again."

Marsha looked at Elodie with a mixture of fear and pity. To her credit, she came up with a nice play of her own.

"No problem, Elodie. You're only human. I think." Elodie let that one glide by.

"Do you want to rehearse together? I bet you have a lot you could teach me." Elodie was laying it on thick and Marsha didn't have it in her to resist. An offer like that from the queen is hard to refuse if you've been a lowly servant all your life.

"Yeah, that would be great," Marsha said.

"Fantastic. We'll meet at my house tomorrow and start with some simple acting exercises. I'll tell the housekeeper to cater it. Do you like crepes?"

"Uh, yeah, sure . . ." Marsha replied, her voice drifting off as she glanced around the room, suddenly aware that all eyes were on her. "I, uh, gotta go to the bathroom," Marsha said, barely audibly, and then she sped off toward the girls' room.

No one said anything for a few seconds as we all tried to make sense of what we had just seen. On the upside, I had forgotten about Joey and Kate's blog. On the downside, Elodie was heading straight for the three of us. And she did not look pleased. Her fake nice had drained away and all that was left was pure concentrated evil.

"Joey, where have you been all day? I've been texting you since eight a.m."

"Sorry, El. I've been a little textually frustrated. We've been busy with our blog. Once it's up and running, you can catch up with me there," Joey responded.

"What does that even mean, Joey?" Elodie bellowed.

"It means if you want to know what's up with us, check us out at Joeynkatergr8.com," Kate offered.

"I'm sorry, was I talking to you, beek?" Elodie sneered. "Enough of this, Joey. I'll see you at pom practice after school." Elodie wasn't asking. She was telling. Elodie and Joey faced off, glaring at each other. Everyone watched, silent. Elodie had never taken Joey on in public.

"I wouldn't count on it, El. Gotta bounce. Catch you later," Joey said. And then she hooked arms with Kate and they rushed back into the computer room. For the first time ever, Elodie and I were united in our mutual distaste for our current situation. We exchanged a look, remembered we hated each other, and went our separate ways. I told myself, *This too shall pass.* And then I repeated it over and over again, until I almost believed it.

Chapter 16

Put a Fork in Me

Mom had agreed to drop me, Joey, and Kate at the mall after school. I was hoping we could put the blog behind us and have some fun. Because I really needed it. I had visions of us all trying on outfits at Forever 21, like in the makeover scene in *Pretty Woman,* with Lady Gaga playing in the soundtrack of my mind. I know, the Disney of it all was pretty lame. Still, it would have been fun. It just wasn't meant to be.

On the way to Forever 21, Joey and Kate decided to take a quick detour to the Apple store to check out some software for their blog. I set off for Forever 21 alone with Joey and Kate swearing up, down, and sideways that they would meet me there in ten minutes. I wandered in the store amid groups of giggling friends who were all dancing to their own rocking soundtracks while I shopped to the sounds of the world's tiniest violin playing mournfully in my head.

I rambled aimlessly through the store for fifteen minutes with no sign of Joey and Kate, and I had pretty much given up when I spotted it: a short-sleeved sequined minidress in a candy apple red. The dress that could change my life. I knew I could rock it in a way that would be irresistible to Alden. It was perfect for the Fall Fling. Forget the fact that I hadn't been asked. Forget the fact that it was twenty dollars more than I had to spend. I refused to let any of that get in my way. A girl should always be ready for anything. And the dress was ready to go, go, go. I snagged it off the mannequin and ran to try it on.

It was perfect. Like it was made for me. I admired myself in the three-way mirror. I looked cool and sophisticated, with a touch of rock 'n' roll.

"That dress looks great on you, Franny." I whipped around to see Naomi smiling at me.

"Uh, hi, Naomi," I said nervously.

"You should get it. It fits perfectly," Naomi offered.

"Uh, yeah. I don't really have enough cash. I was just kind of trying it on . . . for fun, you know."

"Yes. I do know. Sometimes trying on the perfect dress can make your day. Even if you can't buy it."

"Yeah, totally," I said. Because I understood exactly what she meant.

"How are you?" Naomi asked.

"I'm good, uh, I guess," I wasn't really sure how to answer. Because I wasn't very good at all.

"And how's your dad doing?"

"He's, uh, good." Which wasn't true, but what was I going to say?

"I'm glad to hear that." Naomi tried to sound perky but I detected a distinct note of sorrow in her voice. "I'm sorry about the way things turned out that night. I'm not really sure what happened. I would have liked to get to know you better. But things don't always work out the way we want, do they?"

I nodded because I could certainly relate to that.

At that point, two twenty-something guys walked up to Naomi and handed her their business cards. She waved them away and turned back to me.

"I don't know what it is, I must have acquired some kind of weird scent. Certain guys won't stop tracking me. It all started that night with your dad. I had to change my phone number and e-mail, it got so crazy for a while."

"Wow. Weird," I said, because I didn't want to say much else. I was worried that I might somehow let on that I was to blame for her affliction.

"It's kind of turned me off from dating." I guess Naomi hadn't found her perfect mate yet. "So how much is that dress anyway?" Naomi asked.

I glanced at the price tag. "It's fifty dollars."

"That seems like a steal for a dress that makes you look that good."

"Yeah. I guess." She made a good point. It did seem more than fair for the perfect dress. Still, the fact remained, I just didn't have the cashola.

"How much money do you have?" Naomi asked.

"Thirty bucks."

"Tell you what, I'm going to loan you the rest and you can pay me back when you see me next."

"But what if I don't see you again?"

"Then it's a gift."

Naomi, the woman whose love life I had sabotaged, was offering to give me money for a dress my own mother probably wouldn't spring for. On the one hand, I felt pretty terrible for what I'd done to Naomi and knew I didn't deserve her money. On the other hand, I really wanted the dress.

"That would be great, Naomi, thank you so much."

"You're welcome. Let's go check out. I'm buying my daughter some T-shirts. Why don't you tell me what you think of them? She's eight and I know she'd find you way cool."

I couldn't help but smile at that notion. Me? Way cool? I liked the sound of it.

"You have a daughter? I didn't know that," I said.

"There's a lot you don't know about me." Naomi laughed. She was right. I didn't know her at all. And I hadn't bothered to try.

The irony was, Naomi wasn't so bad. In fact, she was pretty great and probably better than most girlfriends a dad could bring home. But she still wasn't my mother. And that, in a nutshell, was the problem.

"Thanks again, Naomi," I said before leaving the store with the dress that would change my life. I owed her. Big-time. "I'll see you around."

Two fifty-something men approached Naomi. She discouraged them with a quick, fiery look. She'd obviously gotten quite dexterous at fending off suitors.

"Franny, here's my new phone number, in case you need me. And will you please say hello to your father for me?"

"Sure," I promised. But the truth was, I probably wouldn't. Helping out Naomi was kind of a conflict of interest for me.

@@@@

"Francisco, wake up!"

I cracked an eye to see Granny's face looming, like, five inches from mine.

"What time is it?" I asked, still groggy.

"Six thirty. Time to get up and have a little chat." Granny was still wearing her sleeping outfit, which consisted of baggy harem pants with Japanese cranes all over them, a ratty old tank top, and (here's the hard part) no bra.

"I don't do six thirty. See me at seven." And with that, I pulled the blanket over my head.

Granny pulled the blanket back down and narrowed her eyes to slits. "We've got a little problem. Last night I took out the Hindi help box because I wanted to lend it to Gladys, and I noticed something very strange. Do you have any idea what that was?" Granny paused, waiting for me to say something. I had no idea where Granny was going with this but I suspected it was nowhere I wanted to be.

"Franny, I know that box pretty well now. I can sense when it's been active, and you've been fiddling with it. Haven't you?"

I sat up. I needed a lawyer.

"We discussed this, Franny. The universe does not take lightly to magical pranks. There is no room in the cosmos for a twelve-year-old girl to be goofing around with powers beyond her control." Granny exhaled loudly, annoyed. "I need you to start talking. What have you said to the box? Did it give you recipes? Did you use them?"

I was going to have to come up with something or risk going down in flames.

"Okay, I'll admit I may have had a little chat with the box." I was speaking slowly, trying to buy myself time as I groped for a plan.

"Aha. I knew it!" Granny exclaimed.

"But nothing happened, I swear. I just wanted to see that world-peace recipe. I mean, you wouldn't even let me peek at it and, well, you know how stubborn I can be—"

"I certainly do," Granny interrupted. Was that really necessary?

"I couldn't stop thinking about what the recipe for world peace looked like. I mean, world peace is a big deal. So I asked for it again. But I didn't do anything with it; that would be irresponsible. I know that." Granny gazed into my eyes, trying to read me. I took a gamble, reached out, and pulled her into a hug. It was a make-or-break move.

"All right, sweet pea. As long as you didn't do anything with the recipe."

"I didn't," I said, crossing my fingers behind my back in an effort to reduce my guilt and minimize my culpability. I knew it wouldn't really work but it was worth a try.

"We need to make sure to keep you on the path to righteousness."

"Totally. I'm all about the path to righteousness. I was thinking of biking it this weekend."

Granny burst out laughing. "Francisco, you crack me up." She stood and walked out of my room, giggling to herself.

Whew. Close call. I was sweaty from the strain of such furious backpedaling so early in the morning. I jumped into the shower to wash away the stench of lying, and I vowed not to use the box again. Unless absolutely necessary.

I got out of the shower to find a text from Kate:

We'll meet u @ skool.

The second week of the rest of my perfect life wasn't going nearly as well as the first.

Joey and Kate were hard at work in the computer room when I got to school. They were huddled together, tapping away on a laptop, wearing matching outfits consisting of black skinny jeans and white T-shirts. They looked like busboys at a fancy restaurant. It made me nostalgic for Kate's crazy suits.

"Hi, guys," I said, determined to stay positive.

Kate and Joey looked up at me as though I'd walked in on them in the bathtub. Did they really need all this secrecy for a blog?

"Oh, hey, Franny," Joey said.

"Hey, *amigo*," Kate said.

Amigo? Did Kate just say *amigo?*

"Actually, we're done here," Joey said, snapping shut the laptop as I tried to sneak a peek, which was a real blow to my positivity. "We were just going to head to our lockers. Wanna come?" Joey asked me.

"Sure," I said. I was grasping at any and all olive branches as I felt myself going into free fall.

James Singer and Alexi Butterworth caught up with us in the hall. James fell in step with Kate. Alexi moved around to walk next to Joey, nudging me out of the way in the process. Had someone stuck a sign on me reading KICK ME WHEN I'M DOWN?

"Alexi and I were thinking that the four of us should all go to Del Anisa for dinner before the Fall Fling," James said.

"What do you think, Joey?" Alexi asked.

"I don't see it happening," Joey said.

"Okay, cool. You'd rather just go the two of us, then?" Alexi said to Joey.

"There's been a change of plans. I'm not going to the Fling with you, Alexi." Joey tossed this off, completely oblivious to how crushed Alexi looked.

"I don't understand," Alexi protested.

"Sorry, James. It's a no-go for me too," Kate said.

James stared at Kate for a beat. His worst fears were confirmed. He had been rebuffed by a beek. And Alexi had lost his hold on Joey. Alexi and James turned to me, as if I could help them. All I could do was shrug. I was just as surprised and confused as they were. Maybe even more so, since it was my recipe that had gone completely haywire. James and Alexi backed away, shaking their heads and staring at the ground.

"You guys aren't going to the Fall Fling?" I could not get my head around this latest news bulletin.

"We're going. Just not with James and Alexi," Kate said.

"We're going together," Joey added.

Together? They were going together. I repeated this information to myself in an effort to make sense of it. What did it mean?

"Are you going, Franny?" Kate asked. At least she cared enough to ask.

"I'm hoping Alden will ask me, but I'm not banking on it."

"You could go with Alexi or James," Joey said, and then she and Kate cracked up.

I turned on my heel and stomped off to English class, hoping against hope that Joey and Kate would realize their insensitivity, catch up with me, and apologize. But it didn't happen. Instead, I walked the halls alone. English was DOA. Ms. Posey had brought in a monitor and a DVD player and had us all watch *Star Wars*. Too weird.

English didn't do anything to improve my mood; I was still in a deep funk about Joey and Kate when I sat down in art. But then Alden slid in next to me and I felt my mood lifting.

We were sitting together, working quietly, when suddenly he turned to me and said nervously, "Franny, I, uh, wanted to ask you something."

Was this it? The moment I had been waiting for? Was Alden about to ask me to the Fling? I will never know. Because Elodie suddenly appeared at Alden's side.

"Hi, Alden, have you seen the paper cutter?" Elodie was about two inches too close to him. Her boobs were practically in his face as she purred in his ear, "I thought I saw you using it." Elodie caught my eye for a split second, long enough to convey her intent: *I will destroy you.* Message received.

"Uh, yeah, it's right here." Alden reached over and handed the paper cutter to Elodie. I felt him slipping away from me. I could see his eyes drawn to her breasts. He was a twelve-year-old boy—it was impossible for them not to be. Even my eyes were drawn to her breasts.

"Elodie, Alden and I were in the middle of a conversation. If you don't mind—"

"Actually, yes, I do mind, Franny. I mind very much," Elodie hissed.

Alden looked at me helplessly. He was playing with the devil and not entirely sure of the game.

Elosie said, "Alden, I have two tickets, box seats, to the Yankees game this weekend. I thought we could go. My dad would take us in the helicopter."

I heard a bell ring. It was over. Put a fork in me. I couldn't compete.

"Wow, Elodie," Alden said, his eyes wide. "That sounds awesome. I'd love to." Poor Janet Scully; she'd never know what hit her.

Elodie squeezed onto the bench between me and Alden, shoving me off and onto the floor. As I stood up, Elodie grabbed my arm and pulled me in close.

"I am crushing you, Flanders. Can you feel it?"

Uh, yeah. I could, actually. But I didn't want to give her the satisfaction so I just smiled and prayed the Yankees game would be rained out. I tried to make eye contact with Alden but he was gone, fully wrapped up in Elodie's force field. I was back in a funk and this time it was worse than before.

Chapter 17

Positively Apocalyptic

"WHAT DO YOU WANT TO DO TONIGHT?" I asked Dad, hoping he'd revert back to his normal self and come up with something fun and exciting. I really needed the distraction.

"I could make us some toast and we could watch MSNBC," Dad offered as he sat at the kitchen table, his head resting on his hand as though he couldn't hold it up any longer.

Toast and MSNBC? Dad was circling the drain. And the timing couldn't have been worse. I really needed his unflagging enthusiasm and perpetual optimism. But he seemed to have permanently misplaced both. I had had visions of a fun evening of Scrabble and Chinese food. Or Wii ski and Mexican. Dad is a crazy Wii sports competitor. I've only beaten him at tennis once, and I think it was because he let me. But it was not meant to be. What was merely sad a few days ago had turned positively apocalyptic. Instead of getting better, Dad was getting worse. Open bags of food, unwashed dishes, and clothes were strewn about the house. Dad looked like he hadn't slept in days. The fact that it was entirely my fault did not escape me.

"I just don't get it, Franny. Everything was so fantastic between us and then, bam, it all went south." Dad's eyes welled up with tears. It felt like a knife to my heart. What kind of cold-blooded daughter causes her loving father to cry? There was a special place in hell reserved for someone like me, right next to Elodie.

"I've e-mailed her repeatedly. But they keep bouncing back."

I should have told Dad about running into Naomi. How she'd bought me the dress. How she wasn't so bad. How she had changed her e-mail to avoid the stalkers I'd sicced on her. But I didn't. Because if I did, I could pretty much kiss goodbye any chance he and Mom had of getting back together.

As I watched Dad struggle with basic tasks like buttering toast and pouring a glass of juice, I was struck by an awful truth: What if Mom and Dad weren't meant to be together? What if Dad really and truly did belong with Naomi? I mean, he was having a harder time getting over Naomi than he'd had getting over Mom. It had been more than a year since their divorce, and Mom and Dad seemed pretty happy now (present moment excluded). Happier than when they were together. I could remember nights of screaming and yelling, when I'd had to turn on my radio and cover my head with pillows to drown them out. I wasn't happy they split up, but now I couldn't decide if that mattered as much as their happiness. My happiness, their happiness; I weighed one against the other. I was fairly dedicated to my own happiness. But then again, how happy could I be if Dad was going to be in a permanent state of depression?

After a half-hour of MSNBC, I left Dad staring at the television and snuck upstairs to my room to paint. I had brought home my canvas from school in order to put in a little overtime. I worked for a solid two hours, and I felt a little better until I snapped open my phone and began reading the backlog of texts from Joey and Kate. Then I felt worse, a whole lot worse.

> Check out our awesome new blog. You're gonna luv it. We will be blogging every day, every way, about all things Joey and Kate! Check us out at www.joeynkatergr8.com. What are you waiting for? Go, go, go

A glutton for punishment, I opened up my computer and logged on. It felt like a cold hard slap across my face as I stared at the screen. It was filled with silly pictures of Joey and Kate mugging for the camera, not one of which included me. But that wasn't all. There was plenty more soul-crushing to come ...

> September 22, 10 p.m. Welcome to the first official Joeynkatergr8 entry. Joeynkatergr8 is brought to you by Joey and Kate, the best friends you can't have. Because three's a crowd. But we're in a generous mood. So we're going to let you experience everything Joey and Kate: our dirty little secrets, our private thoughts, our every move. Because, you know you want it. Sign up now for e-mail blasts before we change our mind ...

I had to stop and take a little breather. I was feeling a little lightheaded.

Check it out, we're both wearing boxers and camis, matching, of course. And we're munching Teriyaki Turkey Jerky. Our fave.

Since when was turkey jerky their "fave"? What happened to Kate's staunch veganism? Now all she ate was meat. Soon she'd be out tracking deer with a bow and arrow. It was all so inane, so boring. It begged the question: Who cared, other than me? And I only cared because I was so enraged at being left out.

We're listening to M. Ward on Kate's Nano with a splitter.

M. Ward? Joey hated M. Ward. At least, the Joey I knew. He was way too alternative for her.

A few critical thoughts before we bounce:

(1) We both want to see the Sahara, the Alps, and the Amazon River, hopefully together.

(2) We would love to keep a panda as a pet but would settle for a Labradoodle.

(3) We think dark chocolate kicks milk chocolate's butt.

(4) Simon Cowell should be put out of his misery.

Ciao for now. We'll blast you soon. So stay ready and be waiting. You won't want to miss a minute of what we've got going on. Because we've got it going on and you don't if you're not a part of Joeynkatergr8.

Yeah. I wouldn't want to miss a minute of these scintillating details. Pandas. The Alps. Chocolate. Simon Cowell. Riveting stuff. Instead of my having two best friends who didn't get along, I had no friends. Two seconds later I got another text.

Joey and Kate are going for Gap-ad cool tomorrow. We'll be wearing khakis and white tees.

Gap-ad cool? Gag me with a spoon. Was there anything left of the Joey and Kate I used to know? I climbed into bed and pulled the covers over my head. This was like a bad dream I couldn't wake up from. I spent the night tossing and turning, feeling bad about what I'd done to Dad and Naomi, feeling bad about what Joey and Kate had done to me, and feeling bad that the stupid box wasn't exactly living up to its potential.

In the dim light of dawn, I finally got up and decided to paint. Taking my frustrations out on the canvas made me feel better, at least temporarily. It was kind of cool, painting in the early-morning light. I'd never done this before and it made me feel like a real artist. Not some middle-schooler desperate to get her lame landscape painting into the Fall River Art Fair. In my sleep-deprived state, I saw myself as a mad artist driven to paint by the emotional turmoil that was turning her inside out. Instead of depicting the grass with peppy green tones, I chose a darker purple, and my painting really came alive. Yellow skies, blue trees, a black sun—this was how I expressed my twisted world. By seven I had finished the painting. I stood back to admire it. Whoa. It totally rocked. I decided to bring it to school to show Call Me Jeff.

I turned on my phone and was assaulted with an endless stream of e-mail blasts from Joeynkatergr8.com.

Joeynkatergr8's Hots and Nots: Joey and Kate are wearing boy-friend jeans but calling them girlfriend jeans because girlfriends are hot and boyfriends are not. Joey and Kate are riding a wave to school today because the wave is hot. Skateboards are not.

Stop the madness. I want to get off.

I went down to find Dad staring into his coffee and nib-bling at a piece of burnt toast. He looked like he hadn't slept a wink. What if Dad got so bad he stopped working? Then none of us would eat, and we couldn't pay the rent, and before you knew it we would be living in the woods behind Dairy Queen, Dumpster diving and braiding bark together to make mocca-sins to sell at the flea market. My world was spinning out of control. And I had no one to blame but myself.

"Morning, sunshine," Dad said, unaware of the irony. "I made you breakfast."

Dad held out a pathetic piece of burned toast that looked about three weeks old.

"Thanks. It looks delicious," I said. "I should go. I wanna get to school early and show my art teacher my painting," I said, offering it up for Dad to view.

"It's great," Dad said, trying to muster enthusiasm. This

tepid response to my work was too much. Since when does a parent not fawn slavishly over his child's artwork, even when it sucks? And my painting was the opposite of sucky. If Dad hadn't been half out of his mind with grief, he would have been blown away by my artistic brilliance. My eyes welled up with tears. I know, I'm twelve, nearly a teenager. I should have just dealt, but the thing was, I really wanted my dad back.

I gave Dad a big hug goodbye, trying to prop him up with love and affection. Then I rushed out the door, painting in hand, and hoofed it to school. Alone. Because Joey and Kate hadn't shown up and they hadn't even bothered to text. It was a new low, in a solid twenty-four hours of lows.

On the way to school I received ten more Tweets from Joeynkatergr8, Inc.

> Besties are hot. Peaks are not.
> The Afghan Whigs are hot. Band is not.
> Sushi is hot. Enchiladas are not.

I deleted the rest before even reading them. Enough already.

When I got to school, the stairs were crazy with activity. At first glance, I thought it was just more of the same, but on closer inspection, I realized that people were pushing and shoving one another, vying for new spots on the steps. What a few days ago was a scene of perfect harmony had suddenly devolved into *Lord of the Flies*. I watched as a smeek and a loner tossed another smeek off the lower landing, and then both dove for his spot. How much longer until they all began eating one another? Was I to blame, or was this just human nature? I had to give myself a tiny break here. Rome wasn't built in a day; thousands of sweaty slaves lent the project some support. I was one girl, trying to change the world. I needed some help. But where to turn? Back to the box, I figured.

As I stared at the steps, Max Clarick approached.

"I knew it was too good to last," Max said. "They need the pecking order. They crave it. Without it, it's a social free-for-all. This could get ugly."

Was Max right? Was middle school impossible to navigate without cliques? Had I turned this working banana republic (we learned about that in history last year) into an anarchy? I marched up the stairs and was met by Alexi and James. Alexi held up his iPhone, and I could make out Joey and Kate's website on his screen.

"What is up with this? 'Girlfriends are hot. Boyfriends are not'?" Alexi asked.

"I, I'm not really sure," I said.

"Did I totally screw up when I wore that green polo shirt the other day? I mean, I know she doesn't like it. It was just that nothing else was clean . . ."

"She doesn't hate you. She's just going through a phase. You know how Joey is. One day she's into French. The next day she's all about Italian," I said, trying my best. But I think we both knew I was just putting a Band-Aid on a cancer. This thing was bigger than the both of us.

"And how do you explain Kate?" James asked. "She was all into me and now she won't even look at me."

Jeez, couldn't these boys see that I was as clueless as they were? "Just give her a little time to come around. She's focused on the blog right now . . ."

I turned and scrambled up the stairs. I really wasn't in the mood for the Spanish Inquisition (fifth grade history). As I had suspected, Joey and Kate were nowhere to be found. I took the stairs two at a time. Toward the top, I nearly fell over Janet Scully, who was curled into a ball, crying. Everyone was steering clear of her, which is exactly what I wanted to do. I mean, what had Janet Scully done for me lately? But I couldn't do it.

"Are you okay, Janet?" I asked.

No response. I tried again. "Janet, what's wrong?"

Janet let out a long, low moan. I dropped to my knees. "Seriously, Janet, you're freaking me out here. Should I get the nurse?"

"Noooooooooo. Get Alden to . . ." And then her voice faded out.

"Get Alden to . . . what?" I asked.

"Ask me to the Fling." And with that, Janet burst into a new round of sobs.

"I'm sure it'll all work out," I said, though I didn't really mean it. How could I possibly root for her and Alden?

"You. Just. Don't. Get. It. Franny," Janet barked at me. Which was kind of harsh. I mean, I didn't see anyone else there trying to help. "He. Already. Asked. Elodie."

What? Wait a minute. Rewind. Alden asked Elodie? I had to restrain myself from slumping down next to Janet and bursting into tears. "That can't be true ..."

"It's. True. And don't pretend to feel bad for me. You're just mad Alden didn't ask you. So go away and leave me alone."

She made a good point.

"Where's Elodie now?" I asked. "With Alden?" I tried to keep my voice neutral.

"No. She's with Marsha. Her new best friend."

Marsha! That couldn't possibly be good. I left Janet splish-splashing around in her puddle of self-pity and hightailed it into the school, lugging my canvas with me. The only bright spot of what was fast turning into a historically bad day (and I was only an hour into my morning) was that Elodie was not doing door duty.

I slipped through the crowd and into the hall, where I found Marta holding a tray of what looked like puke on a plate. She had replaced yesterday's high chef's hat with an even higher one. It was impossible to take her seriously.

"How about a little *amuse-bouche* to get your day started?" Marta asked the passing students as she offered up dollops of the vile mixture on crackers. Everyone backed away in disgust.

"Franny!" Marta called as soon as she saw me. "You've got to try my pâté. It's ground pig tongue mixed with duck liver. It's a revelation." Marta offered me a cracker.

"Uh, no, thanks. I just ate breakfast," I said, inching away. But she was on me like white on rice.

"C'mon, you have to try it," Marta insisted, pushing a cracker my way. "I was so inspired last night I stayed up until three working on my new cookbook. I'm going to try out the recipes at school. Frog legs with succotash and cinnamon for lunch today. Chocolate-covered grub worms for dessert. They're a delicacy in Africa, and I have a feeling they're really going to take off here soon."

Marta was staring at me intensely. She was buzzing like a bee, full of manic energy. She seemed like she'd been pounding espressos, but I knew the truth was she'd been binging on the munchie mix. I would have to do something about Marta later. Right now, I needed to rescue Marsha from Elodie's clutches.

I escaped Marta and found Elodie and Marsha whispering in a corner. I had to stop myself from whacking Elodie right then and there. I knew it wasn't all her fault, but it felt really good to blame her for absolutely everything. I was jonesing for a scapegoat, and Elodie fit the bill perfectly. One good punch to the kisser would have felt so great.

I overheard them as I approached. "I don't know," Marsha told Elodie, her voice filled with uncertainty and wonder. "You really think I need to do all that?"

"If you're going to *play* Maria, you need to *become* Maria. Trust me. There's a reason I've been the star of every school play. I totally know what I'm doing. We'll take care of everything at my house after school today. I'll have Sonya whip up those profiteroles you loved. Just remember to bring the rubber gloves and spatulas."

"Uh, okay," Marsha said, sounding dubious.

What was Elodie up to?

"Hey, Marsha, could I talk to you for a minute?" I asked, hoping to provide her with an exit strategy.

Marsha barely looked over at me. "I'm kinda busy right now, Franny." Even Marsha had no time for me anymore.

"Marsha is taken care of, Franny. Why don't you try taking care of yourself," Elodie said, chock-full of snark. I swear I saw a black tongue flicker out of her mouth.

Elodie pointed to my canvas, which was on full-frontal display. "Is that your painting for the Fall River Art Fair?"

"Yes. It is," I said proudly.

"Well, it sucks," Elodie said, laughing.

"Well, you suck!" I yelled at Elodie, no longer able to disguise my pure unbridled hatred for her. She was meaner than ever. The nog was a wash, the blondies were a disaster, and I was coming undone.

"You're going down, Flanders, pack light." Elodie sneered. "Oh, and Alden and I won't be thinking of you when we're making out at the Fling."

We glared at each other for a beat and then the bell rang. I passed Joey and Kate in the hall and they walked right by, ignoring me. And the kicker was, it barely phased me at this point.

My life was a shambles. I had dreamed of a perfect world and had given it my best shot, but I had failed miserably. And in the process damaged (possibly beyond repair) nearly everyone I loved. What had gone so terribly wrong? Had I been too selfish? Too power hungry? I had messed with the universe and now everyone dear to me was being punished for my mistakes. I just wanted my old life back. Warts and all. I was about to stagger into English, feeling a little like I'd clawed my way there, when Principal Mackey appeared out of nowhere and pulled me aside.

"May I have a word with you, Franny?"

You. Have. Got. To. Be. Kidding. Me. Principal Mackey? Seriously? I would have preferred to be scrubbed down with a pineapple.

"I need a little favor from you," Principal Mackey explained. A favor? From me? "As I'm sure you know, your friends seem to be neglecting their duties with pom and band, and they're sorely missed. I understand you wield quite a bit of influence with Joey and Kate. I need you to talk some sense into them."

"Uh, I'm not exactly sure I'll have much success at the moment," I said, which was the understatement of the year.

"I need you to try. This is the first time Jefferson has ever gotten into the finals. I'm sure I don't need to tell you how exciting that is." Principal Mackey paused here for effect. She needn't have bothered. She was having a huge effect on me by her mere presence. "Your friends need to reconsider their decisions. Because without Joey Chang and Kate Franklin, the pom team and the band don't stand a chance of winning those championships. And that will be a huge blow to Jefferson's morale."

"I know exactly what you mean," I told Principal Mackey. More than she'd ever know. Principal Mackey marched off and I lumbered away, hunched over from the weight of the world on my shoulders.

English was totally surreal. Ms. Posey was whistling show tunes and tap-dancing with a deranged fervor as we filed into the classroom. Once everyone was seated, she announced, while tapping around the room, that there would be a pop quiz. A pop quiz? On what? We hadn't done a stitch of work all week, which at first had been a refreshing change of pace from the daily grind but was fast becoming mind-numbingly dull.

"Before I hand out the quiz, I am going to hand out the answers," Ms. Posey chirped. Say what?

Everyone cheered but me. I'm not a big fan of the surprise quiz, but I didn't want to end up illiterate, and if this continued much longer, I was pretty sure that was where we were all headed.

When I entered art, having lugged my canvas around like it was some crazy suitcase, Call Me Jeff pointed to my painting and exclaimed, "That. Is. Magnificent. A masterpiece."

I smiled my first smile in what felt like a hundred years.

Once everyone was seated, Call Me Jeff put my painting

on an easel and insisted everyone study the shading, the color, the texture, and the "beautifully rendered perspective." He called it "inventive, ingenious, nothing short of brilliant." I was so stoked I was afraid I might pass out.

When Call Me Jeff asked for comments, nearly everyone was really complimentary.

"I love the willow trees swaying in the background, right next to the boat on the ocean, and the snowcapped mountains. It's really cool." That was Alden. He may have asked Elodie to the Fling, but it was my painting he was talking about. Sooner or later talent would trump boobs and money. Wouldn't it?

Elodie raised her hand. "I think it's a mess. I can barely make anything out with so much going on. I thought the Fall River Art Fair wanted a landscape painting, not some collection of totally random pictures in weird colors."

"While you are entitled to your opinion, Elodie, I strongly disagree. I think Franny's brought a very specific voice to her landscape. There are many levels to the collage. It shows a vision well beyond her years," Call Me Jeff insisted. It was nice to bask in the glow of success for once. I could get used to this.

At the end of class, after Call Me Jeff had surveyed everyone's work, he walked over to me, put his hand on my shoulder. "Franny, if it's okay with you, I'd like your painting to represent Jefferson Middle School at the Fall River Art Fair."

"Yeah. Definitely," I said, struggling to keep myself from breaking into a victory dance. My world may have been disintegrating all around me but at least I had my art. I was thrilled that I would be a part of the art fair, but what felt even better was hearing this news right in front of Elodie, who went green with envy. *Take that, Smellodie, and put it in your pipe and smoke it.* Sadly, that was the only high note in a day filled with tones so low, I stopped listening.

No surprise, lunch was bedlam. As I could have predicted, people boycotted the frog legs. Furious, Marta refused to serve any other lunch options. She flung frog legs at the wall as she stood guard over the closed salad bar. Mr. Pandrock attempted to hold back the rioting students as he called in reinforcements. I couldn't watch the train wreck anymore. I was on my way out of the cafeteria when I was accosted by Jane and Owen.

"What is up with Kate?" Jane demanded. "She's barely spoken to us in days."

"When she did talk to me, she called me Owen," Owen said, horrified at the thought of Kate using his actual name.

"She's been wearing . . . khakis." Jane could barely get the word out. "And I saw her eating meat. What. Is. Going. On?"

"You've turned her against us," Owen added accusingly.

I could feel my head expanding. "You think you feel left out! You. Have. No. Idea," I ranted. "At least you two have each other." I stopped, my words caught in my throat. I was afraid I might burst into tears. Owen and Jane didn't even notice.

"We always thought you liked us but you've obviously been waiting for a chance to push us out of the picture," Jane said.

"This will not be forgotten, Franny," Owen promised.

And before I could defend myself, they stalked off. More bad juju. My karma was in serious trouble.

The day seemed to pass in years. It felt like a decade later when the final bell rang. I dragged my weary body from the hallowed halls of Jefferson toward home. I had to get my hands on that box. It was my only option. Something had gone seriously wrong and the only way to fix it was with a brand-new batch of recipes.

On my way home, I passed by pom practice. I caught sight of the pathetic pyramid the poms were attempting in Joey's absence. They wobbled and shook and then toppled to the ground, collapsing in a big blond heap. They were hopeless. Principal Mackey was right. They didn't stand a chance without Joey.

Like a soldier returning from war, I stumbled into the house.

"Mom? Granny?" There was no response. Was it possible that no one was home?

I was in Granny's closet in a nanosecond, scavenging through her stuff. After ten minutes of full-on foraging, I gave up. The box was nowhere to be found. Are you flipping kidding me? Now what was I going to do? My throat tightened, my eyes welled up, and then the tears that had been building inside me for the past two days burst forth. I sank to the floor and let myself have a good long cry.

Chapter 18

Breaking and Entering

"Where's Granny?" I practically growled at Mom as she walked in the front door, her arms loaded down with groceries. The twins trailed behind her, whacking and swatting at each other. I was a crazed fiend who would stop at nothing to get my hands on that box.

"Hi, Mom. How are you? How was your day? Could I maybe help you with those groceries?" Mom said. "I'm fine, Franny. Thanks for asking. And how was your day?"

I felt like my head was going to burst and splatter all over the room but I knew I needed to maintain my composure for Mom. I stared at a spot on the wall, gathering my concentration.

"Look, I don't have time for pleasantries. I really need to talk to Granny."

"I was thinking maybe you could take the twins to the park to go skateboarding," Mom said. "You know how you've been wanting to spend more time with them."

Oh, dear God. I had completely forgotten that preposterous idea I'd put forth.

"Right. Yeah, well, now is not exactly the best time to, uh, start that up—"

"Yeah, let's go skateboarding!" Pip squealed with joy.

"Totally." Squeak seconded the emotion.

"I really need to talk to Granny—"

"Granny's not home, Franny. She's out with Gladys. You can hang out with the twins until she returns."

"Not. Today. Mom. Believe. Me," I said. I felt bad not helping Mom out but things had reached DEFCON 1 level. It was not the time to go skipping off to the park.

"I'm not asking you, Franny. I'm telling you."

"Fine. C'mon," I snarled at the twins and then turned and stomped out of the house. The twins scrambled to keep up. Was there any shred of decency left inside me? I was starting to doubt it. Once I fixed everything, I would dedicate myself to becoming a better sister. A better person. But at the moment, I could not have cared less.

The twins got into a knockdown-dragout fight about ten minutes after we got to the park. Something about who was better on the halfpipe. I tried to put an end to it by noting that neither had ever tried the halfpipe, but that didn't seem to matter. When I finally pulled them apart, Pip had a scratch under his eye and Squeak had bite marks on his forearm. Maybe I should have kept the bracelets on these two barbarians.

I attempted to drag the twins home as punishment for their behavior but they were having none of it. And despite my dark mood, the twins somehow managed to coerce me into a shockingly fun game of freeze tag played on skateboards. So while Rome burned, I dashed around the park tagging the twins. Maybe they weren't so terrible all the time. Just most of it.

When I finally looked at my watch, I realized that it was almost dinner. We had been at the park for more than an hour. I didn't have time for this kind of frivolity. I was dangling over the edge of the cliff. I needed to get home and get cracking.

ⓔⓔⓔⓔ

Granny was doing a headstand in the middle of her bedroom when I barged in. She swayed a bit at my forced entry and then promptly regained her balance.

"I really need to talk to you," I said, trying to contain my panic.

"What can I do you for, Francisco?" Granny asked as she remained upside down.

"Uh, you wanna maybe get right-side up?"

"I can't. I need to stay inverted for another ten minutes in order to achieve the full circulatory benefits of the inversion."

Whatever. "I, uh, wanted to take another go at a recipe for the twins," I said, proceeding cautiously. "Because I, uh, think things are getting worse. And I'm really worried about them."

"You are, huh? Funny. You didn't seem that worried when they lost the bracelets." It was really distracting to talk to Granny while she was upside down. Her loose facial skin was gathered in folds around her eyes, and she was beet red. She looked like a melted scoop of strawberry ice cream.

"I was. I was superworried. I just kept it to myself," I lied, because I was a big fat liar and that's what big fat liars do.

"All right, Franny, if you're that worried, perhaps we'll take another pass at it. But we'll have to wait a bit because I lent the box to Gladys."

"You lent the box to Gladys?" I was losing it. "Why would you do that?"

Gladys Pepperdine was Granny's best friend in Fall River. They met years ago when Gladys and her husband, Harold, lived on our street. The first time Granny came to visit us she met Gladys on her morning walk. We had never spoken to Gladys. We just knew her as the crazy lady from down the street who had about a million exotic birds. Anytime I ever saw Gladys, she had a bird or two perched on her shoulder. Naturally, Granny took to her immediately.

A year ago, Harold died and Gladys moved into Leisure Village, a retirement community on the lake. She had to sell off most of the birds, but she kept Chachi, her opera-singing Amazon parrot, who she brought along to Leisure Village.

"Calm down, Francisco. It's really not that big of a deal. She'll return it in due time. Gladys is highly attuned to the occult. I thought she might be able to help me figure out some kinks."

"The twins are in trouble and you don't seem to care. We need that box. Now!"

"You haven't mentioned the twins in a week. I find it a little hard to believe that their situation is suddenly so dire and, frankly, that you care that much." Granny was still upside down, which was really grating on me.

"How could you say that? They are my brothers. My only siblings. I care. Deeply. And, frankly, I'm hurt that you're questioning my intentions."

"Well, we can work on it in a week or so, when Gladys is done fiddling."

"A week? This cannot wait a week!"

Granny got out of her headstand, stood up, and looked me in the eye. "You want to tell me what's going on, Franny?"

I did want to tell her. I wanted nothing more than to pour my heart out to her, confess my sins, and begin the healing process. But I couldn't. I knew she would never forgive me. I was pond scum, plain and simple, but that didn't take away from the fact that I needed that box. I was going to get it if it was the last thing I did, which it very well might be.

"Nothing is going on," I said. "I just want to help the twins. That's it." And with that, I left Granny to her inversion and went to my room to brainstorm.

In addition to their weekly mahjong and Scrabble games, Granny and Gladys were both taking silk-screening classes at the adult extension center at the high school. As luck would have it, Granny and Gladys were off to silk-screening class that night, which was what prompted me to come up with my foolproof brilliant plan (or reckless stupid scheme, depending on whether you're looking at things with foresight or hind-sight).

ⓔⓔⓔⓔ

I wore black leggings and a long black T-shirt and threw a black cap and scarf in my bag for good measure. I was going old-school thief. I was rocking the perfect look for a break-in, which was exactly what I was planning. I told Mom I was heading over to Joey's to study when in reality I was about to embark on a full-on life of crime. I had been only dabbling in it up until now. I officially fell a rung below pond scum when I headed over to Gladys's retirement village to steal a box I had promised my grandmother I wouldn't use in the first place.

As it happened, there was no need for the all-black getup. I could have worn bright pink polka dots with a sign on my chest that read ROBBER because no one was paying attention. Slipping into Leisure Village was appallingly easy. They should really beef up security. I had had big plans to sneak past the guards by jumping a fence or scaling a wall or two, but there was no need for any of that.

As soon as I approached the building, an elderly guard sitting on a lawn chair out front and clearly bored out of his mind waved at me. "Hey there, little miss. What can I do for you today?"

"I'm, uh, here to see my grandmother ... Gladys ..." I said, suddenly forgetting Gladys's last name. Was I the worst criminal in the history of the world or what?

"Gladys Pepperdine?"

"Uh, yep, that's her."

"Room five-ten, but you probably already know that."

"Sure do. Because, uh, I'm always here visiting Grandma Gladys . . . because I'm, uh, her granddaughter. Like I said." I smiled broadly.

The guard didn't even ask my name. He just buzzed me right in. I made a mental note to make sure Granny never moved here. The place wasn't safe. Any common criminal could just waltz in. I walked down the hall trying to keep a low profile, but old people smiled and waved at me. I wanted to scream, *I'm a common criminal, people. Do not be so trusting. The world is filled with evil.* But that didn't seem prudent. So I smiled and waved back.

I found room 510 with little problem. Unfortunately, an elderly couple was making out right in front of the door. Jeez, guys, get a room. Who knew retirement was so much fun? I waited patiently for them to go. I didn't need any witnesses. I took out my phone to read a few texts, all of which were annoying e-mail blasts from Joeynkatergr8. They were doing homework; they were doing a sugar scrub followed by avocado facemasks; they were having popcorn and watching *Lost* . . . I snapped my phone shut and felt more certain than ever that the ends would justify the means.

The couple wandered off down the hall, his hand squeezing her backside. Did I really need to see that? I tried Gladys's door. *Quelle surprise,* I thought (feeling nostalgic for Joey's forced European-language lessons), the door wasn't locked. This place was an accident waiting to happen. I walked into Gladys's room expecting to find some claustrophobic, stinky old prison cell with furniture sheathed in plastic and lame, rinky-dink mementos all over the place. But Gladys didn't roll that way. Her crib was way cool. It was decked out with sleek modern furniture and had abstract art on the wall and a fully stocked bar. There was a beautiful blue and yellow bird ensconced in a golden cage hanging from the ceiling. Chachi was thriving at Leisure Village. Senior living rocked. Now I understood why Granny spent so much time hanging at Gladys's. Maybe it didn't totally suck to grow old. But that was cold comfort at the moment, because now that I was a card-carrying criminal, who knew if I'd even make it to thirteen?

I didn't have to look for the box. It was sitting on Gladys's nightstand. This was all eerily easy. I shut the door, locked it, and sat down on the bed with the box on my lap.

"We meet again," I said to the box. "Seriously, though, we've got to talk. The stuff you gave me last time didn't work out so well. I'm going to need some better recipes. Like, pronto."

I wanted Joey and Kate back to who they were, friends or not; they had become shells of their former selves and I missed them. I wanted to learn English, even if Ms. Posey had it in for me. I wanted Marta's foul sloppy joes, not frog legs or foie gras. And most important, I wanted my dad to be happy again, even if that meant his being with Naomi. I would just have to deal.

I sat very still and stared at the box, concentrating harder than I ever had in my entire life. My heart was beating super-fast, my eyes were twitching, and I was having trouble catching my breath. I knew what was at stake here and I shuddered to think what would happen if I failed and things were to continue apace. Finally, an image of Kate sporting her crazy "Einstein meets skater gurl" suit popped into my mind. She was hanging with Jane and Owen. Joey sauntered into the picture, arm in arm with Elodie, waltzing right by Kate without acknowledging her. And I didn't even mind.

"Give Joey and Kate their old lives back," I said to the box. And then I waited, and waited, and waited, and waited for that darn drawer to open. But it didn't budge.

"Listen, I am so not amused. This is the second time you've pulled this on me. Just give me my recipe and we're done." I shook the box. And still, nothing. The box wasn't giving an inch. Not one stinking inch.

Furious, I whacked the box on its side like I was slapping it across the face.

"Gladys? Are you in there?" It was a man's voice coming from outside the door. "I've brought some chocolate truffles from Paris. Your favorite. And a bit of champagne to wash it down."

Oh no. Now I'd done it. I was going down. To the big house. Did they put twelve-year-olds in jail? I sat still as a stone, quiet as a mouse. Maybe he'd go away.

No such luck. He jiggled the doorknob. "Gladys, why is the door locked?"

I was barely breathing. I felt like I might pass out from lack of oxygen.

"I hear you in there. Are you okay, Pumpkin? It's me, Sweetcakes." I could hear concern creeping into the man's voice.

I felt bad. He was old. I didn't want him to stress. I would have liked to tell him not to worry, Gladys wasn't here, but I couldn't. Sweetcakes and Pumpkin would have to work things out later without me around. Finally, I heard his footsteps retreating.

I returned my attention to the box and I was trying to recapture the earlier image of my new old life, the irony of which did not escape me, when I heard a key in the lock. Cripes. With cripes sauce. I dove under the bed just seconds before the door burst open. I couldn't see much, only three pairs of fairly large feet. One set wore sparkly clean Stan Smith Adidas (so not hip). And the other two wore army-issue black boots. Uh-oh. This did not bode well.

"Maybe she's out," said a low, husky male voice.

"I heard a noise." It was Sweetcakes from earlier. Darn him and the horse he rode in on. "And Gladys never locks the door, even when she goes out."

"Let's take a look around." Wow. A woman? Awfully big feet for a woman.

I didn't dare move. I didn't dare breathe.

"No one's here, Mr. Santos," said the big-footed woman.

"I know I heard someone. Or something . . ." Sweetcakes was really starting to get on my nerves.

"Everything looks okay," said the husky-voiced man.

"Something's not right. I can feel it," said Sweetcakes, and then I heard him walk to the other side of the room. "Did you hear something?" Sweetcakes asked. Who was he talking to? "Can you understand me? Was someone in the room?"

"Yes," replied someone who sounded remarkably like a bird.

Oh. Please. No. Chachi. The bird talked. I was totally screwed.

"Bed. Yes. Bed. Yes," the bird bellowed. *Okay. We get it. I'm under the bed.*

I was dripping in sweat as I looked up and into three pairs of eyes.

"Uh, hey there, guys" was the best I could manage.

"What are you doing here?" asked the husky-voiced man.

"Who are you?" asked Sweetcakes.

"My grandmother is friends with Gladys—"

"That doesn't give you the right to go breaking into her room," said the woman.

"I know, you are absolutely right. I have a perfectly good explanation for this . . ." I said as I racked my brain for a perfectly good explanation.

I crawled out from under the bed. It seemed more dignified than remaining there. I stood up and faced my firing squad.

The guy was meaty and pretty scary-looking. The woman was small and unassuming, but then again, she had those big feet. I supposed there was more to her than met the eye. And then there was Pesky Santos, AKA Sweetcakes, a distinguished-looking gentleman with gray hair, pressed jeans, gold cuff links, and an ascot tucked into his open collar. An ascot? Please, spare me. What was this, *Pride and Prejudice*?

"What's going on, miss?" asked the meaty guard as he stared down at me.

"Yeah, it's kind of a funny story . . ." I laughed nervously. No one looked amused.

"I'll bet," said the woman. "You can explain it all at the security station."

"Wait. Don't I, uh, get to make a phone call or something? What about reading me my rights? Due process and all that?" I tried to remember every possible thing I'd gleaned from all those episodes of *Law and Order*.

"You'll get your due process, little missy," said the woman as she put her hand on my neck and guided me toward the door. She and the big guy flanked me, carting me off like a common criminal. Sweetcakes walked in the opposite direction, tsk-tsking all the way down the hall. I looked back fondly on the time when I was merely pond scum, because I had now sunk to a whole new low, some primordial sludge that existed far below the surface of the earth.

Chapter 19

Another Stop on the Road to Ruin

W<small>HEN YOU'RE</small> a typical suburban twelve-year-old girl, the last place you want to find yourself is in a holding cell at a retirement village. Actually, it wasn't really a holding cell. It looked more like a doctor's waiting room, with a few plastic chairs, a water cooler, and some magazines. But it might as well have been a maximum-security prison the way everyone was staring at me, like I was Hannibal Lecter or something. This couldn't be good for college admissions.

Two more security guards showed up.

"Is this the perp?" one of them said to the woman. She nodded affirmatively.

"They start young these days," said another one of the guards.

"Tell me about it. It's a crying shame," the woman added.

People, I'm right here. I can hear you. And let me tell you, I feel awful enough already. I don't need the peanut-gallery commentary.

All five of them stared at me. Five security guards? I was eighty-five pounds. Wasn't this overkill? And where had these guys been in the first place? Maybe all this could have been avoided if security had been a little more on top of things. Maybe they could have saved me from myself. Although I'm not sure anyone could have done that. I had been on the road to ruin for a while already. This was just another stop.

I waited for the questions to start, but nobody asked me anything. They just stood there, occasionally shooting me disapproving looks. One of the guards took out a box of Tic Tacs and passed it around. No one offered me any. I started to get scared. Were they trying to break me down through silence? Was waterboarding next? Or stoning? Who knew what they had in store for me. I was working myself into a tizzy. My imagination was spinning out of control. I had visions of myself banging out license plates in the basement of some prison, seeing Mom and Dad and Granny once a week, with us having to talk on phones separated by a glass partition. I wouldn't finish middle school. I'd never see the twins grow up. What had I done? Why hadn't I listened to Granny? Wet, hot tears soaked my cheeks. Take me away. Lock me up. Throw away the key. I don't deserve your pity. I'm bad to the bone ...

"Franny, what in heaven's name is going on?" I looked up to see Granny and Gladys standing in the security-office doorway, framed in the bright fluorescent light. Granny looked pissed. I'd never even heard her raise her voice; it was always peace, love, and yoga. But now I saw anger, betrayal, and disappointment etched on her face.

"Granny, I-I thought you were at class. Wh-what are you doing here?" I stammered.

"I think the more salient question is, what are *you* doing here?"

"And in my room, with the door locked," Gladys added.

"Yes, that does seem to be the burning question," the female guard put in.

"We'd like answers," Granny said. "Now!"

"It's sort of a long story . . ." I hedged. "Maybe we should talk later. At home—"

"We're going to talk now," Granny said.

"We've got plenty of time," Gladys offered. And then she and Granny plopped onto chairs on either side of me and fixed their eyes on me with a red-hot intensity.

With little choice, I launched into my story, warts and all. Everyone listened, rapt. No one was eating Tic Tacs now. In fact, as I continued on about the magic recipes, the monk, Joey, Kate, Dad, Naomi, Elodie, Marsha, Ms. Posey, and Marta, several other Leisure Village staff members wandered in to listen. I was a very bad person, but at least I was entertaining. What felt like two days later, I finally stopped talking. It felt good to get the whole ugly mess off my chest. I had been living under a dark shroud of secrets and lies for so long, I had forgotten what it was like to breathe the fresh air of truth, despite the consequences. When I looked into Granny's disheartened face, I knew there were going to be grave consequences.

No one said anything for a while. And then finally the meaty guard spoke up. He turned to Granny. "You've got a box of magical recipes?"

"Uh, not really . . ." Granny groped for a response. It was all my fault for spilling the beans on her otherworldly secrets, the beans I had sworn up and down I'd never spill.

"Could I maybe get a recipe from you? There's a girl I really like but she's not interested in me. If I could make her some brownies, or cookies. Or whatever. Then, you know, maybe she'd change her mind . . ."

The female guard turned to Granny. "There are these gold hoops I've had my eye on, but they never go on sale. Maybe you could find me a recipe for the store manager."

"Here's the thing," Granny said, summoning her authority. "There's no magic box. I just made it all up. I thought it might help Franny get through some tough times. It's a grandmother's trick, to offer the idea of magic to a child. It's related to Jungian analysis." Granny was laying it on thick. Now I knew where I got it from. This lying thing seemed to be deeply embedded in my family's DNA. "It's really just a silly old box filled with useless recipes. But Franny's a young girl, prone to tall tales. She likes to believe there's magic in the world, and, quite frankly, don't we all?"

"I wouldn't mind trying one of those recipes, just for the heck of it," said the meaty guard.

"I'm sorry. But it's just a bunch of hooey," Granny said, shooting me a look.

The guard turned to Gladys. "You wanna press charges, Ms. Pepperdine?"

"I think I'll leave the punishment to her grandmother,"

Gladys said. "If you don't mind, I'm going to find Mr. Santos and see if I can't rustle up those truffles and champagne."

Gladys leaned into Granny and pecked her on the cheek. "See you at tai chi tomorrow?"

Granny nodded. And then Gladys stood up and approached me. She folded me into her arms and whispered in my ear, "As I recall, middle school can be hell; sometimes you need a little outside help. Hopefully, your grandmother won't be too hard on you."

☺☺☺☺

"Granny, I'm so, so sorry. I totally screwed up. I was just—"

Granny put her hand up, kind of in my face, to stop me. As in *Talk to the hand*. I shut up immediately and we drove home in silence, the box between us.

Granny seemed deep in thought. Was she ever going to speak to me again? Would she just ignore me as we passed each other every day in the house? Would we have to communicate through Mom? Mom! Ugh! I hadn't even begun to think of the Mom of it all. This wasn't going to be pretty.

When we got home, Mom was in the kitchen playing Battleship with the twins.

"B-six, B-six, B-six," Pip roared.

"One second, Chase," Mom said, and then, turning to me, she asked, "Did Granny pick you up from Joey's?" Mom looked confused since Mom was supposed to pick me up from Joey's.

"Yes. I picked her up," Granny said without missing a beat.

"She called me on my cell." Now Mom looked thoroughly bewildered. While Granny carries a cell phone with her, she never actually turns it on. It's just for emergencies.

"You turned on your cell, Mom?" Mom asked Granny.

"I'm not an idiot, Anna. Of course I turned on my cell phone," Granny shot back.

"Okay. It's just, I've never actually seen you use it."

"Well, as it turns out, you don't know absolutely everything about me. I'm quite the cell phone user these days."

Mom wasn't sure what to make of Granny's sudden attitude. And then she noticed the box. "What's that you're carrying?" Uh-oh.

"Just a little homemade gift from Gladys. It holds pot pouri, sachets, you know, that kind of thing," Granny said, playing the old-lady card.

"B-six, B-six, B-six, B-six, B-six, B-six, B-six." Pip was losing his mind.

"One minute, Chase. Franny, you need to shower and clean your room."

"Actually, Franny and I need a little quality time together this evening, if you don't mind," Granny said.

"C'mon, Mom, B-six," Pip yelled at the top of his lungs, throwing all of his sixty pounds into it.

"Chase Baldwin Flanders. I will not tolerate that kind of behavior. Time out."

Pip marched out of the room. Squeak turned to Mom and in a sweet, gentle voice asked, "Is it a hit? B-six?"

"Yes. It's a hit," Mom said.

"Sunk ya! Sunk ya! Now we're gonna dunk ya." Squeak threw his hands in the air. "We won, dude," he shouted to Pip, who was sitting on the fluffy red time-out chair in the living room. Pip let out a muted squeal of glee as Granny and I slipped away into her lair.

I took a seat on the bed. I knew I was in it for the long haul. Might as well get comfortable. Granny sat down next to me and put her arm around me. I was surprised and touched by this gesture. Maybe she wasn't going to hate me forever.

"I have sensed something was wrong for a while now," Granny said. "I could see it in your aura. Usually it's light blue with a few streaks of pink. Lately it's been brown. That's never good."

"If you knew something was wrong, why didn't you say anything?"

"I was waiting for *you* to say something. I gave you numerous chances to come clean but you never did," Granny said. "You never talked to Joey and Kate, did you?"

"No. I lied."

"Yes. Many times. I'm very disappointed."

I was waaay beyond ashamed.

"I was hoping you would own up to what you'd done. Because the only way to fix anything is to admit that you made the mess in the first place," Granny continued. "I entrusted you with a lot of responsibility. Probably too much for someone your age. What upsets me more than your lying is that once you realized you needed help, you chose to break into my friend's home instead of coming to me. I thought we had forged a bond, a friendship. I thought we trusted each other. But I was wrong . . ."

Tears began streaming down my cheeks, for like the tenth time that day, because there is no worse feeling than realizing you let down someone you love.

"You weren't wrong, Granny. We have forged a bond. And a friendship. I mean, totally," I said between sobs. "I'm so sorry I've disappointed you. I was selfish, thoughtless, inconsiderate—"

"And reckless. Very, very reckless. You're lucky. Things could have been a whole lot worse with the way you abused the magic."

Lucky? I certainly didn't feel lucky. "I got a little carried away with the powers the box gave me."

"Yes. You certainly did. But they're not your powers. Or my powers. Those recipes are meant for people in need. The holder of the box is simply a conduit, charged with a higher purpose."

I had gotten heady with power. I was no better than Elodie. "I really messed up. I know that now, Granny. You should punish me. To the best of your abilities."

Granny smiled, which felt like a tiny sliver of light piercing through the dark dungeon that had become my life. "To the best of my abilities. All right, I think we're going to start with some daily meditation for the next week. Every morning before school, to give you an opportunity to reflect."

Okay, I deserved that.

Granny heaved a huge sigh. "You've really gotten yourself into quite a jam."

"I know. I was hoping that I could fix everything and you wouldn't notice."

"Yes, well, quite a few people have noticed now, haven't they?" Granny said. "I'm going to need some kind of recipe to make those guards at Leisure Village forget everything."

Granny was quiet for a beat and then she whipped out her cell and punched some numbers into it. She held it to her ear for a moment, put it down, looked at it, shook it, punched in some more numbers, put it back to her ear, and then finally turned to me, frustrated. "Okay, I give up. How do you get it to work?"

"You have to turn it on first," I said gingerly.

"Right. Got it. And how would I do that?" I took the phone from Granny, turned it on, and then handed it back to her.

"Who are you calling?" I asked.

"Lama Tensing Pasha. The monk. We need to bring in the big guns. Hopefully, Lama will know what to do because I haven't got the darnedest idea. I just hope he'll have the time for us."

Granny punched about a million numbers into the cell

and waited for what seemed like hours until finally I heard a booming voice on the other end of the line.

"*Tah-shi de-lah,*" Granny said. Her whole being seemed to light up as she connected with Lama. "*Khe-rang khu-su de-bo yin-peh?*" Granny was fluent in monk?

They chatted away forever. I watched, mesmerized by the sight of my granny talking monk and totally taking charge. My ship was probably sinking but I felt relieved that at least some-one was finally at the helm.

"*Kah-leh phe. Sahng-nyi jeh yong,*" Granny said, and then hung up and turned back to me. "Lama is going to borrow Oprah's plane and he'll be here tomorrow."

"Tomorrow, as in *tomorrow* tomorrow? Like, the day after today?" I said, aghast. Lama was coming here, to Fall River? I was pretty sure he was going to be seriously pissed at me. I re-ally wasn't looking forward to that. And then, because it had just registered, I said, "I'm sorry, did you say *Oprah's* plane? As in *Oprah* Oprah?"

"Yes. He's her spiritual advisor. Actually, Oprah, Lama, and I were all quite close in Spain in 1540. That was a wild time." Granny chuckled, shaking her head.

I said nothing because, well, how could I possibly respond to that?

"Apparently, Lama knew something was wrong here. He's highly attuned to cosmic shifts. His left ear was aching all week and that usually indicates astral distress. Or a serious inner-ear infection."

"What exactly are you going to tell Mom when Lama shows up on her doorstep?"

"I'll have to think of something, especially since he's bringing a few deputies. Could be tricky. They'll need to assess things at the house and at Jefferson before making a formal plan."

"At school?" I said, horrified. "My school?"

"I'm afraid so, Franny. You've really stepped in it, my dear."

I was going to bring a monk and his entourage to school with me tomorrow. I was about to become a social pariah the likes of which had never been seen at Jefferson. But that was my penance. That, and a whole lot of early-morning meditation. Frankly, I thought I was getting a fairly light sentence, considering the offense. Granny could have come up with a whole lot worse. She was pretty cool, as grannies go.

Chapter 20

Justin Timberlake Knows My Name

I SPENT HALF THE NIGHT reading up on Bhutanese monks on the Web. The fact that these guys can spend fifteen hours a day in total silence made me nervous. I spend fifteen hours a day talking. The likelihood that Lama and I would hit it off seemed remote.

I dragged myself out of bed at 7:00 a.m. It was the second all-nighter I'd pulled in a week, and I was starting to feel the effects. My left eye was twitching, my hands were shaky, and my legs felt wobbly. I looked into the bathroom mirror and discovered, to my horror, that I had bags under my eyes the size of grapefruits. I was aging in dog years. At this rate, I wasn't going to make it to my teens.

I was on my way downstairs to breakfast when Granny appeared out of nowhere and pulled me into the hall closet. She was dressed all in black with a ski cap pulled low over her head. She shut the closet door and the two of us stood in the dark.

"Granny, what are you doing?"

"I'm looking for the stupid light switch," she said. "Why must everything in this house be so complicated?"

I reached up and pulled a cord, illuminating the tiny space. We were standing so close together our noses were practically touching. Granny smelled of patchouli; her foot was in a bucket, and a mop grazed her head. She looked absurd but she was my leader.

"We need to stay above suspicion, at all costs."

"Everything we're doing looks suspicious. You're dressed like a thief and we're hiding in a closet."

"Who got us into this mess in the first place?" Granny looked at me indignantly. "I'm just trying to get us out of this. I suggest you zip it and pay attention."

Granny was right. This was not the time for snark or sarcasm. This was the time to bite my tongue and go along with Granny no matter how crazy her plan seemed.

"We're meeting Lama at an undisclosed location and then going straight to school. I don't want your mother slowing us down with questions. You'll exit through the front door and head toward school, just like always. I'll exit through the garage and pretend to drive to tai chi. This way, your mother won't suspect a thing. We'll meet on the corner of Pineoak and Osage." Granny stuck out her arm. She wore an old sports watch. "Let's synchronize our watches. What time do you have?"

"I don't wear a watch." Granny looked bummed. It was the first hiccup in her plan. "But my phone has a clock," I added helpfully. I took out my cell and checked the time. "It's seven thirty-one."

Granny stared at her wrist. "That's weird. My watch says four thirty." She held her watch up to her ear. "The darn thing's not working."

"Your cell also has a clock."

"Really? Good to know. I can't quite remember where I put it . . ."

"I think we'll be okay. I've totally got the plan. I'll have breakfast—"

"Good thinking. I hadn't factored breakfast in."

"And then at eight, I'll grab my stuff, exit through the front door, and meet you, like, five minutes later."

"You're good at this, Francisco."

Granny opened the door a sliver and checked to make sure the coast was clear before releasing me. I headed into the kitchen just in time to catch the tail end of yet another pancakes-versus-waffles discussion between Mom and the twins.

"I'm not eating this," Pip insisted as he stared at the plate of waffles in front of him. "I want pancakes."

"They're made out of the exact same batter. They just look different," Mom urged. "C'mon, just try one."

Mom handed me the plate of waffles. "You still do waffles, right?"

"Sure," I said, taking the plate. I shoveled in the waffles and was just grabbing my stuff for school when Granny waltzed into the kitchen. "I'm off to tai chi. Toodles, everyone," Granny said, winking at me.

"Mom, why on earth are you dressed like a bank robber?" Mom asked Granny. I stifled a laugh.

"It's my new tai chi outfit. Black is the new Zen," Granny offered on her way out the door. It was a pretty good comeback, right off the cuff.

"I'm off to school. Bye." I kissed Mom and exited the house.

At the corner I jumped into Granny's car and she peeled out like a maniac, weaving in and out of traffic.

"Slow down," I said. "You're going to get us killed."

"Don't be such a cautious Carol. I've got it under control."

"Where are we going?"

"I can't say. You're lucky I didn't throw a hood over your head. Just don't pay attention to the route I'm taking."

About ten minutes later we pulled in to a tiny airport just in time to watch a sleek silver jet land on an empty runway. We got out of the car and stood on the tarmac as the jet taxied to a stop. I wasn't so nervous anymore. I was actually kind of psyched. This was so unbelievably cool. Now I wished I'd dressed for this kind of adventure, maybe a metallic Lycra jumpsuit with a small knife attached to my ankle. My jean skirt and T-shirt weren't cutting it.

The door of the plane opened and what looked like a small moose stumbled out and descended the stairs.

"Tell me that's not Lama?" I said to Granny, figuring anything was possible.

"It's a *dyiong-gyem tsi*. It is believed they're magical creatures and Lama goes pretty much everywhere with his," Granny said.

It sure was ugly. I hoped we weren't taking it to school. Explaining Lama was one thing; explaining a butt-ugly moose was a whole 'nother thing.

Next, a black and white crane waddled down the stairs.

"A *thrung trung karmo*. Sacred species of cranes, unique to Bhutan," Granny offered.

It was like Noah's Ark. Were there any people on the plane?

Two bald men in red robes with orange sashes emerged.

"Is one of them Lama?" I asked.

"No, those are his deputies Merpa and Guppa. Guppa plays a mean game of Ping-Pong, and Merpa is a very talented chef. His specialty is Tex-Mex," Granny said.

After the deputies, a man who looked like Justin Timberlake came down the stairs. Exactly like Justin Timberlake.

I turned to Granny. "Is that Justin Timberlake?"

"I don't know who that is, darling."

The man who looked exactly like Justin Timberlake walked toward us.

"Franny?" said the man who looked exactly like Justin Timberlake.

"Uh, yeah," I said, because that was pretty much all I was capable of saying as I stared at what was either Justin Timberlake or his identical twin.

"I'm Justin Timberlake," said the man who looked exactly like Justin Timberlake. No way! No way! Justin Flipping

Timberlake was standing, like, two feet away from me. And he knew my name. My mind was officially blown.

"Lama's a bud of mine. I hitched a ride with him and he told me all about your situation. Man, you really messed with the universe, huh? That sucks."

"Uh, yeah," I said again. I was talking to Justin Flipping Timberlake. Or, rather, not talking to Justin Timberlake. Because I couldn't form a proper sentence. Jeez, even Justin Timberlake knew how royally I'd screwed up. This was becoming a global embarrassment. Did Oprah know as well?

"It's really nice to meet you. I've got to roll, but here." Justin pulled some tickets out of his pocket and handed them to me. "I'm performing at the Meadowlands next week. Hopefully, I'll see you there."

And then, before I could say anything remotely intelligent, Justin Timberlake disappeared into a waiting limo.

"Oh. My. God. I. Am. Totally. Flipping. Out," I said to Granny. "That was Justin Timberlake. And he knows my name! And he gave me tickets to his concert!"

"That's nice, dear," Granny said, not really listening because she was focused on a short bald man who had just stepped off the plane. Granny's whole face lit up. She was bobbing up and down excitedly and waving furiously.

The man wore a shiny black Adidas tracksuit with neon yellow basketball shoes. This was the famous Lama? He didn't look like a monk. He looked like he should be selling stereos.

Lama took both of Granny's hands in his. "It is divine to see you, Mathilda. The light in me honors the light in you." Lama and Granny stared into each other's eyes, perhaps communicating telepathically, I wasn't sure. It was all a little wacky. But who cared? I'd just met Justin Timberlake. Justin Flipping Timberlake. I could die happy.

Lama began to take off his pants. Yikes. What was this turn of events? I shut my eyes. I didn't even want to know what was going to happen next. To my great relief, Lama was wearing a pair of red cotton pants underneath the Adidas tracksuit. He removed his jacket to reveal a saffron-colored robe. This was more like it; now he was starting to resemble a monk. But he still had on those blazing yellow shoes.

"The AC on that plane is out of control. Justin lent me these, thank goodness."

Lama turned his gaze on me. "Hello, Francine."

"*Kuzo zangpo la,*" I said haltingly.

Lama laughed, his eyes twinkling. "Granny said you were clever. How long have you been studying Bhutanese?"

"'Hello' and 'Where is the restroom?' is all I can say." I had memorized that off the Internet. "I'm, uh, so sorry I messed with the universe. I know it was a really bad idea."

"Yes, well, it certainly wasn't a good one. You've really gotten yourself into quite a bind. You didn't listen to your grandmother, did you?"

"Uh, no," I said, bracing myself for yet another well-earned lecture.

"Listening is a muscle, Francine. We must continually work it or it will become weak and useless." Lama passed his hands over my head ever so lightly, without touching me. They just sort of hung above my hair like antennas, searching for a signal.

"I'm going to become a better listener, I promise. If it's the last thing I do."

"It will not be the last thing you do, Francine. Far from it." Lama smiled. The deputies smiled. Even the moose seemed to smile.

"Okay, we should hustle. I've got to fly to LA tonight. I have to be at a fundraiser at Brad and Angelina's." I didn't need to ask Brad and Angelina who? because by now it was pretty clear how Lama rolled.

Lama promised he'd have an airport employee take Granny's car to our house, and then we all climbed into a waiting Lexus hybrid and hightailed it to school. I was starting to get sweaty with nerves. The deputies and I sat silently while Granny and Lama caught up on their current and past lives. Moosie curled up in the far back and licked his hooves. The crane seemed to have disappeared. I couldn't believe this was really happening. I was bringing a monk, his deputies, a moose, and my granny to school. God help me. I could pretty much write off the rest of the year.

As we got closer to school, Lama turned his attention to me. "Franny, how many recipes did you use? Over what period of time? Did you administer any of them on a Monday? And do you have any gum?"

Whoa. That was a lot of questions. "Uh, I used two recipes on Joey and Kate, over three days, I think. The second recipe was on a Monday . . ." I stopped for a moment because the last question really threw me. "Do I have any gum?" I repeated.

"Yes. I love gum and it is so hard to find in Bhutan but you Americans always seem to carry it with you wherever you go."

I handed Lama a piece of Bubblicious. He popped it in his mouth and savored it like I'd just given him a chocolate truffle.

"Delicious." Lama turned to Merpa. "Make a note to pick up twenty packs of this . . . Bubblicious," Lama said, reading the wrapper.

Merpa nodded solemnly.

Chapter 21

Karma Bites

We pulled up to Jefferson and idled by the side of the building. This gave us a vantage point from which I could identify all the key players for Lama and explain what had gone so terribly wrong in each case. Joey and Kate were sitting outside on the grass, hunched over a laptop.

Lama listened carefully as he took in the scene on and around the stairs. You didn't have to be a monk with a thousand years of experience to see that life at Jefferson Middle School was in bad shape. The bickering, shoving, and maneuvering of the previous day had reached critical mass. There was an air of danger about things as geeks, beeks, smeeks, govs, loners, juvies, and peaks eyed one another warily, protecting their new spots with an intense ferocity.

"Until I can meet these people, Franny, and feel their energy, I won't know the extent of the damage. So, like you say in America, let's roll." And with that, Lama hopped out of the car, and we all followed. Me, the deputies, Granny, and Moosie. We were quite the motley crew.

We approached the stairs, and everyone stopped what he

or she was doing and stared at us. Several people pointed to Moosie and laughed. Granny, never one to shy away from attention, waved to the curious masses. I grabbed her wrist.

"Please, Granny, I'm begging you, stop waving," I whispered. "Don't make this any worse than it has to be." Which was the understatement of the year because it was already much worse than it had to be. I was pretty sure that I had secured my place in the social dungeon for all eternity. No Fall Fling, no more border crossing, no more anything. In time, I could start anew at a college far, far away.

We approached Joey and Kate. "Hey, guys," I said.

They didn't even bother to respond as they tapped into their laptop, oblivious to the monk and moose I had brought to school. I shouldn't have been surprised. This was just a natural extension of their complete and total self-absorption. I rolled my eyes and started to walk away. Lama touched my arm to stop me.

"Talk to them. I need to get a read on the situation," Lama instructed me.

I cleared my throat. "What are you guys doing?" Lama stood by my side. He closed his eyes and started humming.

Joey looked up. "Hey, Fran, can't really talk."

"We're working with a designer on our new website," Kate offered. And then they turned their attention back to the laptop. They didn't even register Lama, whose humming had drawn the attention of everyone else standing nearby. I felt heat rising to my cheeks. I was deeply wounded by the complete and utter lack of acknowledgment by my two former besties. Yes, it was all my fault. But that didn't make it sting any less.

"Website?" I said, confused. "You mean the blog?"

"The blog was just to get us started," Kate countered.

"Yeah. You can't get enough hits without a real website," Joey added.

Blog, website. Whatever. It was all ridiculous, and yet I would have given my left arm to be included. How would our friendship ever recover? Things seemed beyond repair at this point. Even with Lama working overtime.

Lama nudged me. "Time to move on, Franny. I've got what I need."

Lama started up the stairs. We all trailed after him, running into Marsha Whalley on the landing. I nearly fell backwards when I saw her. Her long, dark frizzy hair had been shaved off. She had a buzzcut, colored a vibrant green. This was my fault too.

"Marsha, what happened to your hair?" I asked, not sure I wanted to know.

"Elodie gave me a makeover last night. It's fab, right?" Remarkably, Marsha seemed pleased with her new green do. "Elodie thought Maria would be much more modern as a punk rocker and I have to agree. The whole prissy English thing is so done."

"Yeah, totally," I said, thinking just the opposite. Spiky green hair was so not the way to go for *The Sound of Music*. I was pretty sure Marsha would be fired on the spot, which had most likely been Elodie's evil plan all along. Mr. Sheeplick would have no choice but to give the part to Elodie, who would be waiting in the wings.

"Hey, Franny, who are your friends?" Marsha waved to my crew. "Hi. I'm Marsha." She leaned over and nuzzled Moosie, who whinnied a bit. "Cool, a moose."

"These are, uh . . . a few of my grandma's friends. They're here from Bhutan on a peacekeeping mission." I had to smile at the realization that I wasn't actually lying, for the first time in forever.

"I love the hair, sweetie. It's a marvelous shade of green. It really suits you," Granny interjected, offering her hand to Marsha. "I'm Mathilda, Franny's granny."

"Hey, that rhymes." Marsha laughed.

Jeez, this was pride-swallowing. Could we please lose the rhyming couplets?

"Nice meeting you. See you later, Franny." Marsha scooted off to hang with the theater geeks, who had of late embraced her as their new queen, despite the fact that she looked like Shrek.

After Marsha left, Lama turned to me with a smile. "That's the one you gave the Fix-It Formula to, no?" I nodded. "You have done good with her. You used the recipe properly and with the right spirit. You have helped to bring joy to her heart. No need to worry about her. She will light her own way."

When we got to the front door, Elodie appeared, blocking our entrance. Standing next to her were Alden and Samantha Ross. Alden was holding Elodie's hand, a sight that sent a sharp stab of pain through my heart. Lama gently placed his hand on my arm, and a soothing pulse of energy shot through my body. Weird. Had Lama sensed my pain?

Alden looked from me to Granny to Lama to the deputies to Moosie and back to me. I hoped he was thinking that life with me would be a whole lot more interesting than life with Elodie and her breasts. But most likely he was thinking what a complete and total nut job I must be. And at that moment, I kind of had to agree with him.

"Is that a . . . moose, Franny?" Samantha Ross asked, quick as ever on the uptake.

"No. It's a *dyiong-gyem tsi*," Granny said.

"I don't want to talk about it," I said to Samantha.

"I see you've made some new friends, Franny." Elodie cackled. "It's official, you've become a total loser. We'll have to come up with a new name for you because you're definitely no longer a border crosser." At this, Elodie and Samantha high-fived. Alden turned away, probably too weirded out to even look at me.

I balled my hands into fists and dug my nails into my skin. I wanted to turn the emotional pain into physical pain in the hopes that it might fortify me instead of reducing me to tears, which is where I was headed.

"Well, well, well, we meet again. You never know who you're going to run into," Lama said. He was right up in her face, but Elodie was unable to meet his gaze. What was going on?

"I have no idea what you're talking about," Elodie replied in her snarkiest voice.

"The last time I saw you, you were leading your men into battle, preparing to slaughter an entire village, burning everything to the ground. You were Genghis Khan. I was just a small black crow at the time, but I'll never forget you. You were the scariest creature I'd ever seen and you haven't changed a bit." What? Elodie was Genghis Khan in a former life? That was the craziest thing I'd ever heard, and yet it made sense. I was starting to come around to this whole notion of reincarnation.

"Now I understand how hard things have been for you," Lama said, turning to me. "She is ruthless and will stop at nothing to get what she wants, but her powers have been severely damaged over the years. She is little more than a paper tiger, an empty vessel. She will burn herself out eventually, as she has done throughout the centuries. Just stand by and watch."

"Whatever. Like I care, crazy dude." Elodie rolled her eyes. She tried to hide it, but I could tell she was spooked.

Lama brushed by Elodie and entered the building. Elodie didn't say a word. We all followed. On her way in, Granny stopped and put her face, like, two inches from Elodie's. Their noses were practically touching.

"Karma doesn't lie, my dear, and yours is about to bite you in the butt. Poetic justice is headed your way. Watch out." Wow. You go, Granny.

"Yeah, what she said," I added, looking Elodie straight in the eye. Lama's words had given me a sudden jolt of confidence.

Once inside, Lama didn't really walk so much as glide through the hall, moving with such grace and agility it looked like he was floating. He sniffed the air, ran his hands along the walls, touched a locker and then licked his finger. The deputies and Granny stood back a few feet, watching. Moosie found a chunk of a Snickers bar on the floor and devoured it.

"Point me toward the cafeteria," Lama said. I was about to show him the way when Principal Mackey appeared.

"Franny, what is going on? Who are these people? And why is there a . . . moose in the school?" Principal Mackey looked pissed. "You all need to go straight to the office to sign in and I'll need IDs—"

Lama offered his hand to Principal Mackey, interrupting her tirade. "Hi. I'm Lama Tensing Pasha, a friend of Franny Flanders and her grandmother. We are in town from Bhutan, where I live and teach. I have heard talk of your fine institution and your innovative teaching methods and I was compelled to stop by and see for myself."

Principal Mackey's expression transformed. She went from

pissed to puffed up as Lama extolled the virtues of Jefferson. If a monk could occasionally lie, then maybe I wasn't all *that* bad. As Lama spoke, he took Principal Mackey's hand in his and quickly tied a yellow string around her wrist.

"What is this?" Principal Mackey said, staring at the string. Good question. I was wondering the same thing.

"A gift from Bhutan," Lama said. Moosie sniffed Principal Mackey's skirt. I worried she was going to freak out. I once saw her chase a cat out of school with a baseball bat. But she just rubbed Moosie's head and smiled at Lama.

I saw a flicker of a spark jump from the string. Principal Mackey didn't notice. But it confirmed my suspicions: The string was magic. Lama was doing magic. I was both relieved and troubled at the thought. More magic? Could Fall River handle it?

"Let me take you on a tour," Principal Mackey said, hooking arms with Lama. "Where should we begin? The biology lab has the latest equipment, and I'd love to show you our AP Latin class. They now speak the language. We don't consider it dead at all."

"To be honest, I'd like to begin in the cafeteria, if you don't mind. We have a saying in Bhutan. 'The cafeteria is the heart of a school's soul,'" Lama said, winking at me. I had to suppress a giggle.

Principal Mackey had trouble digesting this odd request. "Interesting. I've, uh, never really heard anything about that in all my years in education."

"You underestimate the importance of the cafeteria." Lama smiled at Principal Mackey. "Will you lead the way?"

Principal Mackey did as she was told. It was Lama's world; we just lived in it.

We reached the cafeteria. Marta looked wild-eyed and deranged. She wore a white robe cinched at the waist with a belt that contained about a hundred deadly-looking knives. She'd completely lost her grip. With a machete, she was deboning what looked like a small mammal. Even Lama looked alarmed at the sight. He approached her, took her wrist in his hand, and tied a yellow string around it.

"Marta, it's so nice to meet you," Lama said. Moosie nibbled at the mammal while Lama talked to Marta.

"Are you here to deliver the curry? Because you're late," Marta said. She didn't even notice the string around her wrist. And then, mere seconds later, the intensity in Marta's eyes seemed to dim. She looked down at the fleshy animal in front of her, disgusted, and swept the entire thing in the trash.

"Can you grab me a can of mushroom soup from the shelf? And the peaches?" Marta asked Lama. Lama obliged willingly. "I am so not in the mood to make lunch."

The old Marta was back, as uninspired, cranky, and lazy as ever. Flip me out! Lama was a miracle worker. And whatever they were, those little yellow threads were potent and quick-acting. I could barely contain my excitement. Maybe all was not lost. Maybe Lama could actually fix absolutely everything I had totally screwed up. Maybe.

Next up, Ms. Posey. We entered the classroom to find Ms. Posey standing on her desk, bumping and grinding to Katy Perry's "I Kissed a Girl," which was blasting from an old-school boom box.

"C'mon, people, if you're happy and you know it, shake your groove thing. What are you waiting for?" The class stared at her in abject horror.

"Franny, you've really outdone yourself here," Granny whispered to me, chuckling. And then, unable to stop herself, Granny started to sway her hips, moving to the music.

"Stop it," I snapped at Granny, yanking on her arm.

Just as with Marta, Lama managed to maneuver the string around Ms. Posey's wrist, and within minutes she had morphed back into her old grumpy self.

"Who brought in this, this . . . monstrosity," Ms. Posey said, pointing to the boom box. "The entire class will pay for this. I want a paper that compares the themes of *Jane Eyre* with those of *The Odyssey* on my desk Monday morning." The class groaned. Personally, I couldn't have been happier.

That string was the answer to all my prayers. But why hadn't Lama tied them onto Kate's and Joey's wrists?

"This is fantastic, Lama. Thank you. We need to find Joey and Kate so you can give them the yellow strings—"

"Franny, minor alterations like Marta and Ms. Posey are easily accomplished. But there are some things I can't fix so easily." This was not what I wanted to hear. If Lama couldn't fix Joey and Kate, who could? Were they beyond repair?

"Franny Flanders!" Ms. Posey barked. "Why is there a moose in my classroom? And a bunch of . . . Hare Krishnas?"

"Uh, well, you see . . ." I searched for something to say that wouldn't land me in detention. Luckily, Principal Mackey came to my rescue.

"They are monks. Not Hare Krishnas. And the moose is a sacred and magical creature," Principal Mackey said sternly. "And I don't appreciate that tone in the classroom, Helga. It does not set a good example for the children."

Ms. Posey turned beet red and looked chastised. It was a lovely sight to see. I savored the moment, which I knew wouldn't come again any time soon.

"Furthermore, they are with the Bhutanese Department of Education. I've brought them to your classroom hoping they could learn from your teaching methods. But honestly, I am not so sure at the moment," Principal Mackey said.

"I . . . I'm sorry," Ms. Posey said, taking a seat at her desk. "You are right. I will try to speak to the children with more respect. It's just . . . sometimes I get so frustrated."

"That is not the children's problem. That is yours. Deal with it!" Principal Mackey snapped, and then she turned on her heel and left the room, motioning for Lama and crowd to follow her.

Whoa. Was that the magic or just plain old-fashioned justice? It was hard to tell.

Lama pulled me aside before following Principal Mackey out. "Franny, I've seen what I needed to see, and there's nothing more I can do right now. I need to rest and refuel. This takes a real toll on my psyche. We will meet again this afternoon. Hopefully, I will have more answers for you." Hopefully? I needed a lot better than that. But what could I do? You can't exactly argue with a magic monk.

Chapter 22

There's Magic All Around

I WALKED INTO THE HOUSE to find Granny, Lama, the deputies, and Mom sitting around the kitchen table having a grand old time. Moosie and the twins were out in the backyard. Everyone was chowing down on macaroni and cheese and yakking away like old friends. Mac and cheese? Couldn't Mom have provided a more exciting culinary experience? No one even noticed my entrance.

"If memory serves, Anna, I think Mathilda and I met for the first time in Egypt in A.D. 15," Lama said to Mom, in all seriousness.

"Yes. At the time we were both alligators," Granny chimed in, as if this were the most normal thing in the world. Mom just nodded.

"As a Buddhist, I have made my way up the animal chain. I'm happy to have finally achieved human form. Though I do have very fond memories of burying myself in mud at the foot of the Nile with you, Mathilda." Granny laughed and blushed. "It's truly remarkable how many times throughout history Mathilda and I have ended up together. The Peloponnesian

War, medieval Spain, and now here, in Fall River, New Jersey . . ."

I cleared my throat. "Hi, guys." It was time for everyone to veer off memory lane and hit reality road.

"Franny, have you met Granny's friends?" Mom asked. "They're visiting from the East. This is Lama, Merpa, and Guppa."

I smiled at everyone. Lama stood up.

"It is a pleasure to make your acquaintance," Lama said, winking at me.

"Yeah, you too," I said.

"Anna, thank you so much for your kindness and hospitality. I'd like to show Mathilda some things I've brought for her and then we're off to Los Angeles to . . . visit with friends," Lama said.

Friends? Is that what he called Brad and Angelina? That was pretty cool. I wanted to call Brad and Angelina friends too. I wondered if Lama had a string for that.

"May we come visit again sometime?" Lama said.

"Does the Buddha poop in the woods?" Mom giggled like a schoolgirl and blushed. I don't think you make Buddha jokes to a monk. But Lama took it in stride. Nothing seemed to fluster him.

"I hope you'll come again soon. Very soon." Mom smiled at Lama.

Was she crushing on him? How embarrassing. Luckily, he'd be gone soon. I didn't want to have to think about Mom dating Lama. Wait. Monks can't date. Thank God. I erased the thought from my memory bank. Things were way too full in there.

Lama pointed to the mac and cheese. "What was that tasty delicacy called again?"

"You mean the macaroni and cheese?" Mom asked.

"Yes. That's it. It is the most magnificent orange color, and the taste is so sumptuous, the texture so velvety rich. It is unlike anything in Bhutan." Lama turned to his deputies. "We must get many boxes to take home."

The deputies nodded solemnly, pulled out their iPhones, and made notes.

"I have dreamed of this . . . mac and cheese ever since I had it a few years ago in Chicago at the Obamas'. Thank you for taking the time to prepare it for me," Lama said.

"The Obamas?" Mom asked, surprised. "As in Barack and Michelle?"

"Yes. They are lovely people."

Mom stood up. She offered her hand to Lama. Instead of taking it, he placed both of his hands on her shoulders. "The light in me honors the light in you."

"Yes, uh, my thoughts exactly," Mom said, swooning.

Granny shot me a look and then she and Lama, followed by the deputies, exited the room and disappeared down the stairs.

"I've got a ton of homework," I said, grabbing a granola bar and rushing out of the kitchen. I checked to make sure Mom wasn't looking and then made a quick U-turn and snuck down the stairs into Granny's room. The door was closed. I knocked quietly. Granny opened the door a sliver and I scooted inside. More covert ops.

The deputies stood silently by the window. Lama had disappeared.

"Where's Lama?" I asked Granny.

"In there," Granny said, pointing to the closet.

The closet door was shut, but I could hear knocking, banging, and chanting coming from inside. It sounded like Lama and the box were really going at it.

"After we returned from school, Lama took a nap and then spent the better part of the afternoon communing with the box," Granny said. "We just took a quick mac-and-cheese break to fortify him."

"Kraft mac and cheese is most wonderful," said Guppa. That was the first full sentence I'd heard from him. I didn't realize he could speak. It seemed mac and cheese really brought out the best in the Bhutanese.

"It is like tasting the sunrise as it creeps up over the mountain and through the clouds," Merpa added. "Almost as good as a chicken enchilada from Taco Bell."

We all stood around, waiting patiently for Lama to re-emerge. Granny gave herself a manicure. I plopped onto the floor and played with the shag carpeting. Moosie wandered in and settled on the bed.

After about fifteen endless minutes, Lama emerged from the closet and took a seat on the bed. He sat in a lotus position, legs crossed, hands at his sides, eyes closed. I stared at him, my breaths shallow and quick. Slowly, Lama opened his eyes, raised his hand, and opened his palm to reveal a piece of paper. It was the familiar-looking frayed parchment that I had seen so many times over the past couple of weeks, a recipe from the box. I rushed to grab the recipe but Lama closed his fist around the paper and pulled it away.

"Not so fast, Franny," Lama said. "Patience is the better part of virtue."

"So true, Lama. It's what I always tell her," Granny added.

I'd been hearing a lot about the upside of patience lately. But honestly, I wasn't feeling it. If I waited much longer, who knew what kind of funk Dad would work himself into, or how far Joey and Kate would disappear into the blogosphere? Still, I understood what was at stake here and I knew not to mess with Lama. I was going to have to sit tight.

I took a seat on the rug at Lama's feet. "I can be very patient, when I try."

Lama smiled at me. "I'm sure you can, Franny. You can be a lot of things, when you try."

Granny laughed. "You read her like a book, Lama."

Lama and Granny shared a look. These two were beginning to get on my nerves.

"The box holds many mysteries. There is much still to learn about it. We must be cautious as we proceed. Administering antidotes is a tricky business. I can't be entirely sure of the results or ramifications."

Yeah, yeah. Whatever. Could we just skip to the recipes?

"Your intentions were not entirely selfish. You wanted harmony among your friends and family; you enjoy good food; you wanted what is just and fair, socially and intellectually. You just went about it the wrong way. The box is meant to be used only as a last resort. Did you attempt to the best of your abilities to fix your problems through the proper channels of communication?"

"Uh, sort of . . ." I said, withering under Lama's watchful gaze.

"Did you talk to Joey and Kate about how you feel?" Lama asked.

"I tried . . . I think . . ."

"Really and truly, Franny?"

"No." I looked up at Lama, remorseful. He was right. I hadn't tried to solve anything. Instead of telling Kate and Joey how much it bothered me that I had to shuttle back and forth between them all day, I had taken the easy way out. I was beginning to realize that a real friendship is one of give-and-take. I had been giving way too much to both of them, and they had been taking a little too much from me. We needed to get things more in balance.

"You must speak your mind, allowing the truth to shine a light for those who need to find their way in the dark. I was able to easily antidote some of the other recipes with the yellow string, but Joey and Kate have suffered an overdose of magic with both the blondies and the bracelets, which is why remedying the situation is so tricky. We will try this recipe but it won't solve everything. You must still talk to your friends."

Talk to my friends? Why did that seem like the hardest part?

Lama read from the piece of paper in his hand. "'As-It-Was Energizing Facial Mask.' This must be administered to Joey and Kate immediately, and hopefully, order will be restored. They will forget what happened to them under the influence of this recipe, and for the most part they will return to their former selves. But full harmony can only be achieved by you, Franny."

"But what about Dad and Naomi? Where's their recipe? I've seriously messed up my dad's life. He can barely function. And Naomi is followed by a swarm of men wherever she goes. And how can I stop Elodie? C'mon, you've got to give me a few more recipes. Or some of those yellow strings. Those things were amazing. And then I'll never, ever use the box again. I promise—"

"Joey and Kate are the only ones who require a recipe to remove the excess magic from their systems. A single string will cure Naomi of the aphrodisiac but it can't bring your dad and Naomi back together. Only they can do that, for themselves. And you must trust me on Elodie. She will take care of herself in time."

"But Dad's a wreck . . ."

"The magic has forced his life into a different direction, for better or worse."

"In Dad's case, it's definitely worse."

"The question of love is up to fate. Otherwise you will enter a vicious cycle and where will the magic end?" Lama asked. "Franny, there's magic all around. The answers lie within you. You have the power to move mountains." Okay, now Lama was starting to sound like a self-help book.

"What Lama is perhaps trying to say is that she who made the mess must have a hand in cleaning it up," Granny suggested. "You have the power to fix things, Franny. You don't need the box."

I definitely needed the box. "Well, maybe you shouldn't have brought that box into our home in the first place, Granny. Have you considered that?" I was mad now and fighting back. I needed cold hard answers. And recipes. Not all this talk about self-empowerment. Lama got up and put both hands on my shoulders.

"The world is a strange and mysterious place and its secrets reveal themselves to us in complicated ways," Lama said, smiling beneficently at me. He was one cool customer. I could see why Justin, Oprah, Brad, Angelina, Granny, and probably a lot more people were so enamored with him. His words resonated. His presence was powerful. He had a weird, calming effect. I wasn't sure exactly what he was talking about but I knew that he had more wisdom in his pinkie than we had in all of Fall River.

"Seven words keep coming back to me as I spend time in your world. I myself am not sure what they mean. But maybe in time their meaning will be clear to you. *Candlelight, janitor, dinner, closet, Smart Car, kiss.* Hopefully, that will help you in your journey," Lama offered. "Now I must go. Brad and Angelina are expecting me at six. Wheels up."

Candlelight, janitor, dinner, closet, Smart Car, kiss? Seriously? That was it? "How are those words going to help me?" I asked Lama.

Lama placed his hands on my head and hummed quietly for what seemed like hours. "Franny, it's all going to work out. And you'll be stronger for figuring it out on your own. Let me tell you, middle school in Bhutan isn't any better. I remember the day three boys filled my locker with rice and then gave me a wedgie."

"There are wedgies in Bhutan?" I asked.

"Where there are butt cracks, there are wedgies," Lama responded. Excellent point. I hadn't considered that.

"Your light shines very bright, Franny. The world is waiting." Lama gave me a quick kiss on the top of my head, and turned to Granny. "We will meet again in this life and in many others."

"I look forward to it," Granny said. "The light in me honors the light in you."

"The light in me honors the light in you," Lama repeated. And then Lama went into the closet, grabbed the box, and handed it to me.

"Why me?" I couldn't believe Lama was entrusting me with the very thing I had used to wreak so much havoc.

"I think it's in good hands here. I can see you have learned your lesson today. Someday, you may really need it. You have a special place in this universe, Franny. The box is a part of your destiny."

It sounded suspiciously like he was encouraging me to dip my hand right back into the cookie jar. I didn't know if I could handle the temptation.

"What if I mess up again? I don't think the universe would be very happy with me then. And the last time I tried to use the box, it wouldn't actually give me any recipes. Maybe it doesn't want to work with me anymore."

"You asked a lot of the box. Like anything, it can only process so much at one time. It was a little overwhelmed by your requests."

I had freaked out a magical box? That couldn't possibly be good for my karma.

"Keep in mind that the box is there to solve problems only after you've tried to solve them yourself. One day you may not need the box at all. Until then, be prudent." Lama took my hand in his and placed some yellow threads into my palm. "One for Naomi and then keep the rest in a safe place, just in case."

And then he was gone, with the deputies and Moosie in tow. Granny and I went to the window and watched as they all climbed into the waiting car.

"I'm gonna miss that monk," Granny said.

"Yeah, me too."

Chapter 23

If There's a Will,
There's a Way

I took a seat on Granny's bed. "So what happens next?" I asked her.

"We get cracking on that facemask."

"I don't have a clue how I'm going to get Kate or Joey to put it on. I mean, they've barely spoken to me in days. What am I going to do? Pin them down and slather them with goo?"

"We'll figure something out. If there's a will, there's a way. The question is, is there a will?"

"But what if they won't put the mask on? What if they do, and it doesn't work? What if something goes wrong, like it did with the blondies? Or what if—"

"Hold up there, Francisco. You're working overtime. One problem at a time. Why don't you put your concerns on ice and let me handle things for the moment?" Granny glanced at the recipe. "All right, easy-peasy. This is going to be fun. I think we've got most of this stuff. I just need to find the clary oil."

Why couldn't things be easy? Why must everything be so fraught? I looked up at Granny and realized at that moment how much I loved her. I was relieved she'd forgiven me. She was pretty awesome and just having her around was an adventure. Sure, this particular adventure sucked big-time, but life with Granny was a lot more interesting than life without her.

I decided to chill and let Granny sail this ship. I just hoped she knew what she was doing. Granny went into her bathroom. I followed and stood behind her, watching as she got down on her hands and knees and began scrounging under the sink for ingredients. Granny lifted bottles, jars, and pots of stuff, squinting to read the labels.

"Does that say clary sage oil or cod-liver oil? You don't want to screw that kind of thing up. Cod-liver oil can really turn you inside out. I took it once and had the runs for a week. Clary sage, on the other hand, is very calming." The last thing this situation needed was a case of the runs.

Granny was now sprawled on the floor, her yoga pants slipping precariously down her backside. "Granny, let me look. I can read the small print a little better."

I got down on my hands and knees and quickly spotted the clary sage oil. I handed it to Granny.

"Can't I just see what happens if I put the strings on Joey's and Kate's wrists?"

"What you fail to understand, Franny, is that sometimes even magic has its limits. Lama left you with a lot more than recipes. He encouraged communication, which can work wonders. And he offered you seven words to help you in your quest."

"Oh, right; *candlelight, janitor, dinner, closet, Smart Car, kiss.*

Very helpful. I mean, I totally get it. He had to roll. If I had the choice of hanging with me in Fall River and trying to solve this astral disaster or going to some fab party in Malibu at Brangelina's, I'd be outta here too."

"Franny, they're clues. Lama wouldn't have mentioned them if he didn't think they were important." Granny gave me a hug. "We're going to figure everything out. Now, are you ready to rock it out?"

"Rock it out? What are we rocking out?"

"Isn't that what you young kids say?"

"Yeah. It is." I laughed.

"Like I told you, I try to keep current."

I realized this was one of those moments in life that could determine everything. Either I could gather my strength and fight or I could fold and continue to be miserable. I decided to buck up and do this thing.

"We're going to have to trick Joey and Kate into putting on the masks because I can't just ask them to pop by for facials, like I could a few weeks ago." I just wasn't sure how to do that. I was hoping maybe Granny would come up with something.

"Trick them! Yes. Fantastic. I'm in," said Granny. "How?"

"I have no idea," I told Granny. She just gazed at me patiently.

I stared back at her and racked my brain. Neither of us said anything for about fifteen minutes, and then an idea came to me. Something I had seen on *The Simpsons*. It was so crazy, so outrageous, it just might work.

"I think I've got it," I said.

"I love it," Granny said before she'd even heard the idea, which was so Granny.

"What if we were to go on their blog and tell them they've won a free in-home beauty treatment by a world-renowned beautician?"

"Where do we get the beautician?"

Granny was not being so helpful. Did I have to do every-thing myself? "Well, you can't do it. And Mom can't do it. But . . . Gladys could. They've never met Gladys. She'll go to Joey's house when Kate's there and she'll administer the face-masks. It's perfect."

Before I knew it, Granny was on the phone with Gladys explaining the scheme. I could hear Gladys squeal with de-light. And then Granny got busy whipping up the As-It-Was Energizing Facial Mask. The ingredients were surprisingly basic—lemon juice, egg whites, avocado, honey, bananas, and a few drops of the clary sage oil. The tricky part was holding a backbend for the first two minutes while the mask jelled.

I e-mailed Kate and Joey a fake announcement that read:

Congratulations. You have won our Best of Blog contest. We sifted through over 10,000 blogs and chose yours as the most rockin' blog in the blogosphere. As first-place winners, you are invited to a day of beauty with Svetlana Ourzinsky, beautician to the stars! Today! In your own home! RSVP ASAP or the prize will go to the second-place winners.

I sent it from Granny's e-mail account and then sat back and waited.

It felt so clearly like a scam I was a little embarrassed and started to mentally backpedal, but within minutes, I received a response.

We accept! We love that you love us. We love us too.

"Okay, Granny," I said, shutting my computer. "It's on."

☙☙☙☙

Granny and I wore trench coats, sunglasses, and baseball caps. We looked absurd but I didn't want to argue with Granny. She really wanted to go incognito. In our matching disguises, we didn't look the least bit incognito.

Gladys was waiting for us two blocks from Joey's house. She had on a white lab coat over a pink tennis dress. Her hair was held back in a matching pink sweatband.

"Gladys, why would a Russian beauty expert be wearing a tennis dress?" I asked.

"No idea. But I've got a tennis date with Luc Santos later today, which is why *I* am wearing it. Don't worry. I've got it under control. Velma Boriskovitz, who lives next door to me, helped me with the accent. Your friends won't know what hit them," Gladys promised, obviously sensing my concern.

Granny and I crouched in the bushes by the side of the house as Gladys approached the door. We had a good view of the backyard, where we could see Joey and Kate in the midst of what looked like a photo shoot. Joey's little sister, Jemma, who considered herself a budding stylist, had set up a whole Victoria's Secret thing on the lawn out by the pool. Joey and Kate were lying on lounge chairs in bikinis. I did a double take when I saw Kate wearing a teeny-weeny string bikini, obviously one of Joey's. Kate never wore anything but surfer shorts and a sports bra to swim. It tripped me out. Jemma was shooting pictures of Joey and Kate with a digital camera.

"That's right. Make love to the camera. C'mon, give it to me. Work it. Work it," Jemma commanded. My God, she was eight years old; where did she learn stuff like this? I made a mental note to limit the twins' play dates with Jemma.

Joey and Kate were vamping it up on the lawn, so self-absorbed it was obscene. They both seemed so far removed from who they used to be I started to worry they were past the point of no return. Could I really bring them back with some lame facial mask?

When they heard the doorbell ring Joey and Kate jumped up and disappeared inside the house. A second later, they were at the front door greeting Gladys.

"Vell, hello, dahlings. I am Svetlana. You gorgeous creatures are Joey and Kate, no?"

"That's us," Kate said.

Gladys put a hand beneath each one's chin. "Vhat young beauty. Makes me miss my youth in Minsk. Aaah, ve vould chase the butterflies around the garden at the czar's palace. It vas so fun and free back then ..."

The czar? Wasn't he overthrown at the beginning of the twentieth century (sixth grade social studies)? Hopefully, Joey and Kate weren't paying attention that day.

"I know just ze thing to bring out ze freshness in you. And good werk on ze, how do you call it? Blog? Iz zhat how you say it?"

"People, I don't have all day," Jemma yelled from outside.

"Jemma, chill," Joey barked. And then she turned to Gladys. "This won't take long, right? We're in the middle of a photo shoot to bring our blog to the next level."

"It's going to be major," Kate added.

"Zis vill only take one half-hour of your time. Ve go outside and ve vill begin."

I had to hand it to Gladys: she may not have rocked the right look but she certainly had the accent down.

Gladys, Joey, and Kate disappeared into the house and then reappeared in the backyard a few minutes later. From our perch in the bushes, Granny and I had a perfect view.

"Lay back on zis chaise and I vill spread ze mask onto your face, and ze pictures you take after zis vill be ze most beautiful pictures zhat you have ever seen. How you say . . . photofantastico! You must lay perfectly still for thirty minutes or your skin vill look like tree bark."

Joey and Kate blanched at this.

"Gladys used to do dinner theater. She's got a real gift," Granny whispered.

"Thirty minutes seems like a long time . . ." Kate said.

Gladys ignored Joey and Kate's protestations. She guided them both onto the lounge chairs and slathered the masks on their faces before they could say much more.

"After thirty minutes, clean ze mask off, and zen look in ze mirror. It vill be amazing. I can't vait to see ze pictures on ze blog. I am big fan of ze blog. I love ze, how you say? Hots and nots?"

"Thank you, Svetlana," Kate said. "We think it's one of our best features."

"We should send out a quick e-mail blast," Joey said to Kate. And then she said, turning to Gladys, "Is it okay if we use the iPhone? We won't move much. It's just, people need to know we're doing the masks."

"Just for a minute, zen no more moving. And I mean zat!" Gladys barked.

"Totally. What's the mask called?" Kate asked.

"It iz . . . um. It iz called, um . . . zat is an excellent question." Gladys looked flustered. "I must clear my brain so zat I can remember vat it is called. I vill just valk a bit and zen it vill come to me. Excuse me for a minute," Gladys said.

Oh no. Gladys had forgotten the name of the mask. Nightmare. I should have tattooed it on her hand. The next thing I knew Gladys was heading straight for me and Granny. Why couldn't she just make something up? Luckily, Kate and Joey were too wrapped up in sending out their e-mail blast to notice.

"Energizing Facial Mask," I hissed to Gladys as she approached. "Now go, go!"

"Right-o. Thanks." And with that, Gladys hurried back to Joey and Kate.

"It iz ze world-famous Energizing Facial Mask. It iz used by kings and queens," Gladys said to Joey and Kate.

"Great." Joey tapped into her iPhone.

Gladys snatched the iPhone away from Joey. "No. More. Movement! Now, dahlinks, I must go. I have an appointment vith the czar's daughter," she said.

Again with the czar?

"You are both very special. Do not forget zat," Gladys added.

"We know," Kate and Joey said at the exact same time. And then "Jinx." Followed by gales of giggles. I had to hold back the urge to bring up my breakfast.

Gladys met us outside. We scurried down the street and away from the scene of the crime. Once we were at a safe distance, we all had a group hug. Even I got caught up in the excitement of the moment. We had done it! Granny and Gladys high-fived. And then fist-bumped.

"You were brilliant, sweetie. I am impressed. You really need to get back to your work with the the Players," Granny said to Gladys.

"I know. It felt good to be acting again. I think I'll give the Players a call this week," Gladys replied.

"I really appreciate your help, Gladys. Especially after the break-in," I said. "I'm really sorry about that, by the way."

Gladys smiled at me. "I know you are, sweetie."

"Do you have time for a celebratory mix-in at the Sweet Spot?" Granny asked.

"Sure. What the heck. Sweetcakes can practice his serve, God knows he needs to. I beat him six–love last week," Gladys said.

We headed to the Sweet Spot. Granny and Gladys went a little crazy with the mix-ins. Butterfingers, gummy bears, Reese's, bananas, and white chocolate chips. It looked disgusting, but after one taste I realized my modest mint chocolate chip with M&M's was pretty sad. These ladies knew how to party. Too bad they weren't about a hundred years younger because they'd be fun to hang with. More fun than my current crew, that was for sure.

Outside we group-hugged again. "Goodbye, dahlinks. Zis vas more fun zan the George Clooney movie marathon at Leisure Village," Gladys said, back in character.

Granny and I got in her car and headed home, or at least that's where I assumed we were going.

"You think it's going to work?" I asked Granny for, like, the five hundredth time.

"I'm sure it'll work. It just needs a little time," Granny responded.

"I'm running out of time, Granny! Pom and band competition are tomorrow. And if Joey and Kate don't show up, everyone will blame me. And the Fall Fling is next Friday. And it won't be any fun if Joey and Kate aren't there. And what are we going to do about Dad and Naomi and Elodie, and then there's Marsha . . ."

"It took some time to make this mess; it's going to take some time to clean it up."

"*Candlelight, janitor, dinner, closet, Smart Car, kiss.* I haven't gotten any closer to figuring out what it means."

"Well, I can help you with at least one of the clues," Granny said as we pulled up to a storefront on the edge of town. The sign read SAVE THE PLANET SMART CARS.

What? Wait a minute. "Smart Cars. What are we doing here?" I wanted to know.

"I actually bought a Smart Car a few days ago and have to pick it up. They were just detailing it for me," Granny said. "There's no way Lama could have known about it, so it's interesting that he mentioned Smart Car, don't you think?"

I stared suspiciously at Granny. "Are you just buying a Smart Car so it won't seem like Lama is wacked out of his mind?"

"Of course not. I bought it a few days ago. I swear. I'm trading in this gas-guzzler," Granny said, meaning the Cutlass Supreme she was driving at the moment. "I've always wanted a pink one."

A pink Smart Car? Pink? Seriously?

Granny hopped out of the car and into the store. I followed. "Wait till you see the detailing. As you kids would say, it's pretty sick."

A pink Smart Car sat in the middle of the store. In shiny green script, scrolling across the body of the car, were the words THE LIGHT IN ME HONORS THE LIGHT IN YOU.

"Oh no you didn't, Granny."

"Oh yes I did, Franny." Granny jumped in. She was wearing yellow yoga pants, an orange T-shirt, and bright green Crocs. She looked like a tutti-frutti sundae.

Granny left her old car with the store owner, who was going to trade it in, and the two of us zipped home. It was like being inside a tiny space capsule.

"And what about the rest of the words?" I asked Granny.

"All in due time. Patience is the better part of virtue, Francisco."

"Yeah. So I've heard."

As-It-Was Energizing Facial Mask

1 banana
½ avocado
1 tablespoon lemon juice
1 tablespoon honey
2 egg whites
  A few drops clary sage oil

1. Mash banana and avocado together in a big bowl until creamy.
2. Add lemon juice, honey, egg whites, and clary sage oil. Mix until consistency is smooth.
3. Do a backbend for 2 minutes as mask jells.
4. Apply mask thoroughly to whole face and leave on for 30 minutes.
5. Rinse with warm water. Follow with cold water to close pores.

Chapter 24

Candlelight and Dinner

"If I were her, I wouldn't be so keen to speak to me either. I was a jerk. I jumped to conclusions and started accusing her of crazy stuff. Anyway, Franny, I'm better off alone. Now I can really throw myself into some projects around the house."

I'd gone over to Dad's to see how he was faring. And the unequivocal answer was this: not well. Dad wasn't throwing himself into anything but despair. As he spoke, he sat on top of a pile of wood, staring off into space. He was supposed to be putting together the new outdoor table he'd just bought at Ikea, but he wasn't making great progress. Dad's an engineer and he's usually great at fixing and building things, but he seemed completely stymied by the pathetic little picnic table.

"I think you should try one last time. You always tell me never to give up. Don't be a quitter. I mean, I've been wanting to quit piano forever. But you keep saying stick with it and eventually I'll be happy I did."

"You know what, quit piano," Dad said, which really threw me for a loop.

"Look, I don't want to quit piano. I just want you to call Naomi."

"I didn't even think you liked her."

"That's not true. It wasn't about Naomi. It was more about seeing you with someone other than Mom. It was just a shock to my system. So I didn't really give her a chance. But I will this time," I said. "You guys seemed great together. I mean, you both like, uh, popcorn and, uh, pancakes . . ." I was really reaching here since those were the only two things I'd seen Naomi eat. The truth was, I knew very little about Naomi except that she made Dad happy, and, really, that was all that mattered, especially when he was so miserable. "And she's the perfect height for you. Not too tall, not too short, which is important because you can hurt your back if you're always bending—"

Dad interrupted me. "Franny, it's over. I screwed up. There's nothing left to do."

I had tried six ways to Sunday to convince Dad to call Naomi but nothing worked. If Dad wasn't going to call her, I was going to have to call her myself. I had to get them together. I owed it to both of them.

@@@@

"Hello?"

"Hi, Naomi? This is Franny, remember me from—"

"Of course I know who you are. What a nice surprise. How are you?"

"I'm fine. I'm calling because I really wanted to pay you back for the dress and I was wondering if we could meet up, for, uh, coffee and I could give you the money."

"Franny, you don't have to—"

"I insist. How about we meet at the Orange Rabbit tonight at seven?"

"Well, uh, I kind of have plans tonight. What about tomorrow?"

Tomorrow? Dad was hanging on by a thread. This couldn't wait until tomorrow.

"Naomi, I know this is a lot to ask, but please can you meet me tonight? I want to thank you, but I also really need someone to talk to. Mom and Dad are so distracted with work lately. I'm not getting along with my best friends and I thought we really connected at the store that day. I could use a friend right now."

"Of course I'll meet you, Franny," Naomi said quickly. Wow. She was a saint, which was why she and Dad should be together and why I was pond scum.

It wasn't hard to convince Dad to meet me at the restaurant too. He didn't have any plans for the rest of his life.

Game on.

Suddenly, I remembered two of the words Lama had mentioned: *candlelight* and *dinner*. Maybe those seven words did have deeper meaning.

I knew just what I had to do. I hopped on my bike and sped over to the Orange Rabbit, where I proceeded to hand over half my life's savings to the manager, who, by the way, was more than happy to take money from a child and then conspire with said child. His name was Fernando and I liked him immediately, despite his loose morals. Fernando knew exactly what to do. He would save the most romantic table, pick out the most beautiful flowers, choose a fine wine, light candles, and place a violin player in the corner nearby. It would be the perfect setting for love to bloom all over again.

At about five minutes to eight, I found myself crouched in the bushes for the second time that day, waiting for Dad and Naomi to arrive. I had a rash of mosquito bites, but if this was my punishment, I was happy to take it on the chin (and the leg, and the arm). Fernando was going to seat whoever arrived first and tell them I had called to say I was running late and would be there soon. Fernando would then usher in whoever came second, and hopefully, as soon as Dad and Naomi saw each other, they'd forgive and forget and the fireworks would begin.

Unfortunately, that plan went up in smoke when Dad and Naomi arrived at the exact same moment, literally running into each other in front of the restaurant. They both just stood there, staring. Neither of them said a word. I held my breath and waited.

"Hi, Mark." Naomi was the first to speak.

"Naomi . . . uh . . . Naomi . . ." Dad finally spat out. It was not his finest moment.

"It's nice to see you," Naomi said.

"Uh, yeah. You t-too," Dad managed to stammer.

"What a funny coincidence. I'm meeting Franny here for coffee. Did she mention it to you?" Naomi was handling things with far more ease.

"Uh, no. She didn't," Dad said suspiciously. And then Dad paused. Because he knows me so much better than Naomi does. "But I'm sure she's behind this. I'm so sorry, Naomi. Franny asked me to meet her here for dinner. I think she probably dragged you here with the idea that she could get us back together. I told her it was hopeless but you know what kids are like when they get something into their heads . . ."

Things had veered way off course. I slipped into the restaurant to fetch Fernando. Hopefully, he could intervene. When Fernando and I came back outside, Dad was walking away. Naomi was standing in front of the restaurant surrounded by four guys, all of whom she was attempting to fend off. Oh no. I had completely forgotten to take into account the aphrodisiac. Fernando made a beeline for Naomi.

"Hello, beautiful lady, would you want to have dinner with me this evening?" he asked her.

What? Fernando was about to spend my hard-earned cash on a candlelit dinner for himself and Naomi? I don't think so. I marched over and swatted Fernando.

"This is my dad's girlfriend, dude. What do you think you're doing?"

"You didn't tell me how lovely she was. Now that I have

seen her, it is impossible for me to imagine her with anyone else," Fernando said.

"Franny, there you are," Naomi said.

"Step back, Fernando. I'm warning you," I said. And then I called after Dad. He stopped, turned around, and stared at me.

"Franny?" Dad said.

"Naomi, I brought you this bracelet. Can I put it on your wrist? We're, uh, handing them out in school to, you know, fight breast cancer," I said. I was pretty sure my nose had grown, like, four inches in the last week. But before I could get Dad and Naomi together, I really needed to wash away the stench of the Sensationally Sexy Smoothie.

"Sure. Though I thought the breast cancer bracelets were pink," Naomi said, holding out her wrist.

"Yeah, well, everyone does pink. Which is why we're doing yellow. Dare to be different and all that." I was sweating like a construction worker in the heat of summer.

"Franny, what is going on here?" Dad demanded.

"Funny all of us running into each other like this." I laughed nervously.

Fernando attempted to stroke Naomi's hand but she shooed him away like a gnat.

"Franny, did you ask Naomi and me to come here and meet you with the intention of tricking us into having dinner together?" Dad wanted to know.

Lama was right. Time to bite the bullet and tell the truth. "Yes. I did. And what's so wrong with that? Neither of you was going to do it yourself. You were both just going to stay miserable. And maybe never, ever see each other again. Which would have been an awful thing because you two are meant to be together."

I turned to Naomi. "My dad is in love with you. He misses every little thing about you. How you spread your raspberry jam on bagels, how you eat peanut butter mixed with Nutella, how you fold your T-shirts into thirds."

Naomi turned to Dad. "You remembered all that?"

"I remember everything," Dad said.

"I ran into Naomi at Forever 21 recently and it was obvious to me that she still cares about you. And would probably be willing to forgive you if you could just pull your junk together and apologize," I told Dad.

"You're right, Franny. I'm sorry, Naomi. I acted like an idiot," Dad said.

"Yes. You did. But everyone makes mistakes. Even me. On occasion." Naomi smiled. She was funny too, this Naomi. She really had it going on.

"So, how about you both give it another chance? You owe it to yourselves. Because love doesn't just walk in every day. Most of the time, it walks right by. Trust me, I know this from experience. You've got to grab it with both hands and hold on for dear life." I had no idea where all this lyrical prose came from. Maybe I was Emily Dickinson in a former life. Whatever it was, I was on fire. And the funny thing was, I meant every word of it. For the first time in two weeks, I wasn't manipulating or spinning or bending the truth. I was telling it like it was. Straight up.

Dad and Naomi gazed at each other. Within moments, they were lost in each other's eyes. It was sweet, but also a little icky. I mean, after all, it was my dad.

The other suitors, including Fernando, fell away. I don't know if the string was working or they just sensed the futility of the situation.

Dad took Naomi's hand in his with a renewed sense of something. Confidence, courage? "Franny is absolutely right. I am in love with you. And I don't want to live another minute without you."

And then they started kissing. Big-time. I was happy that everything was hunky-dory again, but I had no interest in watching my dad suck face. Too much information.

"Okay, okay," I said. "Break it up. Enough PDA. You guys can do that in the privacy of your own home."

Naomi and Dad pulled apart. Dad took me in his arms. He hugged me for what seemed like three days. Before he let go of me, he whispered in my ear, "Nicely played."

"Right back at you," I said. I turned to Naomi. "Are you busy tonight?"

"Actually, I've got plans with you," Naomi said.

"Yeah, as it turns out, that's not going to work. Something just came up," I said. "But Dad is free. How about the two of you have a nice candlelit dinner inside? There's a corner table with your names on it."

"I'm in," Dad said.

"Me too," Naomi added.

And then I slipped away, because my work there was done. At the very least, I could check *candlelight* and *dinner* off the list.

Chapter 25

I Know What You've Done

I RODE UP TO MY HOUSE to find Elodie sitting on my doorstep. Elodie? On my doorstep? Just when things were finally starting to turn around. Didn't I deserve a tiny little break here? I'd been working my butt off all day to put the universe back on track and this was my thanks?

I jumped off my bike and marched up to Elodie. If she wanted a fight, she'd picked the perfect moment. Fortified by my latest triumph with Dad, I was ready to tussle.

I balled my hands into fists and punched at the air. "Okay, Elodie, bring it. Hit me with your best shot. I'm ready to fight you."

"Oh, please, don't be such a drama queen. I'm here to negotiate, Franny."

"I don't negotiate with terrorists," I said, which I thought was pretty clever.

Elodie rolled her eyes. "Real original. Like I haven't heard that one before. Listen, Franny, I'm not going to beat around the bush. I seem to have lost my power at school, and I want it back. I know you can help me and I'm willing to make it worth your while." Elodie said this in a remarkably straightforward way, minus her usual snarl. Still, I didn't trust her one bit.

"I don't know what you're talking about, Elodie," I said, heading into the house. I wasn't making any deals with the devil.

Elodie grabbed my wrist. "Franny, I know what you've done," she growled.

"Wh-what do you mean?" I asked, trying to hide my growing concern.

"I know about the box. And I want to use it. To get my power back. And a few other things as well. We can work together . . ."

"Like I said, I have no idea what you're talking about," I repeated, except this time with less conviction. Elodie knew about the box? How was that possible?

"Franny, let me ask you a question. How do you think I got so powerful?"

"Uh, you're rich and you have big boobs and no morals?"

"So funny, Franny. You really should be a comedian."

"Thanks. I'll keep it in mind."

"Don't," Elodie said with a sneer. "Anyway, I don't know if you remember but I wasn't very popular in lower school."

I did remember that. Besides Joey, who had known Elodie since birth, Elodie hadn't really had many friends. She was always mean, but no one had taken her very seriously. Or paid much attention to her.

"It was at the end of the summer after fourth grade when

I found the box at my dad's office. I was hanging out there one afternoon, going through his stuff while he was in a meeting, and I found this bizarre box in his desk. Madonna, who was one of my dad's clients, had brought it back from Asia. My dad was holding on to it for her while she was on her world tour."

Oh. My. God. Was it possible? Could Elodie be making all of this up? It was a little too coinckydinky. Madonna had a box? That made total sense. I mean, no one could look that good at fifty.

"It was kind of by accident that I discovered its power. I must have said something out loud that somehow connected, and then the next thing I knew, I was holding a recipe. I never really figured it out, but I was able to get four recipes out of it before it stopped working. And by the time fifth grade started, I had boobs, popularity, power, and poms." Elodie paused and stared at me.

"Is this sounding familiar, Franny?"

Yeah. All too familiar. But I didn't say anything because I had a feeling that anything I said could and would be used against me. Cripes. What were the chances? Only a few of these boxes existed in the whole world, and two middle schoolers in Fall River had used them. Me and my worst enemy. It was flipping me out.

"I wanted to try to get more recipes from the box. Maybe ask for As for the rest of my life, some fab bling. But when I went to my dad's office a week later, it was gone. Madonna had taken it back. My dad agreed to call Madonna and see if I could use it one last time because my dad will pretty much do anything I ask. But Madonna told him she didn't have it anymore. She had returned it to some monk in Asia. I figured she was lying. Then I saw your monk friend in school and I put everything together."

"If the other recipes worked on you, why didn't the nog work?" I asked.

"I'm allergic to ginger. I threw up the whole thing after lunch."

So that's why Elodie hadn't been affected. Strange as it was, it all made sense. Elodie's rise to power had been a little too swift; her breasts were a little too big for a seventh-grader's; her pom appointment a little suspicious, considering how uncoordinated she was. She could barely do a cartwheel. Thank God the box had stopped working for her or who knows what would have happened. Elodie might be ruling the world by now.

"I pretty much forgot about the box because I already had mostly everything I wanted. Until now. You have totally messed with my mojo."

"Too bad," I said. "Deal with it." Elodie had messed with everyone else's mojo. It was high time someone messed with hers.

"I don't think so, Franny. If you don't let me use the box, *you're* going to have to deal with it. Because I'm going to tell everyone what you've done."

"Good luck. No one will believe it," I said. I was bluffing.

What if people did believe it? Granny and Lama were not going to be pleased. But what choice did I have? I couldn't actually let Elodie have access to the box. It was waaay too scary a thought.

"What about money, or clothes? You've got to want something I have," Elodie offered, trying a new tack.

"You don't get it, Elodie, this isn't a negotiation. Tell people whatever you want." I was still bluffing but now that I knew the recipes would probably work on Elodie, I was pretty sure I could find one that would make her forget all about the box. I just needed Granny's help.

"What if I make Alden ask you to the Fling?"

"The only way I would ever want to go to the Fling with Alden is if he asks me himself because he really, really wants to go with me. Not because you made him."

"Oh, don't be so lame, Franny. Everything is a negotiation. Name your price."

"I want you to leave my house. Now."

"Franny, either give me access to the magic or I will tell everyone what I know, including my dad."

"Right now I control the magic. If I were you, I'd watch my back." I brushed past Elodie, marched into the house, and shut the door. I fell against the wall. My body was trembling. I had put up a brave front but Elodie had shaken me to the core.

I rushed down to Granny's room. She was sitting on her bed meditating when I barged in. I knew she hated to be interrupted but this was an emergency.

"Granny, we've got a big problem," I said.

"Elodie?"

"Yeah. How did you know?"

"I saw her outside."

I told Granny the whole story and she didn't even flinch.

"It figures that little witch once had the box. Well, it'll be over my dead body before she ever gets her hands on it again!" Granny exclaimed. "I've got the perfect idea."

Granny got up, went into the closet, and came out with a plate of fudge.

"What's that? And how long has it been in your closet? I don't want to kill Elodie."

"Forget-It-Fudge. I made it the other day. I used it on the guards at Leisure Village. Works like a charm. Luckily, I've got some left over. We'll have Mr. Santos deliver it to Elodie. He'll say he's from the Chocolate Bar and it's a gift from Alden. Women love to receive chocolate. Mr. Santos will handle it with aplomb. He oozes respectability, with the ascot and all. She'll never suspect a thing. Trust me."

I felt bad using Alden but Granny was right. It was the best way to get to Elodie.

"Alden will be doing the universe's work. If he knew, he'd thank us. And, Franny?"

"Yeah?"

"If Alden is worthy of you, he'll see Elodie for who she is. Think positive thoughts," Granny advised.

Yeah. Right. I had a magic box. But as it turned out, Elodie had had it first. What was next? Raining frogs? This was all a little much for a suburban preteen from New Jersey. I just wanted to jump ahead to where everything miraculously worked out. But I wasn't so sure that was going to happen. There were still so many moving parts, all swirling around me ominously—Joey, Kate, Elodie, Alden, pom and band competitions, the Fall Fling, and the Fall River Art Fair. I was dizzy thinking about it all.

Granny put her arms around me and pulled me in close. "Sweetheart, I know this is all coming at you fast and furious, but it's a privilege. In time, you'll see that. I have a lot of faith in you." I hoped I could live up to Granny's high expectations. At the moment, it didn't seem likely.

Granny called Mr. Santos and gave him his instructions. He was happy to help. Naturally, Gladys wanted to tag along as well. She would play Mr. Santos's wife and they would pose as the couple who owned the Chocolate Bar. I crossed my fingers and hoped for the best as I dragged my weary body off to bed.

☻☻☻☻

I slept until nine the next morning, and when I came downstairs, Kate was sitting in the kitchen. The twins were tossing mini marshmallows into her mouth from six feet away. Kate was wearing her "Einstein meets skater gurl" uniform, her lime green scooter was by her side, and Joey was nowhere to be found.

"Too easy, brah. Step back," Kate said to Squeak.

"Hey," I said to Kate, hesitant to get too excited. But. Oh. My. God. It sure seemed like Kate was back.

Kate looked up at me. "Hey, homey, what's the hap?"

"Uh, nothing much," I said, which was the understatement of the year.

"The wackest thing just happened. I ran into Joey on my way to Jane's, and she was all up in my bizness. 'Where are you going? We have to work on the blog.' And I was like, 'You're tweakin', girlfriend.' Blog? 'Sup with that?"

"I, uh, don't have a clue what's, you know, up with that," I said.

Kate was back. There was no mistaking it. But why wasn't Joey back? That was the question. Still, I was 50 percent there, which was a lot closer than I'd been last night. Like Granny said, I needed to think positive thoughts.

"Anyway, I got to Jane's and she and Owen totally dissed me. Hard core. They said I wasn't in band and I was bush league. And then Owen shut me down, just slammed the door on me. Battle of the Bands is today, and without me ..." Kate's voice faded off and her lower lip started to tremble.

It was September 25. Band and pom competitions were today. No. Flipping. Way. I'd completely forgotten with everything going on. Just as I was trying to figure out a plan of attack, Kate burst into tears, something I hadn't seen her do since preschool. The twins stared at Kate in horror as she sobbed. She was their hero. And she was crying? They didn't know what to make of it.

I threw my arm around Kate's shoulders and led her out of the kitchen and up to my room. The twins didn't need to see her in this state. Truthfully, I didn't need to see her like this either. Kate was always in control, no matter how much things got her down. She got mad or she got even or she took a stand, but she never fell apart. It broke my heart to see her like this, hyperventilating, tears streaming down her cheeks, her face red and blotchy. And I was the one who'd brought her to this sorry state.

"I don't understand what's going on, F." Kate continued sobbing.

I needed to explain things to her. But how? What could I possibly say that would make any sense? And then the doorbell rang.

"Franny, it's Joey," Mom yelled up to me.

Oh no, no, no. Say it isn't so. I could only deal with one crisis at a time.

"Just go," Kate said, wiping her eyes.

"I'll be right back," I promised as I headed for the stairs.

Joey was standing at the door, looking forlorn.

"Franny, I think I'm going crazy. You've got to help me."

"Wh-what happened?" I asked, a little afraid of the answer.

"I'm not exactly sure. It's been the *très* weirdest hour of my life. First I found myself yelling at Kate that we needed to work on some blog. And then Kate blew me off and I stood there, wondering what I was talking about. A blog? With Kate? Do I have a blog with Kate?"

"Uh, it's kind of a long story . . ." I said gingerly.

"And then I went to pom practice and Elodie told me I was off the team. Off the team? I'm the captain. *I* decide who's on the team, and today is the citywide pom competition, she knows that . . ." And then Joey burst into tears. Nightmare!

Joey was back but not exactly at her best.

Mom appeared, sensing trouble. "Everything okay, girls?"

"Yeah. We're fine, thanks," I said, not wanting to involve Mom since I knew there'd be more questions than I was prepared to answer. With little choice, I steered Joey up to my room, where she was mighty surprised to find Kate.

"What is *she* doing here?" they both said at the exact same time.

"Uh, jinx?" I said, laughing nervously and trying to lighten the mood. Neither of them even cracked a smile.

Kate stood up. "I'm gonna bounce, dawg. Catch you later."

Joey and Kate stared at each other with thinly disguised annoyance. They both wanted a part of me, and as usual there wasn't enough of me to go around. Watching them, I realized I couldn't do it anymore. Something had to give.

"You. Are. Not. Going. Anywhere," I said with a conviction that surprised all three of us. "Sit. Down. Kate. And. You. Too. Joey."

Kate sat. And so did Joey. They both stared at me, stunned and speechless. I'd never raised my voice to either of them. We never really fought. Because I always went along with everything. Until now.

"We need to talk," I said.

"Okay," Kate responded.

"Yeah, totally. Let's talk," Joey added.

Looking at them sitting next to each other on the bed, I was hit by a rush of emotions: sadness that the recipe hadn't worked out as I'd planned; happiness that Joey and Kate weren't lost to me forever; anger that things couldn't ever be easy. Then, and this is totally humiliating, instead of rising to the occasion and finishing what I started, *I* burst into tears. Soon we were all sniffling and wiping our eyes.

I pulled it back together, took a deep breath, and launched in. "I am so sick of running interference for you guys. I hate being a border crosser. It's a total freaking bummer of a buzz kill every single day. I don't want to spend my life bouncing between your two groups; it's giving me the most gigantic headache of my life." I turned to Joey. "You have the poms and the peaks." And then I turned to Kate. "And you have band and the beeks. And I have nothing, *nada,* zilch to call my own."

"You have us—" Joey protested.

I put up my hand to shush Joey. "When I joined the fencing club, I couldn't watch pom or band practice and you guys got upset. When I joined the soccer team, I couldn't make the football games and you guys got upset. Neither of you has even noticed that all I do is watch your activities instead of doing my own. Why doesn't anyone ever watch *me* do anything? I've been so busy trying to meet *your* needs that *my* needs got lost somewhere. I don't tell you guys what to do or who to be friends with and I don't want you to tell me. If I want to join the chess club and miss pom and band practice, I should be able to. And if I want to have lunch one day with Kate, I want you to understand that, Joey. And if I choose to walk home with Marsha Whalley, I want you both to understand. And if I want to walk to school with Joey one day, you're just going to have to deal, Kate. And on occasion I want to be able to do things with both of you, outside of school. Like on my birthday. Or during the summer. I'm not asking you guys to be best friends, I just want you to get along, for my sake. Are. We. Clear?"

"Totally," said Joey and Kate at the exact same time. They looked shell-shocked.

"Good. I'll be right back," I said, because at this point I was maybe ten seconds away from complete hysteria and I needed reinforcements. I left Joey and Kate on the bed looking woozy from my outburst, and headed down to Granny's room.

She was watching *Oprah*. As soon as she saw me, she turned off the television, which was a big deal, considering it was *Oprah*.

"Are you okay, Francisco? I'm sensing a lot of unusual energy around you."

"Lama was right. I should have talked to Joey and Kate a while ago," I said.

"What happened?" Granny asked.

"I told them everything I was feeling and stuff I didn't even realize I was feeling."

"What did they say?"

"I think they got it."

"And how do you feel?"

"Actually ... pretty good." I did feel good, come to think of it. I felt like I'd just unloaded a fifty-pound sack that had been strapped to my back.

"Do you think *janitor* is a metaphor and my talk with Joey and Kate was like a thorough housecleaning of my soul?" I asked Granny.

"I think it means a person who cleans a place of business as their job. Don't worry, the meanings of the rest of Lama's words will reveal themselves soon enough," Granny promised. "I talked to Gladys this morning and it's, how do you kids say ... all good. Elodie took the bait, hook, line, and sinker. She'll still be a mean and nasty soul, but she won't remember anything about the box. Unless, of course, the recipe wears off ..."

"Why would it wear off? Most of the other recipes didn't."

"They might have eventually. We didn't have the time to wait around and find out. I told you, it's an inexact science. But let's think positive thoughts, shall we?"

Right. Positive thoughts. "But wait—what am I supposed to tell Joey and Kate about the box? And their behavior? And why they may be missing the most important events of their lives today?" I asked Granny.

"You can't tell them anything about the box. You've seen what happens when people learn about magic. It's chaos. Just try to avoid their questions and figure out a way to help them get to their competitions."

"And what if other kids from school have questions?"

"I just made a new batch of Forget-It Fudge. There's plenty to go around. For now, focus on getting your friends where they need to go. Things have a way of working themselves out if you nudge them in the right direction. Positive thoughts, sweet pea."

I went back upstairs to make sure Kate and Joey hadn't killed each other. As I approached the door I could hear them talking softly inside. At least they weren't fighting. I pushed open the door, walked in, and found them on the bed. Joey had a pad of paper on her lap on which she had scrawled a bunch of notes.

"Franny, Kate and I heard what you said and we're sorry. You're right, we've been selfish and childish. Kate and I cannot promise to be friends with each other all the time, but we want to do whatever we can to make your life easier," Joey said.

Whoa. Weird and wild in the best possible way.

"Here's the deal, F. Mondays and Wednesdays you roll with me. Tuesdays and Thursdays you roll with Joey. Fridays are a free day. We'll all three rock out your birthday, dawg. We'll switch off summer vacations every year. Every other Sunday, we'll hang as a threesome, and, uh, what else . . ." Kate turned to Joey.

"We'd also like to offer you a few bonuses to sweeten the deal," Joey said, sounding more like a CEO than the head pom. "We're going to ask my *madre* to teach all three of us how to make crème caramel because we know it's your favorite. The next time it snows we'll all go sledding at Kill Hill because we know how much you love it. And we are going to try superhard not to say a mean word about each other to you. *Jamais. Jamais. Jamais.*" Joey turned to Kate. "It means 'never' in French."

"Tope," Kate said. And then she turned to Joey. "It means 'tight and dope.'"

"Got it," Joey said.

This whole thing was tripping me out.

"I think we've covered everything," Joey said.

"Are you down with this, F-ster?" Kate asked.

"Totally, but does it have to be so . . . official?" I asked.

"For now, dawg," Kate said.

"Until we get the hang of it," Joey added.

It was all a little formal for my taste but whatever. It was incredibly touching. They'd mostly given me exactly what I'd asked for and I was grateful. Hopefully, in time, we'd relax and slip into it. Positive thoughts.

I jumped up and pulled them into a group hug. They were stiff with each other but it still felt good to hang on to both of them.

Forget-It Fudge

2½ cups sugar
½ cup butter
⅔ cup evaporated milk
7 ounces (1 jar) marshmallow cream
2 cups semisweet chocolate chips
   Dash of cardamom

1. Combine the sugar, butter, and milk in a saucepan. Bring to a boil over medium heat.
2. Boil 4 minutes. Stir constantly.
3. Remove from heat and add marshmallow cream and chocolate chips.
4. Blend until mixture is smooth.
5. Add a dash of cardamom and stir.
6. Line a 9x9-inch square pan with foil, making sure the foil extends over the sides of the pan.
7. Butter foil.
8. Pour fudge mixture into pan.
9. Place hands above pan for 2 minutes while repeating, "Forget what you know. Forget what you saw. Forget what you heard. Forget it. Forget it. Forget it."
10. Allow fudge to cool to room temperature.
11. Cut into squares while still in pan and refrigerate until firm.
12. Remove fudge from pan by lifting foil and pulling pieces apart.

Smart Car, Dumb Car

"We'll never make it. Pom competition is in Galick Arena in an hour," Joey said.

"Yo, give it up, dawg. Battle of the Bands is in Laskey Park in two hours, and I don't even have my uniform," Kate said, looking pretty forlorn. "And Owen and Jane were trippin' on me. It's phat-free. No one wants me."

"Or me," Joey said. "Why *am* I off the team, Franny?" Joey asked, suddenly realizing that I had neglected to explain that part of the story.

"Yeah, 'sup with that, F?" Kate asked. "You said it was 'a long story.'"

"I, uh, just meant *long* as in 'not short.' But it's not really *long* long. More medium-size . . ." I fumbled, clueless as to what to say at this juncture. They stared at me, confused. Granny had told me to avoid their questions. But that was pretty hard with their eyes boring into me. Maybe one day Granny would give me the okay to let my two besties in on the magic. But certainly not now, when things were still so precarious. How was I going to explain things? I was struggling to come up with something plausible when Granny appeared at my door just in time to save the day.

"Girls, girls, girls, what are you doing lazing about? You've got places to go, things to do. Let's hustle," Granny said, winking at me.

"Granny's right. You guys cannot miss the competitions. You deserve to be there! You won't be able to live with yourselves if you just give up without even trying," I announced with newfound conviction. Granny had shown me the way and I had rediscovered the will. I was praying Kate and Joey wouldn't notice that I'd glossed over their questions.

I went to the bed and grabbed Joey and Kate by their hands and pulled them up. "You guys are going even if Granny and I have to drag you there kicking and screaming." I turned to Granny. "Right, Granny?"

"Righto, Frannyo." That was a little lame, but I had to give Granny room to express herself, even if it was a little embarrassing. "You heard Franny. Let's go, girls." And with that, Granny was out the door and down the stairs.

Then, as if shot through with divine inspiration, Joey and Kate rallied. I saw fiery glints in their eyes and I knew I had gotten through to them. They were born to compete. Their spirits returned in force.

"You're right. Let's rock it out," Joey said.

"Yeah, let's do this thang," Kate agreed.

We all raced down the stairs and followed Granny outside. We waited in the driveway as Granny emerged from the garage with her Smart Car. Uh-oh. What exactly was the plan? There was no way, no how, room for four.

"Yo, is that your ride, G?" Kate asked.

"Yes. You like?" Granny said.

"I'm totally feeling it," Kate responded.

"We're all getting in there?" Joey wanted to know.

"They fit thirteen gymnasts in this car," Granny said. "Although no one was actually driving it at the time. But we'll be fine. Have faith."

This Smart Car was called Smart Fortwo. For good reason. I mean, do the math. But Granny wasn't going to let something like extremely limited space stop her. Granny angled Kate onto Joey's lap and then stuffed me onto the floor at their feet. The clowns who pour out of cars at the circus would have been proud of us.

"Let's rock and roll, ladies," Granny said as she revved the engine.

I cannot emphasize this enough: *Do not try this at home.*

Granny weaved her way through traffic, whooping and hollering as we sped toward Joey's house. Granny was having a blast while Joey, Kate, and I were holding on for dear life.

We pulled into Joey's driveway, plowing over her mom's rose garden in the process. Joey jumped out and reemerged seconds later with her uniform, and we were off to Kate's. At Kate's place, we took down two bushes on the front lawn. After Kate propped them back up and got her stuff, we were off again, whizzing along the back roads of Fall River, Granny yodeling with glee. It all seemed potentially suicidal but I kept reminding myself that there was a larger purpose here. We were saving the day, and that came with its share of risks.

We pulled up at the Galick Arena, parked the Smart Car, and hustled inside. The place was a madhouse. Pom teams from all over the city jammed the halls, their brightly colored uniforms and giant pompoms jostling around. We found the Jefferson team just as they were stepping out of the locker room, Elodie leading the troops. Joey approached Elodie. Granny, Kate, and I stood behind her like bodyguards.

"Joey, what are you doing here? With your loser friends?" Elodie barked.

"In case you've forgotten, I'm the captain of this team, Elodie," Joey said.

"Not anymore. You haven't been at practice for weeks. I'm the new captain."

Molly Hastings, pom co-captain, spoke up. "That's not true, Elodie. No one actually agreed to that. Technically, I should be in charge—"

"Molly, you don't have it in you to lead this team. You'll always be number two, which is why I've put myself in charge," Elodie said.

"I made this team, I created these routines. You can't win the competition without me," Joey countered.

"Yo, you heard her, dawg. Step off," Kate said to Elodie. Trip me out. Kate was sticking up for Joey in public. I guess there really was magic all around.

"I'm sorry, was a beek talking to me?" Elodie asked.

"Yeah, get used to it," Joey said, getting up in Elodie's face.

Molly stepped forward and took Joey's hand in hers. "We want you back, Joey."

Gillian Walsh, a short, stocky redhead freckled to within an inch of her life, turned to Elodie. "You suck as pom captain. You're always yelling at us and you can't even do the pyramid. All we ever did was fall down. I have a bruised knee and two sprained fingers because of you."

"Yeah, you're totally uncoordinated. I don't even know how you made the team," Molly added. Uh-oh, the tide was turning and Elodie was getting swept away.

The rest of the team murmured their agreement, and within seconds a revolution had occurred. Joey was in, Elodie was out.

I tried not to gloat but I couldn't resist. I smiled broadly at Elodie, who sneered back at me.

"I guess we can cross the Smart Car off the list," I whispered to Granny.

"Yep. That monk really knows his stuff." Granny smiled at me.

Molly and Gillian pulled Joey off to the side and quickly sketched out the routine on the back of a napkin. Joey studied it carefully. But she didn't have long because the next thing we knew the loudspeaker was calling for the Jefferson poms.

The poms burst onto the main stage. Kate, Granny, and I watched from the stands. It was a nail biter. At first, Joey was on three-second delay as she tried to keep up. Kate and I shared a concerned look. But then, like, a minute into it, something clicked and Joey hit the ground running. It was like her body suddenly remembered exactly what to do. And she took over the stage. She was riveting to watch. With the music pumping and the crowd cheering, the team managed to create three pyramids in record time, Joey flipping her way down each pyramid like a flying monkey. Girls were cartwheeling across the floor and somersaulting through the air like cannon-balls. Granny was yelling and screaming and jumping up and down with such vigor, I worried we might have to call the paramedics. In an act of newfound solidarity, Kate climbed to the top of the bleachers, stomped her feet on the metal stairs, and pounded on the back wall to the beat of the music.

The poms ended up winning third place, which wasn't at all bad, considering the circumstances. Joey graciously accepted the trophy while looking over at me with the biggest, warmest smile I had seen from her in forever. For about the hundredth time that day, my eyes welled with tears. But there was no time to revel in the sentimentality of it all because we had to get to Laskey Park. Stat. To my surprise, Joey insisted on coming with, for moral support.

Kate, Joey, Granny, and I were back in the Smart Car, snaking through traffic at an alarming speed. At one point we passed a policeman, who, after doing a double take, hopped in his car to pursue us.

"Hang on, girlies," Granny advised. "This could get a little dodgy." Granny put the pedal to the metal, zigged down a one-way alley, zipped around the back of a mall, then came out the other side, completely losing the cop. It was insane. But a total blast.

"Big up, G-force," Kate said.

"Thanks, sweetie, and, uh, big up to you," Granny replied.

G-force. I liked it, which was ironic since Kate's slanguage usually drove me crazy. It suited Granny.

"Your granny is tight, dawg," Kate said to me. And I had to agree.

We heard Laskey Park before we saw it. Dozens of marching bands were warming up, and the sound of squeaking horns and booming drums filled the air.

When we found Owen and Jane they were so happy to see Kate dressed in her uniform, ready to rock, that they both burst into tears, immediately welcoming Kate back into the fold. The beeks really were a different breed from the peaks. No wonder they steered clear of each other.

"I'm sorry I called you bush league," Owen said.

"We're so happy you're here," Jane said. "We really need you."

My eyes welled up as I watched all three embrace. I swallowed hard and stifled an urge to throw myself into their group hug.

Head held high, Kate led the band onto the field and into a rousing rendition of "Sgt. Pepper's Lonely Hearts Club Band" and then through a medley of show tunes, none of which I recognized, all of which Granny sang along to at such volume that a boy from a competing band had to tell her to pipe down. Kate was magnificent, standing tall, stomping across the field like a general. A few more bands performed but it was clear to all who the winner would be.

Kate held the first-place trophy in the air and then pointed to me in the crowd.

"This one's for my homegirl Franny," Kate shouted into the microphone. For the first time in forever, it was all good. As good as it gets.

ⓒⓒⓒⓒ

I must have passed out after Granny and I got home from the band competition because the next thing I knew, Mom was shaking me awake.

"Wake up, honey. Your art teacher, Jeff, called and he can't find your painting for the art fair. Did you bring it home?" Mom asked.

I rubbed sleep from my eyes and tried to get my tired brain to focus. It was September 26. I had survived September 25, but clearly more drama lay ahead. There would be no kicking back, resting on my laurels, and basking in the praise and glory of the Fall River Art Fair. No. I was going to have to claw my way to the finish line.

I bolted up in the bed. "No, I didn't bring it home!" My painting was missing? My buzz from yesterday was killed on the spot. RIP.

"Do you have any idea where it could be? Jeff needs it now, he's on his way to set up. He thought you might have gotten cold feet and pulled out," Mom said and then added, "You call your art teacher Jeff? That's wild. We never called our teachers by their first names when I was in—"

I put up my hand to stop Mom. This was so not the time to saunter down memory lane. "I left it at school. In the art room. Where could it be? What could have happened?" I was getting hysterical.

Mom took a seat on the bed and put her arm around me. "I'm sure there's a logical explanation. Let's head over to the art fair and talk to Jeff, see if we can't figure this out. C'mon, let's get you dressed."

I was in no state to be making critical fashion decisions so Mom picked out a moderately cool outfit and helped me get dressed. I remained comatose as Mom led me downstairs. My brain tried unsuccessfully to process the impossible. But it just would not compute. Had my painting been eaten by a raccoon? Had it been sucked into the heating system? Had it been stolen by an art thief? They all seemed to be unlikely scenarios but what else could have happened?

I sat at the kitchen table in a fugue state waiting for Mom to gather the twins, which is when I glanced down at my phone and discovered the text from Elodie.

Karma bites, Flanders.

I gaped at the phone. What did it mean?

"Elodie Blain is a nasty piece of work."

I looked up to see Granny standing over me, staring at the text.

"You don't think—"

"I do," Granny interrupted.

"She couldn't—"

"She could. And she would. Are you thinking what I'm thinking?" Granny asked.

Oh God. I was. We were a little too in sync, Granny and I. It was flipping me out.

"There are three words left: *janitor, closet, and kiss,*" I said.

"I've got a sneaking suspicion the painting has something to do with the first—"

Before Granny could finish her thought, I was up and racing for the door, Granny in hot pursuit. We were climbing into the Smart Car when Mom came running out to the driveway.

"Where are you two going?" Mom wanted to know.

"To look for Franny's painting. We'll meet you at the art fair," Granny said.

"You know where Franny's painting is, Mom?" Mom asked.

"Unclear," Granny said mysteriously.

"Mother, I hardly think this is the time for a wild-goose chase. Let's just go to the art fair, talk to Franny's teacher, and see if we can't figure this out. Franny has a responsibility to be at that fair, with the painting or not," Mom said.

"We're going on a feeling. You're going to have to trust us

on this one, Anna. If we're right, we'll see you in a half-hour."

Wow. Granny *was* the G-force.

"And what if you're wrong, Mother?"

"Then that will be a darn shame."

And with that, Granny and I pulled out of the driveway and hit the road.

When we got to school the doors were locked, but we were able to jimmy open a window to the basement and climb inside. Since I had no idea where the janitor's closet was, we stumbled around in the bowels of the school for quite some time. Just as we were about to give up, the universe reached out and lent us a hand. We came upon a door sign that read JANITOR'S CLOSET.

It was bolted shut, but in an act that might have been magic or perhaps just a singular instance of control over her body's untapped powers, Granny gave the bolt a monumental whack with a flying karate-style kick that snapped it off.

"Tae kwon do extension classes can come in mighty handy," Granny said.

We flung open the door and immediately spotted my painting among the mops and bottles of bleach where Elodie had stashed it. The whole thing would have made Nancy Drew proud.

A half-hour later, thanks to Granny's mad-crazy driving skills, we arrived at the Fall River Art Fair, which was being held in a supercool old warehouse near the river.

We burst through the doors and hurried over to Call Me

Jeff, who was standing with Elodie by the student artwork. Call Me Jeff was holding Elodie's painting and seemed just about to place it on display when we approached. Elodie looked positively postal upon seeing me. And my painting.

"It may be too late, but here it is." I panted, out of breath. I handed my painting to Call Me Jeff. "And for the record, I would never bail on something I'd committed to." I didn't even look at Elodie. I didn't want to give her the satisfaction.

"I am so relieved you found your painting, Franny. I was heartbroken when I went to the art room this morning and it wasn't there. Where was it?" Call Me Jeff asked.

Before I could answer, Granny answered for me. "It was in the janitor's closet. Where Elodie stashed it. Hi. I'm Mathilda. Franny's granny."

Either I was going to have to change my name or Granny was, because I simply couldn't have her introducing herself like that anymore. I mean, I was a real live exhibiting artist, not some cartoon character on Nickelodeon.

"This is crazy. You don't actually believe them?" Elodie asked Call Me Jeff with righteous indignation. She was a very good actress, I had to give her that.

Call Me Jeff thrust Elodie's painting at her. "We will talk about this later, Ms. Blain. For now, I would appreciate it if you would take your painting and not say another word because, frankly, I do believe them. I wouldn't put it past you."

Granny turned to Elodie, grinning from ear to ear. "I think

you put it best, my dear, when you said karma bites. I couldn't have expressed it better myself."

Elodie stared daggers at Granny.

Mom, Dad, Naomi, the twins, Joey, and Kate made their way over and gathered around to watch as Call Me Jeff took my painting and placed it on the shelf next to the other students' works. He picked up a very official-looking nameplate that read FRANCINE FLANDERS and set it underneath the painting. Wow. Flip me out. I was a famous artist at the Fall River Art Fair, not some lame spectator.

As this all unfolded, Alden came sauntering over and joined the crowd admiring my work. Elodie charged forward and grabbed Alden by the arm.

"Let's get out of here. This is totally a waste of time."

Alden ignored Elodie and turned to me. "Your painting is beautiful, Franny."

"Did you hear me, Alden?" Elodie was getting kind of frantic.

"Chill, Elodie. And let go of my arm." Alden took a huge step away from Elodie. "It looks even better here than it did at school, Franny."

I felt a warm heat rise up from the tip of my toes to the top of my scalp.

Elodie tried again. "Alden, my dad's waiting in the limo with Nets tickets."

"You go, Elodie. I'm staying here. With Franny."

He might as well have said *Will you marry me?* My heart melted, pooling at my feet on the floor. Elodie glowered at me. But it was all posturing. She knew she'd lost. There would be many more battles in this war, but for today, I was declaring victory. Elodie exited with her signature huffing and puffing.

And then it was just me and Alden. Mom, Dad, Naomi, Kate, Joey, the twins, and Granny had all slipped away, leaving us alone.

"Maybe we could go to the Met sometime. The Vermeers there rock," Alden said.

"That would be awesome," I said.

Alden and I gazed at each other for what seemed like two years. I could get lost in those green eyes and never find my way back home. And that would be okay by me.

"Franny, would you like to go to the Fall Fling with me?" Alden asked.

Yes, yes, yes, yes! A thousand times yes! Of course I didn't say something totally lame like that. I just barely held my junk together and squeaked out, "Sure, that would be cool." But there was a huge party going on inside my body, with a live band, fireworks, and a full-on buffet.

Chapter 27

Sometimes Words Fall Short

HOME SWEET HOME. I was relieved to be back in the place I had so desperately wanted to escape nearly a month ago. Would my life always be this rich in irony? I hoped not.

By the following week, mostly everything had returned to normal. Geeks, smeeks, beeks, juvies, loners, govs, and peaks had happily retreated to the safety and comfort of their old familiar spots on the stairs. The caste system was back in place. Turns out, kids rely on the social structure that's been a carefully cultivated part of middle school since the dawn of time. Who was I to mess with that?

Joey and Kate drifted back to their separate worlds of peakdom and beekdom, and I still shuttled between them. Ms. Posey was back with a vengeance. We had pop quizzes, essays, and book reports coming out of our ears. Though, for the most part, she stayed off my back. Marta's food had, against all odds, managed to get worse. Lunch last week hit a new low. We had mystery meat in a grayish broth that tasted suspiciously of shoe leather. Angus Braun ended up with food poisoning the next day. But bad cafeteria food, like a first kiss (which I'm getting to), is an adolescent rite of passage. And at this particular moment in time, I was embracing every middle school convention I could (boys, BFFs, bras).

I still had my small victories. Elodie was barely clinging to the fringes of popularity. People stormed by her in the morning, nearly trampling her as she attempted, with no success, to guard the door. She was forced to eat at the juvie table last Wednesday when the peak table was full up.

Joey and Kate had totally held up their end of the bargain. I joined not only fencing club but knitting club as well. And we went bowling together and they both let down their guard enough to have a really fun and relaxed, uh, ten minutes. During the rest of the time, they were a little stiff and uncomfortable. But, whatever. I'll take ten minutes and turn it into fifteen next time. Just watch me. Because I'm thinking positive thoughts these days . . . except when I'm not. And just in case, I've got the box, stored away in the deepest recesses of Granny's closet.

Now, back to the kiss. The final clue from Lama. It was going to happen, I was certain of it. It was just a question of timing and location. It's weird and a little scary when you know someone is going to kiss you and you want them to, but you've never been kissed before and aren't entirely sure how it works. I hadn't gotten a lot of sleep in the past week, worrying about it. Would I be good? Or would I suck at it? Would Alden be good? Or—and this was the worst possible scenario— would he suck at it? I just wanted it to happen. Get it over with. It was starting to feel like a cavity. I just wanted to get to the dentist already.

The night of the Fall Fling was exactly five nights after the Fall River Art Fair. In that time, Alden and I had gone out for soft tacos at Señor Rosa's twice, while Mom waited in the car. We had gone to the movies once, and he had walked me home from school three times. But there had been no kiss. I waited for it; I watched for it; I even moved in close once; but it didn't happen. At this point, I assumed it was going to have to happen at the dance. I mean, a kiss was part of Lama's prophecy, and everything else had come to pass. The idea that Lama could have made a mistake on this one critical issue was too awful to contemplate.

By the night of the dance, I thought I was going to implode from the sheer force of my anxiety. Luckily, Kate had patched things up with James, and Joey and Alexi were on again, so at the very least, even if I went down in flames I would be surrounded by my peeps, who could douse the fire, throw a towel over me, and cart me off.

I was ready and waiting for Alden an hour early. I was wearing the cherry red sequin dress that Naomi had helped me buy and my first pair of heels—strappy black sandals that Dad and I had picked out together at the mall. I felt about two feet taller and ten years older. Mom had applied blush, mascara, and lip-gloss and then put my hair up in this twisty bun that looked superchic, very Kate Moss. I don't want to overstate things, but I looked hot. Hotter than I'd ever thought possible.

I was vibrating with energy, and I started pacing through the house to calm my nerves. Granny got so tired of my pacing, she forced me to sit with her and watch *Oprah* until Alden arrived.

Dad, Naomi, Granny, Mom, Pip, and Squeak rushed to the door when the bell finally rang. It was so embarrassing, I shooed them away and answered the door alone.

"Franny, you look amazing," Alden said, his eyes wide in appreciation. "Uh, here, this is for you." He handed me one of those flower corsages you wear on your wrist, which kind of poked me due to a stray thorn from a rose, but I worked through the pain and swore I'd never remove it. It was the most beautiful thing I'd ever seen.

Alden, thank God, was not wearing a tuxedo, which I think is major lame for boys under eighteen. Instead he had on a crisp blue suit with a white shirt and plaid Vans. He looked so handsome I had trouble breathing. When I walked him into the living room, my entire family pounced on him. Oh man, how humiliating. But Alden was grace under pressure, which made me love him even more, if humanly possible. Mom and Dad insisted we pose for about a thousand pictures. It got completely out of hand when Granny started filming us with her Flip and the twins took pictures with my iTouch. I finally had to put my foot down.

We met Kate and James and Joey and Alexi in the school lobby. Joey wore a long silk dress and a cashmere shrug. She looked regal, like the Jefferson Middle School queen she was.

Kate had on her usual uniform: a black man's suit hacked off at the knees and elbows. But instead of her bowler hat, she had on this incredible velvet fedora from the twenties, with a long striped feather wrapped around its brim. The best part of all was that James was wearing a similar outfit. He had cut off the arms of a suit, in solidarity. It was a beautiful thing. I teared up. Jeez, I was such a weepy Wendy these days.

"Hey, Franny!" Marsha Whalley rushed toward me.

"Marsha . . . Oh my God, you look . . . amazing," I said. She did look amazing. I just wasn't sure if it was in a good way or a bad way.

Her hair was still a shocking green but she had taken the punk look to a whole new level. Her eyebrows were shaved off completely. And she had pierced her nose. A gold stud protruded from her left nostril. It kind of looked like a booger. She wore a neon yellow micromini with ripped stockings and Doc Martens.

"Uh, Marsha, are you here with a date?" I asked. And then, as if on cue, Elodie came around the corner.

"She's here with me. Aren't the eyebrows rad? So *Sound of Music,* right?" Elodie was loving this. She had failed to bring me to my knees but she wasn't done trying to destroy Marsha.

Once we entered the gym, I forgot all about Elodie because the place was totally rocking! There was a live band, and people were flinging themselves around with abandon. Alden and I dove right in and danced for two hours straight. He knew how to move, which was a relief because the worst thing in the world is being stuck with a guy who dances like a duck. We stopped once for some punch and then hurled ourselves back into the mix.

At one point in the evening, Principal Mackey shimmied over to me and gave me a little hip bump. "Franny, I don't know what you did, and I don't want to know. But I owe you a huge thank-you. I've got my two trophies. And I couldn't be happier." And then she boogied off, singing to the music, hands in the air, fingers snapping.

A little while later, I caught sight of Marta and Mr. Pandrock dancing in a slow groove all their own. It was cafeteria love. And it proved there was someone for everyone, which was a comforting thought.

The most shocking part of the night was when Marsha Whalley charged out on stage and launched into a hard-core punk version of "My Favorite Things" from *The Sound of Music*. Marsha attacked the song, winging her microphone in circles and lunging at the audience like a wild animal. Elodie stood off to the side, certain that Marsha's performance would be the final nail in her theatrical coffin, allowing Elodie, at long last, to take over the role of Maria. But this just wasn't Elodie's year. Because instead of going down in flames, Marsha was rocking the house. Everyone cheered and clapped and then Marsha dove into the crowd. People held her up and carried her along as they chanted her name. She had gone from recluse to royalty and it was flipping me out, in the best possible way. Mr. Sheeplick, the drama teacher, was cheering along with everyone else. It was pretty clear that we were in for a very punk *Sound of Music* this year. And I, for one, was totally psyched.

I watched Elodie as the full impact of the situation hit her. She staggered away from the scene like she'd been in a car crash, and she sat on a chair, alone in the corner, staring out at the crowd. Maybe this would be a learning experience for her. Maybe she would realize that being a total bitch wasn't the way to go. Maybe her soul would heal. Positive thoughts. But, honestly, I seriously doubted it. Most likely, she was just gearing up for the next attack.

Then, just when I least expected it, when I'd almost forgotten about it, it happened. The dance was over and Alden and I were waiting to get our coats. He put his arm around my waist and gently pulled me toward him, then kissed me lightly on the lips. His lips lingered on mine; they fit perfectly, like we were made for each other. It felt like everything in the world was right. I didn't want the moment to end. But I had to pull away, because I had stopped breathing.

"Was that . . . okay?" Alden looked worried.

Sometimes words fall short, so I took a few deep breaths and then pulled Alden toward me and kissed him again. This time, I lingered a lot longer. I was getting the hang of it now, breathing and everything.

"That was . . . awesome, Franny," Alden whispered in my ear. His breath felt warm and tingly on my skin.

"I know," I said. I had goose bumps all over. My first kiss. And it was waaaay better than I would have expected. If only every single moment of my life could feel like this. But I guess if it did, I wouldn't know how special this one was.

When I got home, Mom and Granny were waiting for me on the stoop. Seriously? On the stoop? I mean, why not just come out to the car and say hi to Alden's dad? If I was going to have a love life, we were going to have to establish some boundaries.

I hustled them both inside and filled them in on all the details.

When I finished, Mom pulled me into her arms, tears in her eyes. "A boyfriend. I can't believe it. You're so grown-up. Seems like just yesterday you were a tiny little baby and now you've got a boyfriend. A boyfriend . . ." Uh-oh, Mom was having a moment. I just needed to smile and hope that it passed quickly.

"I knew it was going to be a great night. Your stars were perfectly aligned," Granny said.

Still a little weepy, Mom shuffled off to bed while Granny and I went down to her room to watch *America's Got Talent*. Granny pulled out a massive box of doughnuts from her closet and offered me one. Man, what else did she have hidden in that closet?

"What happened to purifying and detoxing your system with beet juice and parsley?"

"It's not good to be too pure. I need a little toxicity every now and then. At my age, you've got to shake things up. Keep moving upstream, or you end up a dead fish."

I wasn't entirely sure what she meant but I got the gist of it.

We were both silent for a while as we watched a set of triplets throw a monkey back and forth over a burning hoop. Scary. Is that what America calls talent?

"I got an e-mail from Lama this evening telling me his ear had stopped aching. I guess the universe has settled down, no?"

"Yep. Things are pretty calm, for the moment."

"But who knows what the future will bring, right?" Granny smiled slyly. "Good thing we kept the box."

I laughed. "I love you, Granny."

"I love you too, Francisco."

"I'm really glad you moved in."

"Me too, sweet pea."

☙☙☙☙

A really long limousine with tinted windows cruised through the streets of Fall River, an unusual sight in this sleepy suburb. Pedestrians stopped to stare, trying to get a glimpse of the fabulous, famous, important people inside. But they couldn't make out anything through the smoky glass.

Had they been able to see inside, they might have been surprised. It wasn't your typical limo crowd. It was a pretty crazy collection of people: Alden, Kate, James, Joey, Alexi, Dad, Naomi, Mom, Granny, Gladys, Mr. Santos, Lama, and I were crammed into the car, heading to the Meadowlands to see Justin Timberlake in the tricked-out limo Justin had sent over.

Against all odds, everyone was getting along like a house on fire, as Mom would say. Lama and Mr. Santos had discovered their mutual love of Mongolian BBQ, and Lama was talking up a little spot in Bangkok that had the best ribs in the world. James, Gladys, and Kate spent most of the ride alternately creating a rap song and watching *American Idol* on the flat-screen TV embedded in the back of the front seat. Naomi had once been the captain of her pom team, and she and Joey were deep in conversation about how to execute a round-off backflip from someone else's shoulders. Dad and Mom had yet another batch of questions for Alden. But he actually seemed cool with them so I let them do their thing while I chilled and enjoyed my little moment of bliss. It didn't hurt that Alden held my hand the entire ride.

Once we got to the concert we didn't have to wait in line like the commoners. A guy who works for Justin met us at the door and swept us through the back halls of the stadium until we were in the VIP area. I'm not 100 percent certain but I think Heidi Klum and Seal were there and that guy from *Grey's Anatomy* who died in the second season, and I thought I saw J. K. Rowling. The music was crazy loud and we were so close to the stage that Justin's sweat hit Kate on the arm. She swore she'd never wash again. Everyone was grooving like mad. Lama was pumping his fists in the air and singing along. He knew every word of every song.

At one point, I happened to glance up at the glassed-in skyboxes ringing the stadium, and I caught sight of Elodie, all by herself. When she saw me, she pounded her fists on the glass and screamed. She looked like a mental patient locked in an asylum. Karma bites, huh, Elodie?

I didn't know whether to feel sad or satisfied. I think I felt a little of each. Lama tapped me on the shoulder and pointed to Elodie in her little prison.

"I have it on good authority that her next life will be spent pushing a very large ball of excrement in a very small circle."

"What does that mean?" I asked.

"She is going back down the chain. She'll be a dung beetle."

"Really? How do you know that?" I wanted to know.

"I texted her name to my assistant at the monastery and he put it into the system. That's what came out."

"No way. You have a reincarnation computer? That's crazy."

"It's not exactly a computer. It's the pattern the rain leaves on a series of cliff walls near the monastery. When you come to visit, I'll take you there."

"So . . . what will I be in the next life?" I asked, terrified of the answer.

"I won't tell you that. But I will tell you to keep true to yourself and others, and you'll be happy and move up the chain." Lama smiled at me with just his eyes. It was weird how he could do that.

It was past midnight when we all climbed back into the limo. As we coasted along the highway, the dark world flashing by, I started to fall asleep. Alden was by my side, holding my hand, and I laid my head on his shoulder. This must be what heaven feels like. Just as my eyes began to close I looked around one last time. I wanted to take a mental picture. Joey and Kate were sleeping peacefully on Alexi's and James's shoulders, respectively. Dad and Naomi were gazing out the window, arms around each other. Granny was foraging through the minibar, nibbling on pretzels, Skittles, and gummy bears and sipping a Red Bull. Man, when Granny went toxic, she gave it her all.

Granny and I locked eyes, and she lifted her Red Bull in a toast. "To the light in you, Francisco," Granny said.

"To the light in you, Granny."